THE DEVIL IN MARYVALE

A Maryvale Cozy Mystery

Book One

Jackie Griffey

Book and Cover design by eBook Prep
www.ebookprep.com

October, 2016
ISBN: 978-1-61417-687-9

ePublishing Works!
www.epublishingworks.com

CHAPTER 1

Two of Sheriff Cas Larkin's officers, Deputy Doug Freeman and Deputy Haines, drove slowly, Doug keeping his eyes on the road and the underbrush that lined Highway 220 north of Maryvale. Doug was the youngest of Sheriff Cas Larkin's deputies.

"We'll have to cut through the woods and cross that narrow stream of water to get to the back of The Roadhouse. I'm glad I've got my boots on," he said.

Senior Deputy Randal Haines nodded his head in agreement. The Roadhouse, a local barbecue joint, had reported trouble with a drunk customer taking someone hostage. Just another routine call for the Pine County, Tennessee, Sheriff's Office.

The two officers were to approach from the rear, backing up Sheriff Larkin who would take the front entrance. The place and most of the underbrush around it had been there since Hector was a pup, and the Roadhouse property backed up to a small branch of the river.

Haines sighed. There was no other way to get through the wild, thorny growth on the old fence at the back of the place. Both Freeman and Haines philosophically accepted local conditions as the price you had to pay for living in a small southern town in general and Pine County, Tennessee, in particular.

Haines nodded as he warily eyed his side of the road. "Looks pretty overgrown here. But it's been cleared a little farther on and a couple of picnic tables put back by the tree line. You can pull off there." He paused and smiled at his young partner. "We're probably in more danger from ticks drinking us dry than drowning," he teased Doug.

Freeman soon spotted the picnic tables and pulled the car onto the shoulder far enough to clear the road. He was as leery as his boss, Cas Larkin, about dust or mud on his car, and looked a little encouraged as he and Haines got out.

"This is better than I was expecting. Hope our luck holds and the water isn't very deep." He grinned and held up one hand with his fingers crossed. Freeman, at twenty-five, was not only the youngest of the Pine County deputies, he was the most optimistic.

"Shouldn't be." Haines spoke as he walked, his long legs covering the ground quickly. "The growth on that old fence in back of the Roadhouse is so thick you'd never get in that way. It wouldn't be worth your uniform to try and bully your way through it. Not to mention what all that holly and wild roses would do to your hide. Makes the water sound downright good. And I'm permanent press from the skin out."

"Yeah. I am too. My wife's as practical as the county about anything that has to be ironed or dry cleaned."

They walked single file on a path local fishermen must have worn in the weeds. Randal Haines was the oldest of the Pine County deputies and retiring soon. With his head turned to admire the scenery and part of his mind on his retirement plans, Haines bumped into his young partner.

"Hey! What's the idea? You didn't signal you were going to stop! You traffic hazard, you!" Haines chuckled good-naturedly.

There was no answer. Deputy Freeman stood rooted to the ground. His eyes stared ahead and to the right of the path. Haines followed his line of vision as Doug raised his arm and pointed a not too steady finger.

"Over there," Doug managed to get out. "The other side of the path. There's, there's something or someone behind that tree."

Meanwhile, at the Roadhouse, Sheriff Cas Larkin stood outside questioning the manager of the restaurant as Senior Deputy Rhodes watched.

"You called this in? About some trouble-makers?" Cas nodded toward the closed door.

"Yes, sir. I made it to the outside phone there and called you. Never thought I'd be so glad to see one of your cars pull in here." Heavyset, wiping perspiration from his brow with his apron, the man certainly looked miserable enough to be telling the truth.

"How many of them are there?"

"There were four of them that came in together. Two of them left when they saw the sign that said they couldn't get beer on the weekend. Then of the two that are still here, one of them was too far gone for anything that happened to make any difference to him, but the other one must have been watching too much television." He shrugged, "Turns out he had a gun and he's holding four of the other customers hostage until he gets a beer. He thinks he's a big guy and it's a big joke to him. But he's drunk and he's waving a gun around."

His worried eyes pleaded for help. "He could hurt somebody."

Cas knew it was a personal sacrifice for the Roadhouse owner and manager to call for help. He knew how hard he tried to keep anyone from calling about trouble there because he was trying hard to put up a good, safe front and keep the local churches off his back. There were rumors about how hard the churches had to lean on him to get him to quit selling beer on weekends. This wasn't going to help the place's reputation any.

Cas looked around the place, picturing about where his back-up deputies were at the moment. The Roadhouse was in a building so old Cas couldn't remember when it was built or what it was originally for. And every change of owners seemed to make a difference only on the inside, not the grounds around it.

"You said it's a hostage situation in there?"

The manager nodded. His hands twisted his apron, his worried eyes going to the closed door.

"Is there only one of them in there with the hostages? The one you said has a gun?"

"Yes, Sheriff Larkin. I mean, well, as I said there's one of his beer buddies in there with him. But I don't think he knows what's going on if you know what I mean."

Cas pinned him down. "Dead drunk?"

"Yeah, out of it. And," he quickly added. "He was that way before he got here, too. I didn't give them, any of them, anything to drink. Not getting any beer was what set them off."

Cas nodded. "Do you know for sure how many people he's holding in there?"

"Four. There's four of them. Two men who came in alone and a nice elderly couple." He shook his head. "I feel bad about that. The old folks come here often for the barbecue. I'd hate to see them get hurt. Having a gun waved at them is scary enough, without being held hostage. I feel bad about it," he repeated.

He looked down at his scuffed up shoes as if he meant it.

Cas raised the manager a notch in his estimation for his concern but made no comment. He waved him back and warily approached the closed door.

Standing to one side, Cas drew his gun. With his other hand he knocked with loud authority on the battered looking door of the restaurant.

"This is Sheriff Cas Larkin," he called in his no-nonsense voice. "Open this door and let those people in there with you come out. Now!"

The answer was a shot which lodged in the wooden door near the bottom, and a derisive guffaw. Cas also heard a feminine scream that was quickly cut off.

Inside, the husband of the woman who had screamed at the shot held his wife in his arms, her white head cradled on his chest.

"It'll be all right, Annie. It'll be all right," he told her softly.

The gun swiveled around to cover the two of them. "That's right, it'll be all right. You just keep your mouth shut so they won't think they've got to come chargin' in here shootin' or nothing! You hear?"

The woman made a little moaning sound and her husband nodded.

"Why don't you just let them out," one of the other hostages reasoned. "You'll still have two to bargain with." The speaker was in his middle twenties and the other hostage about his age nodded agreement.

"You're so smart, maybe I should just hand you this gun and see if YOU can get us some beer." The hostage taker sneered. He looked at the bar as if he hated it. "Might know the stingy crud would have all his stock locked up in the back room and the taps shut off. All of you just keep your mouths shut, you hear?"

No one said anything. Both the young men were wearing khaki work clothes and had come in alone. The one who had made the suggestion gave a slight shrug, glancing again at the other one. Both appeared to be cooperative, waiting out this crisis. They looked away from the gunman, not wanting to set him off again. The hand with the gun in it looked pretty shaky. They watched apprehensively as he went a little closer to the door and shouted again.

"Sheriff, you want these people out there, I'll swap them to you for beer. And since I'm holdin' all the aces, I want a six pack for these four citizens, you hear me?"

Cas held his gun steady, his eyes raking the scene to make sure no one was too close to the door before he spoke again.

"Yeah. I hear you, and I know you can hear me. What do you think the odds are on you getting that beer?"

"Not too freakin' great from what I hear about you. But what's the big deal about a little beer?"

The beer and the stress were beginning to tell on the heretofore brave, self-styled bandit. He began to whine as he got to the begging stage. Beginning to sober up a little he realized he'd caused himself worse trouble than he'd bargained for. The game wasn't funny any more. The two men in khaki were afraid of what he might do on purpose or accidentally as his general condition degenerated. He was still waving the gun around. As the hostages watched, braced to duck bullets any minute, he faced the door and yelled again.

"If I let these people come out, what's going to happen to me?"

The answer was immediate and positive. "The same thing that happens to any disorderly drunk that threatens people's lives and takes hostages." Cas glanced at the Roadhouse manager who was as familiar with all the drunk stages as he was.

"There are a few other things I could charge you with too," Cas warned. "But those are the main ones. You'd be doing yourself a favor to get those people out of there."

The Roadhouse manager nodded hopefully at that, his face still crumpled up with worry.

"Maybe they won't want to come out now," Cas called a little louder. "Maybe they'll all want to sue you. You'd be better off in jail. You'd better give your situation some serious thought."

"Aw, gee!" The wail was almost crying. "I don't know how we got to this! All any of us wanted was a little beer to wash down our barbecue."

"All I know is those people are still in there. There's no progress being made as far as I can see, and you're getting in deeper trouble all the time."

"Supposin' I was to let them come out. How long would I have to stay in jail, assuming you're going to put me there just soon as you get a chance?"

"You assume right." The answer was chiseled in stone. Cas remembered the scream that was so suddenly cut off. He'd heard no other voices besides that and the self-styled bandit demanding beer. "Are any of them hurt?"

"No! I never hurt nobody, never meant to hurt nobody. They'll tell you that themselves."

"In that case, I'll charge you with being drunk and disorderly and let you out in twenty-four hours. First, open the door and scoot that gun out with your foot. Then let those people in there with you come out. Then you stand in front of the door with your hands where I can see them. Your brain too pickled to understand all that?"

"Yes, sir. I mean, no, sir. I understand. I will. I'll do that." Thirst and desperation seemed to be working on his manners.

A few seconds later the door opened a few inches and a small hand gun was put gently on the asphalt outside the door, the hand quickly withdrawn.

Cas eyed the weapon. "Little twenty-two pistol," he told the manager.

"Probably got it at some knife and gun show." Rhodes looked it over from where he stood.

The manager raised his eyes and held his breath, watching as the door opened wider. They heard footsteps inside.

He, Cas, and Rhodes looked closely at them as the hostages filed out. They seemed to be all right.

Cas noted there were four of them as the manager had told him. An elderly man and woman were closely followed by two men who were wearing khaki work clothes. There was the trace of tears on the woman's cheeks. None of them looked happy, but they were all right.

Rhodes moved to stand beside Cas, his eyes on the door, waiting for the trouble maker.

As soon as the hostages cleared the door the Roadhouse manager hurried to meet them, talking fast. He promised all of them vouchers for complimentary meals and apologized for the unpleasantness.

"I'm so sorry...." Cas heard the manager's voice like background music while he watched the door.

Now he could see the would-be bandit standing just inside. He had both hands over his head, a worried look beneath the five o'clock shadow on his face. He stood still, waiting for whatever fate Cas had in store for him. The expression on his face showed he knew it wouldn't be good, but he stood there silently, his hands over his head. Cas and Rhodes could see the feet of his friend who was lying on the floor beyond him as they went in to handcuff the hostage taker.

"You drive a hard bargain, Sheriff Larkin." The hostage taker found his voice again. "All I wanted was a couple of beers for me and my friend here."

He put on as pitiful a face as he could at the injustice of it all. Self-pity oozed from every pore.

"Um-hum, your buddy there sure seems to be in need of another beer." With his foot, Cas nudged the man lying on the floor. He slept on, blissfully unaware of any problems at all.

"He looks as comfortable as a hound dog under a porch." Cas almost grinned at the open mouth and comical expression.

Rhodes touched the vertical drunk's shoulder. "Turn around and put your hands behind you."

"Before you do that, help your buddy up. He's going with you." Cas jerked his head toward the docile dreamer.

The hostage taker got his friend up with a little help from Rhodes. The groggy buddy roused a little as they worked to get him on his feet. Slumping, half awake, he leaned unsteadily against the wall. He stared groggily around, his attention caught by his friend the hostage taker, who was complaining again.

Then the back door opened and Deputy Freeman came in, quickly sizing up the situation.

Cas motioned to him. He went to help Rhodes get the two drunks cuffed and out to the car. As Deputy Freeman passed him, Cas noted his soaked uniform and the strange expression on his face.

"Where's Haines, Doug? One was enough to cover the back door. Did he stay to drive the car back?"

"I wish that was it," Doug said with feeling. "Now that these guys are in the car I'll go back and get our car and take you over there. Haines didn't have any choice about staying there. I'll hurry."

"No need," Cas cut him off. He remembered the old adage about calamities coming in threes and it did seem his own cases came in bunches like bananas most of the time.

Dread tensed the muscles in the back of his neck as he spoke. "We can go around in this car. It won't hurt these two to wait a little longer to sleep off their beer."

Cas eyed the wet uniform again. "Looks like the water was a little deeper than I thought."

"Yes, sir." Deputy Freeman managed a weak smile. "We've been discussing the advantages of wash and wear."

"Tell me, what is it that's keeping Haines back there?"

Rhodes had come to stand beside Cas, their attention on the young deputy.

"I, we found a body, sir. A teenager." He added sadly, "It's a young girl."

CHAPTER 2

Arriving at the place Haines and Doug had gone into the woods, Rhodes parked behind their patrol car. Cas checked the prisoners. They sat, one asleep with his mouth open, the other looking sullen and mean. But quiet. The mean one's personal war was over. He'd lost and he knew it. Cas spoke to his young deputy.

"Doug, call in and get the coroner's office out here. Rhodes and I will wait here for them. I'll send Haines back with you to take care of these two guests of the county."

"Yes, sir."

Walking behind Rhodes on the path toward the tree line, Cas sighed, remembering the suspicions he had had at breakfast that morning. It was as if fate had let him get that good breakfast to tide him over for what the rest of his day had in store. He hadn't known how well off he was.

The day had started out better than good. It was his weekend to work and the good scents from downstairs had lured Cas to the kitchen earlier than usual for a Saturday breakfast he had not expected. What he expected was a cup of coffee and a doughnut, if he was lucky, at the office. He sniffed, narrowing his eyes at his wife, Connie, as he entered the kitchen.

"Do I smell sausage?"

He paused and closed his eyes to savor the aroma. Then he carefully lowered his six foot frame into his chair at the head of the table. He half expected to wake up, his sleepy head on the table in the break-room.

"Sure do. The best kind of sausage, too."

Connie poured coffee into his cup and smiled affectionately at him. "It's the deer meat package Rhodes brought us the other day." Rhodes was an avid hunter and as generous as he was lucky.

Cas sat without comment as he sniffed the combined aromas of the special breakfast his wife had fixed him. But he was happy only from the neck down. His suspicious nature was setting off alarms in the back of his mind.

Connie poured his orange juice as he unfolded his napkin, too busy for small talk as she hurried to get them fed and him off to work. Cas's suspicious nature was working on him in earnest now. He looked sideways at Connie as she finished putting things on the table.

He wondered what he was in for this time. This had all the classic clues she was up to something. Maybe there was something she wanted him to do or maybe she was up to some matchmaking plot again in spite of his warnings about that. It was Connie's firm belief that everyone should be happily married, and she gave Cupid and Mother Nature a helpful push every chance she got, in spite of his frequently repeated warnings.

He straightened in his chair and regarded her with what she called 'his sheriff's look'.

"All ready." Connie spoke brightly as she sat down opposite him where she could still reach the coffee pot.

His stomach gurgled in anticipation, making Connie smile. He sipped his coffee, "Ah, just right."

"Of course," she agreed complacently. "But it's nice to be complimented once in a while." Obviously, she knew she had set an award winning breakfast before him.

Cas waved his hand at the spread before him, giving up subtlety. "Venison sausage, eggs over light the way I like them, English muffins. My favorite toast, as you well know. And marmalade? Orange marmalade?" He eyed the bottle as if it were gold plated. Connie stifled a giggle.

He sat straight in his chair, the fork in his right hand like a gavel. "Hmm, you'd have to have bought the marmalade yesterday," he mused aloud. "That means all this must have been premeditated. The marmalade was the tip off," he added sagely. "I'm being buttered up for something, right?"

A smile played around Connie's lips. "Uh-huh. I knew you had that figured out when you started taking inventory of the goodies on the table." Connie's dark blue eyes danced with amusement.

"I knew it. There's more here than breakfast, all right." He took a deep breath and braced himself. "Why don't you just put me out of my misery and tell me what's on your mind?"

Connie spread marmalade on her English muffin, taking her time. She let him suffer a while for always expecting the worst. She sipped her juice before she spoke.

"You're right, as usual, Sheriff Larkin."

She spoke politely, playing the game he had chosen. "I do have something I want to talk to you about."

"We've already established that. So tell me?"

Cas started on the good breakfast, waiting to hear whatever it was that was so important it rated a Saturday morning breakfast like this when she could have slept in.

"You've been sheriff here for twelve years now and our house is nearly paid for, thanks to our having a short term loan and it not being a very big loan."

"We're in pretty good shape considering neither of us was born with a silver spoon in our mouths." Cas nodded, agreeing cautiously.

"And aren't you lucky I don't have a lot of expensive tastes?" Connie warmed up his coffee.

Cas smiled affectionately at that. "I guess I'd have been soft in the head enough to marry you anyway, so I guess you can say I was lucky there." Another point conceded.

"So, if we had to we could manage all right on only one salary now."

Cas let out a relieved breath. "I see where you're going. If you want to quit your job and stay home, it's fine with me."

He put his cup down, his expression more serious. "I'd be glad if you did quit. I worry about you going all that way into Fort Craig every day. And the gas and other costs, you have to consider those, too."

"That's what started the idea, looking at the mileage on the car when I was buying gas yesterday."

"I think it's a good idea. Go ahead and quit if you want to."

"And…."

"Oh, there's more?" Cas's face went quickly from comedy to tragedy. "I rejoiced too soon!"

"Cas!" Connie was exasperated. "You've been sheriff too long. You're always waiting for a calamity of some kind. I've been thinking of something else. It's important to me. To us." She looked up to see the worried expression on his face and a wave of sympathy warmed her heart.

Connie patted his hand that clinched his fork like a gavel. "At least wait till you hear what I have to say before you put it on your worry list."

Cas nodded, taking a bite of the hot venison sausage. He regarded his beautiful, petite, brunette wife, whose matchmaking and 'managing him' he put up with because he loved her.

He brooded, wondering what was so important to her, important enough to quit her job for. "Then it's important to me too. What is it you want to do?"

"I'm going to try working here. What I want to do is call on some of the local businesses here in Maryvale and freelance a day or a half day's work when they need someone to help them get out bills or extra correspondence. You know, something that takes more office help than they can keep on regular salaries. Hiring me a few days would be a lot cheaper than having to pay a yearly salary and benefits on another full time employee."

"You're right about that. Sounds like a good selling point to me."

Cas got up and inspected his khaki uniform.

"Did my good breakfast do any harm?" Connie grinned.

"Not a chance. If I'd found any crumbs I'd just have rubbed them in," he laughed.

She came to him for a goodbye hug. "Never underestimate the power of venison sausage."

He kissed her and held her a minute before reaching for his hat. "If it turns out there's no job market here, you can always stay home and fix me deer sausage and English muffins. It will be no problem."

Cas reluctantly let her go. "Missy coming home after lunch?"

"She'll be here around three. Thanks for the input, see you tonight."

No, Cas sighed to himself, remembering Connie's pleased expression, her warmth as he held her. He hadn't really appreciated how well off he was. He dragged his mind back to his current problem as he approached the scene of the crime Rhodes had told him about.

Neither he nor Rhodes spoke, walking single file as the other deputies had.

Haines was standing in the pathway waiting for them. He gave a short wave, turning with them to look at the body.

"Can't have been here long." Cas glanced at Rhodes. "She looks to be about my daughter's age but I don't know her. Do either of you?"

Haines shook his head.

"I do," Rhodes spoke up. "I mean, I know who she is. Her family goes to church where my wife and I go."

"What's her name?"

"Denise Davis. Mother's a widow. They, Denise and her mother and her aunt live together. Aunt's a school teacher. Her mother works in Judge Spruce's office. She's the secretary or something there."

* * *

At home, Connie heard the car stop outside and glanced at the clock. It was five till three.

Missy appeared in the front door. She wore jeans, a short sleeved shirt, and blue denim sneakers. A sweater was slung over one shoulder as she balanced her belongings with a pillow on top. She held the door open with an elbow.

"Hi, mom! This looks like moving, doesn't it?"

"Not even close." Connie wrinkled her nose. "As you'll find out when you have to go to college. Need some help?"

"No, I'll make it." Missy heaved the bedclothes to the front of her burden to close the door. "And I've got a while to go before college."

She stopped at the bottom of the stairs, breathed an exasperated sigh, and rearranged her load again. "Or maybe I'll decide to be a recluse and just stay up there in my room the rest of my life!"

Connie stuck her head around the door, amused at the thought. "I'll believe that when I see it."

Missy smiled too, one foot on the first stair step. "Yeah, on second thought I guess a few moves are worth it to make progress."

Connie stood watching until the pillow sailed from the top of the stairs into Missy's room then went back to her baking.

Missy got back downstairs in record time. A junior in high school, Missy had her mother's pretty face, her father's black hair to frame it, and she was already as tall as her mother. She paused in the kitchen door and closed her eyes. She sniffed the chocolate scent as Cas had sniffed the scent of the venison sausage. Connie laughed at the resemblance.

"What's so funny?" Missy asked on the way in. Without waiting for an answer she went on, admiring the cooling goodies. "These cookies are just right, I don't like them too brown."

"Thanks, boss." Connie checked on the batch in the oven.

"Did you save me some chocolate chips?"

"Yes, though I thought you might be too grown up for such a thing now."

"Never, never, think that," Missy intoned in a chant. "I'm going to eat chocolate chips until I'm a hundred and nine." She quickly amended that. "Maybe ten."

"How was the slumber party?" Connie asked as Missy retrieved the muffin cup full of chocolate chips from the refrigerator and sat down at the table to eat them.

"About what I expected. Most of us had a really good time and of course, there were a couple of fruitcakes who acted like they'd never been allowed out before."

"And nobody tried to crash?"

"No, a couple of cars full of boys cruised by but no one paid any attention or went out. They didn't stop." She added, "Probably because they saw Janet's dad sitting in the porch swing. We had a good time."

"That's good." Connie checked again on her last batch of cookies.

Missy thoughtfully licked chocolate off her fingers. "Mom, what do you know about the devil?"

Connie shut the oven door carefully and turned a surprised face to her daughter. "Not very much, I guess. I wouldn't want to meet him in a dark alley, as the saying goes."

"And you wouldn't buy a used car from him." Missy grinned around a mouth full of warm cookies and melted chips.

Connie contemplated her daughter, thankful she was still more child than woman, grateful for that. "Why in the world do you ask?"

"Oh, one of the Brainless Ones mentioned something about the devil last night and I happened to overhear it. That's all."

"What did she say?" Connie was curious.

"She said the devil was going to punish somebody for something. I didn't hear all of it. I just noticed it because I thought it was a funny thing to say."

"Trying to get attention, no doubt." Connie dismissed it, taking the last batch of cookies out of the oven. "We're having chicken for dinner tonight. These chocolate chips are for dessert and to munch on."

"Good. I like crockpot chicken, too." She gave Connie an approving nod. "Your job's safe, for now."

"That's a load off my mind!" Connie rolled her eyes heavenward.

The last two sheets of cookies were still cooling. Missy got up and began stacking cookies on a paper towel to take upstairs with her.

"Guess I'll have to eat the overflow." She carefully picked up her cookies and started out but paused to kiss her mother's cheek. "Please don't ever get a bigger cookie jar, mom."

The ring-ring of the phone in the silent house sounded loud and shrill. Connie ran to answer it, glancing up the stairs.

"Connie," Cas hesitated. "You sound out of breath."

"I ran for the phone is all, I think Missy's asleep. Are you all right?" It was unusual for him to call home. She knew it wasn't just to chat.

"Yes, I'm all right."

She didn't believe it. She knew every nuance that familiar voice was capable of. He sounded distracted or worried about something. Her hand tightened on the phone.

"I called to let you know not to wait supper for me. I don't know what time I'll be in."

Hearing a sound, Connie turned slightly to see Missy standing in the door. She mouthed 'I heard the phone' and stood listening.

Connie finished her brief conversation and replaced the receiver. She sat down on a kitchen chair, looking shaken.

Missy came into the kitchen. "I heard dad's not coming home for supper. What's going on, mom?"

"You'll know tomorrow anyway. They, your dad and Rhodes and a back-up car went to answer a disturbance call at The Roadhouse."

"Oh, a fight or something? Are all of them all right?"

"Yes, they're all right. It was a drunk causing trouble. Dad resolved that. The drunks are in jail where they should be. But the back-up deputies had to go through the woods to get to the back door of The Roadhouse and they found a body in the woods. It was a young girl."

Cas addressed Rhodes, gesturing behind him. "The coroner's van pulled up as I left the car. I sent Haines back with Doug and called Connie. Told her to expect me when she sees me coming."

Rhodes nodded. "That's about what I said on my call home, too. Here they are." Rhodes moved back to let the men from the coroner's office through.

"At least she hasn't been here very long, thanks to our call to the Roadhouse." Cas spoke quietly to Rhodes. "And she's fully clothed."

"Looks like the cause of death is going to be easy," one of the coroner's men said.

Cas winced, looking away from the body. The handle of a large knife protruded from the chest wound.

CHAPTER 3

The microwave dinged and Missy mixed hot chocolate, casting a furtive glance at her mother. She preferred making chocolate from scratch but this was an emergency. Envelopes of ready-mix would do. She poured the contents and milk into a pan then after mixing it, left it on the stove to keep it warm before handing Connie a cup.

Connie took it and sipped. "Thanks, this is good."

"You looked like you needed it." Missy glanced at her, venturing a small smile. "It's a wonder you can still get chocolate without a prescription."

Connie smiled back. "Sometimes simple things are better than prescriptions."

Missy regarded her from the corner of her eye. She sipped her own chocolate and waited.

Connie's disbelief and denial hadn't yet given way to compassion but the warmth of the chocolate took away the chill of the shock. Things like this just didn't happen in Maryvale, not to people you know. She had to get used to it enough to talk about it. She inhaled the comforting steam from the chocolate.

"Tell me what dad said." Missy's voice broke into her thoughts.

Looking at Missy's worried face, Connie was at a loss where to start.

"About the girl they found," Missy prodded. "I guess it wasn't a car wreck since you said they had found her body."

"No. No, it wasn't. And your dad said she looked to be about your age."

"About my age. And not a car wreck," Missy repeated patiently. She frowned, uneasy. "But, if it wasn't a car wreck and not an accident. You—you…. Surely you don't mean someone killed her?"

Connie nodded, catching her lower lip between her teeth at the horror of it.

"It was murder then. Someone was murdered, right here in Maryvale." Her eyes searched Connie's. "Who? Where, mom? What happened?"

"You know where the Roadhouse is. Out by the junction of Harper's Road and Highway 220. They called for help."

"I know, you told me about the drunks."

"One of them, the drunks, had a gun and was holding some people hostage because they wouldn't sell him beer. While dad and Rhodes watched the front the other deputies had to go through the woods and cross that little branch of the river to cover the back. There in the woods is where they found her. Found the girl's body."

"Mom," Missy's face creased with anxiety. "You still haven't told me who she is. Do they know?"

"Dad said one of the deputies knows her family or something. Her name was Denise Davis. It sounded familiar…."

Connie closed her eyes briefly, then shook her head. "I just can't quite place the name. Do you know her? She must have been in your class, or your dad thinks maybe a year before?"

"Yes. I know her, mom."

It was Missy's turn to be shocked. She struggled with the fact that someone she knew had been murdered. "Her mother works for Judge Spruce."

"Oh, that's where I've heard the name. Did you know her very well?"

"Just to speak to, not well. She was invited to the slumber party last night but I heard someone say she wasn't feeling well or something like that."

"But she was invited?"

"Yes, she was. The ones I called Brainless Ones were friends of hers." Missy continued, remembering the party. "I think it was one of them who said she wasn't feeling well. I didn't pay much attention. The three of them have names beginning with D's. Denise, Diane, and Doris. They were always rattling on about some silly thing, never serious. And now, one of them is dead! Oh, mom," Missy shivered.

Connie came and put her arms around her. She poured them both more chocolate and sat back down.

"I hope they find out who did it soon. What happened?" Her eyes sought Connie's. "How, how?" Missy seemed to shrink a little sitting there in the chair beside her mother.

Connie patted her hand. It felt cold under hers, still warm from holding the cup of chocolate.

"They will find out, don't worry about that. But Missy, in the meantime, someone did this, right here in Maryvale. Don't trust anyone or get in a car with anyone except one of us. Me or your dad. It's hard to believe someone here is a murderer but it has to be someone here. Probably someone she knew, possibly someone we know."

Missy sat silent, appalled at the finality of sudden, violent death.

Connie got up to wash the chocolate cups as she talked. "We'll have to take care until we know who it was who did this and put him in jail where he can't hurt anyone else."

"I know, I'll be careful." Missy shook her head. "I can't believe she's really dead. I saw Denise on Friday, mom. She was standing by her locker in the hall. And now she's gone."

Missy dried the cups. "How did it happen, mom? Was she? Did they?" Missy hesitated.

"Oh, I didn't tell you. She was stabbed. A knife wound to her chest. And dad said she was fully clothed, so they don't think she was molested or anything like that. I don't think from what he said that she suffered much. The stab wound was directly to the heart. What scares me is it must have been someone she knew I would think, to get close enough to stab her like that. So just be patient if I seem to be walking on your heels until this is cleared up."

Tired as much from emotional stress as by the hour, Cas tried to be quiet coming in. But Connie heard him and looked at the clock.

Twelve fifteen. She wondered if he'd taken time to get anything besides fast food to eat.

Sliding her feet into her slippers she went down to the kitchen where Cas was making himself a cold supper.

"Hi, want a chicken sandwich?" Cas waved the loaf of bread in his hand. He had shed his boots and was padding around the kitchen in his socks.

"No, but I'll fix us some chocolate." She stole a glance at his tired face as she got out the pan and measured sugar and cocoa. "Missy says it's a wonder you can still get chocolate without a prescription."

Cas didn't answer and Connie stirred the chocolate as she talked. "And there are chocolate chip cookies in the jar over there."

Cas worked on his sandwich from the array of pickles and other things he had laid out on the table with the chicken.

"The hamburger I had didn't even last long enough to get the preliminary paperwork done on the teenager we found."

He looked up. "I guess you and Missy discussed it over chocolate?" He teased her about their well known fondness for chocolate as Connie poured herself a steaming cup too.

Cas went on, his voice tired. "Did Missy know Denise? I figured she might be a little younger than she is."

"Yes, she knew her. But only the way everyone here knows everyone else. She told me Denise was invited to the slumber party she went to. Said Denise didn't go because she wasn't feeling well, or that's what someone at the party said."

"That's interesting. I felt Missy would know who she was." He gave his head a little surprised shake. "Being invited to the same party is closer than I thought."

"No, I still wouldn't call it close. It was just one of those things where everyone in the same age group is invited. Some of her, Denise's, friends were there, too."

"I didn't know who she was when we found her. Rhodes knows the family and was going with me to tell them. But when we got back to the office they were there waiting for us."

"They were?" Connie tilted her head, surprised. "How did they know?"

"They didn't know. They only knew she was missing. They thought she was still upstairs in her room this morning at breakfast time. Her mother checked on her about bedtime last night and thought she was asleep. Then this morning when she still hadn't come downstairs by nine o'clock her mother went up to wake her, and she was gone."

"Gone? And they didn't know she'd left?"

"That's right. She put two pillows under the cover and slipped out the window."

"But," Connie puzzled. "I thought you said her room is upstairs. Is there a tree by the window? How did she get out without their knowing?"

"I asked about that. Her aunt said she had done the same thing about a year ago. The roof is low on the far side of the carport. She climbed out the window, walked over the roof to the lowest side and jumped down. Must have been easy. They just didn't think about her doing that."

"And they didn't know or miss her until nine o'clock this morning." Connie shook her head at the things children and teenagers could think of to outwit their parents.

Cas nodded, talking between bites of his sandwich. "They thought she might come in, so they waited. They called some of her friends to see if she was with them or if they had seen her. When she hadn't come back by four o'clock, they tried driving around looking for her at the mall and other places. They also called Fort Craig to see if she might have decided to visit a cousin there. But they hadn't found her or heard from her. That's when they decided to come and report her missing and see if we could help find her. Dispatch made the report as we were approaching the Roadhouse. Then of course we reported finding the girl's body. Her parents were waiting for us when we got back."

Connie had met Denise's aunt at school and Muriel Davis at the courthouse. She pictured Denise's mother and her aunt looking for her. Cringed at the anxiety of looking for a lost child.

"I feel so sorry for them. How awful. Do they have any idea who might have done this? No," Connie answered her own question. "How could they? How could anyone think anyone we know could do such a terrible thing?"

"They both said they don't know of anyone who would want to hurt Denise. They're as much in the dark about it as we are. I told them if they remember anything, no matter how small or unimportant they think it is, to call me."

Cas poured milk into his empty chocolate cup, his face grim. "The only break we've got is we found her so soon. If those hooligans hadn't raised such a row at the Roadhouse because they wouldn't serve them beer with their barbecues, we might still be looking for her."

Glancing toward the door Cas asked, "Did you tell Missy everything about the stabbing?"

"Yes, I told her everything you told me. She heard the phone ring and came in while I was talking to you."

"It's just as well. Everybody in town will be talking about it tomorrow anyway. At least the victim wasn't beaten or raped."

"And her mother and her aunt don't know of anyone who might have been mad at her or envious, or any other problem?"

"No. We don't know a thing yet. We'll start on the leg work and see what we can turn up. Maybe it was panic," Cas mused. "She might have done something, or known something the person who stabbed her didn't want known. Young people are hot blooded and see situations as more desperate than they are sometimes."

"Do you have the thing, the weapon?" Connie shrank from the picture that word brought to mind.

"Yes, we've got that. It was still stuck in the wound. Stuck fast. Whoever did it did it quickly and with a lot of force to drive it in like that. There weren't any prints on it, of course. And it's a hunting knife like you can buy at any hardware store around here. I can't see anywhere to start except to begin asking questions. Right now, I've got to get my head on a pillow before my eyes close."

He paused at the stairs. "Did you tell Missy you're going to quit your job in Fort Craig and stay home?"

"No, what with the slumber party, cookies, and now this awful thing, I haven't. I don't know how she'll take it yet."

Rhodes Cromwell was getting into his patrol car as Cas pulled into the parking lot Monday morning. Rhodes was a dead ringer for Ichabod Crane and Cas waited until all six foot two of his spare frame settled comfortably behind the wheel before bending down to talk to him.

"Anything new I should hear about?"

"No, been a quiet night. There's a couple of routine reports, I put them on your desk. Haven't got anything that might help on the Davis case but since I sort of know them, Muriel Davis and her sister, we called to express my and Mary's sympathy. I also said you would be calling on them soon in your investigation."

Cas nodded approval. "Good, I'm glad you did."

"After offering our condolences I asked Muriel to make you a list of Denise's friends. I asked her to write their names along with anything she might know about any of them which is in any way unusual, or might have any bearing on this case."

"That should break the ice a little for me. I was going to call before going over there. I dread it, Rhodes. This is one part of the job no one gets used to."

"I know what you mean. And it's always worse when it's a little one or a youngster." Rhodes started rolling up the window. "I'll be calling in."

Cas went inside and stopped at Gladys's desk to pick up his mail.

"Morning, Boss." Gladys pushed several envelopes across the desk.

"Good morning, Gladys, do you have any calls for me? Did Clint call from the coroner's office?"

"No to both questions, but the mail's light. I hope the Davis case Rhodes told me about will soon be cleared up. It's hard to believe we've got a murderer loose right here in Maryvale."

Gladys was nearly sixty but that wasn't known for certain outside that little drawer behind her with the Personnel label on it. She liked her job as much as Cas did his and being healthy, she didn't figure on being put out to pasture as long as she could be of help. Her eyes took on a hopeful gleam.

"There's no chance whoever did this could be a stranger, is there?"

Cas shook his head. "Not much."

He smiled as he dashed her hopes. "We're too far off the beaten path to have many strangers passing through to blame everything on." He picked up his mail and turned to go.

"Anything I can do to help, I'll be glad to. Extra errands or man the phone longer or anything else." Gladys volunteered to Cas's back.

He turned at the door. "Thanks, but I don't know of a thing right now. Might need something typed up for the file later on."

As if he had anything to type up. Feeling gloomy, his bottom hit his chair like a dead weight. The little he had at the moment could be handled very well by his own slow hunt and peck system. He groaned at the lack of any lead or idea where to start as he pulled out the flat file he had set up.

Laying out the pictures taken at the scene he paused, glancing at the handwritten notes. Spreading them out like a hand of cards he set about getting them in order while it was still a little job.

Something not quite right nagged but eluded him until he closed the file. With a sigh, he glanced up at the clock and picked up the phone.

"Gladys, I'm going back out to the scene in this Davis case. Get hold of Doug Freeman for me. Tell him to get a camera in case we need it and some plastic bags in case we find something that was overlooked before. And tell him I'm waiting for him."

While he waited he mentally went over again what he had put in order, still haunted by the uneasy feeling. It wasn't long before he heard Doug speak to Gladys on his way in.

"I'm ready," Cas called, pushing his chair back.

He settled in the car with Doug and the equipment he brought. "Maybe when we get out there and I can see the place again without all the excitement and milling around, I'll know what's bugging me about the pictures we got."

Doug nodded. "It was such a shock, that didn't help." Doug remembered his own feelings.

They drove out Harper's Road then turned and followed county highway 220 to where the deputies had gone into the woods to get to the back of The Roadhouse.

Cas looked around as they parked.

"Is this about where you parked that evening?"

"Yeah, pretty near. We didn't want to pull off very far because it was muddy."

Cas opened the car door, examining the ground. "Be careful when you get out, we'll look for tire prints."

Doug found the place where both cars had stopped and pointed it out to him. "Easy to see. They're the only ones, and plain."

"That's some encouragement. If our car made prints that good, there must be others somewhere here too. This mire doesn't dry up very fast. It's the only good thing I can think of for swampy conditions."

"Yeah, you'd have to be a mosquito to appreciate this much standing water and humidity." Doug's eyes were already searching the side of the road nearest them.

Cas straightened up, pointing. "You go that way and I'll go the opposite direction. If we don't find anything here we'll look on the other side. But I'd bet my shirt on this side unless he stayed in the road."

It was slow work. They were thorough, but had found nothing by the time they got several car lengths away from each other. Cas waved Doug to the other side of the road. Taking their time, they bent to study every irregularity closely but found no tire tracks or anything suspicious.

Moaning, Cas put his hands on his lower back as he stood up straight.

"I'm going to sit in the car a minute," he said, rubbing his aching muscles. "No cracks about old age, please."

"It's not old age, it's the position. I didn't find anything either." Doug sounded as discouraged as Cas felt. They sat in the car, resting, Cas thinking out loud.

"Here is this murderer, or would-be murderer, his victim beside him. He couldn't have found a more likely, deserted place to kill." He shook his head. "He wouldn't have left the car in the road."

"Maybe he told her there was something wrong with the car and conned her into getting out that way. Then he might have left it on the road."

"I don't know,." Cas frowned. "Car trouble is a stale old line for this smarted-up generation. Let's go and look at the scene again. That's the main reason I came out here."

Doug took the lead and was several feet ahead, almost to the tree line. They were angling back towards the scene and had a way to go to where the body was found. Cas slowed his pace as they got closer, looking carefully at the ground and undergrowth as he went in hopes of finding something that might have been overlooked. It would take a lot of tramping around to make a difference in the healthy crop of weeds. The undergrowth here had to be cleared often. There was only a faint visible path and there was nothing unusual until they came upon some of their own tracks near the marked off area.

Both of them stood gazing down in silence at the place the body had rested when it was photographed. Doug swallowed and looked away. The only good thing he could think of was the girl probably didn't suffer.

"Peaceful out here," Doug ventured.

"Yeah." Cas stood listening to mocking birds in the trees and the murmur of water up ahead where a small brook ran into the little branch of the river. He squatted down by the area of flattened weeds. Doug squatted beside him, remembering when he had spotted the body and pointed it out to Raines.

"I couldn't believe it, or maybe it was just that I didn't want to believe it. I just stood there a minute before I pointed and Raines saw her too."

Cas nodded, "I know now what bothered me about those pictures." Cas tilted his head as they both rose. "It was the position of the body. It looked like it had been dropped instead of falling in a natural position. It was turned at an odd angle, on its back, you follow me?"

"It does make sense she would have had her arms out to break her fall or clutch at the knife, now that you mention it. Or maybe to fight her attacker off?"

Doug gestured toward the distant murmur. "You think whoever killed her might have already done it and been carrying her body? Heading for the river to dispose of it?"

"The water's so close that might have been what he had in mind. That would explain why there were no signs of a struggle here. No blood either. But there might not have been much, with the knife still in the wound."

Cas considered the possibility the victim was already dead. "But there should have been some blood, going into the heart the way it did. It seems to me if this is where she was killed there should have been that and signs of the struggle too." He looked up, jerking his head toward the sound of the water. "And remember, that little branch up ahead there, little or not, is a branch of the river."

"I know it's part of the river. It's deep enough in places if he wanted to sink the body. You know, weight it with something to hide it. But, my dad and I came out here a few times to fish for crappie and there's not enough of a current to carry it away."

"Yeah," Cas admitted. "He's got to have known it would be discovered soon. Let's go back to the road, I've got an idea."

He moved faster than he had going in. Doug was panting by the time he caught up with him. He passed the car and went on to where the shoulder was asphalt and was wider. Doug watched for anything unusual as he followed.

Cas stopped, stooping to see something better. He beckoned Doug to him.

Where he stood the asphalt went beyond the wettest part of the shoulder but there were tire prints in the dryer, sandy soil made by the front tires of a small vehicle.

"Must be one of those toy utility trucks or something like them," Doug guessed.

"It looks like he pulled off as far as he thought was safe, it being dark."

Cas squinted up the road. "If he came up 220 instead of Harper's Road he might have pulled in here, trying to stay on the asphalt. The underbrush doesn't start till farther back. It would be a good place to go in toward the stream."

"There's not too many places he could have come from out that way." Doug hesitated, scratching his head. "Assuming it's one of our local people."

"I know. These prints could also have been made by someone just turning around. But we'll take them on the off chance this is our bird."

He called in from the car, motioning Doug to sit down and rest.

"Gladys, we need someone to get casts of some tire prints we've found out here at the scene. Is there anyone there right now?"

"Yes, sir. Rhodes came in just a few minutes ago."

"Good, let me talk to him."

Rhodes had come to the door and stood listening. He took the phone.

"I'm here."

"Rhodes, we've found the prints of a small vehicle out here not too far from where Doug and Haines parked when they found the body. Looks like our killer may have come up the highway instead of from Harper's Road like we thought. Then again it may have been someone turning around and has nothing to do with this. We'll get casts of them just in case. I'm going to leave Doug out here to ride back with you. I've got something to do. Put Gladys back on."

"Yes, sir, I'm on my way. Here's Gladys."

"Yes, sir?"

"Gladys, I'm going by to see Muriel Davis before it gets any later. Call that number on my desk in there and tell her I'm coming."

CHAPTER 4

Cas saw the car in the driveway as he approached the address Muriel Davis had given him. Late model, well kept. The house had a homey air about it, the place and the car were about what he expected. He pulled over to the curb and parked in front feeling sad he hadn't made any more progress on the case. Bracing himself, knowing this was part of his job and not to be shirked. He started up the steps.

Muriel Davis opened the door before he got to it.

"Your office called," she explained. "I was watching for you."

"I need to talk with you," Cas began. "But I can come back tomorrow if that would be more convenient?"

"No, no. It's all right. It was nice of you to have them call first. And I talked with Rhodes Cromwell earlier. He said you would be coming by."

Cas felt better as Muriel smiled. She held the door and gestured for him to come in.

He guessed Muriel Davis to be about fifty-five. Had Denise comparatively late in life, he noted silently. Muriel was a few years younger than Margaret, her schoolteacher sister. She was about Connie's size, five-two, and slender. Her hair was ash blonde and becomingly arranged. She was still a beautiful woman. Cas noticed all these things and with a pang of anger at Denise's killer, also noticed the traces of tears on her cheeks.

For a few seconds neither spoke. Cas glanced around the pleasant room. It was attractively arranged, cozy and comfortable. He put his compassion aside and concentrated on the things he needed to ask.

"Thank you. As I said, I need to ask you some questions. I'm very sorry about this, Connie sends her sympathy, too."

Muriel only nodded. He took the chair Muriel indicated, determined to find out what he could and get this questioning over as soon as possible.

"First, is there anything you can tell me that you think will help us find out how this happened?"

"No, I'm afraid not." Muriel slowly shook her head. Her eyes were dark from crying and lack of sleep but she was composed.

"I've been thinking, trying to remember anything that could have warned us something was wrong. Margaret and I both have. But there was nothing. Denise had friends and acquaintances, some she was closer to than others. And I didn't let her date very much. She was only a sophomore this year...." A tear spilled over and rolled down Muriel's cheek unheeded.

Cas sat listening with patience and sympathy.

"She went out once in a while. It was when there was a play or a game at school. Activities where she would be in a group of friends. There was no special boyfriend and as far as I know she got along well with all of her friends. There was no problem with any of them that I know of."

"As routine investigation, I'm going to have to talk with everyone you can think of in her circle of friends," Cas told her. "I will need to talk with all of them whether they feel they can help or not. We don't have much to go on right now. But rest assured, we are doing all we can to find out what happened and who did this."

Muriel nodded again, her head bowed. Another tear glistened as it spilled over.

"I'm sorry to have to bother you, Mrs. Davis. If you think of anything at all, no matter how small or seemingly unimportant it is, please call me. If I'm not in my office Gladys will let me know and I will get back with you just as soon as I can. Have you had a chance yet to make out that list of Denise's friends for me?"

"Yes." Muriel looked up, seeming to come back from memory to reality. "Yes, I have. I started on it as soon as Rhodes Cromwell told me you would need it. I think I left it in the kitchen, I'll get it." She rose as she spoke.

"Would you like some coffee?" Muriel paused to ask.

"No," Cas smiled. "But thank you."

Muriel left the room and Cas got up too. He paced, looking around the room. He took a closer look at the family pictures displayed on a table and a bookshelf. Some were of her and Denise. There was one of her with her sister, Margaret Avery, another of her sister, and two of Denise at different ages.

Cas was holding a picture of Muriel accepting some kind of award from Judge Spruce when she returned. He set it down carefully on the bookshelf and took the list she handed him.

"Thank you. My home number is written on the back of the card I gave you. You can call me at the office or at home."

At his office, Cas stopped to give Gladys the list of names Muriel had given him.

"Gladys, get the phone book and find numbers for all these students she doesn't have a number down for. You'd better check the others, too, to make sure they're right. And leave three or four lines between each one for notes."

"Yes, sir." She took the list and reached for the phone book.

Cas gave silent thanks for Gladys as he always did. He could hear her voice from his office as he waded through his mail, checking something with the operator. He wasn't expecting miracles but some of the friends on Muriel's list might know something they didn't realize was important. Right now there was absolutely nothing to give him a start on the case. His innate logic kicked in to reassure him. Murder had been done and somebody had to know something.

"If no concrete facts turn up, maybe I'll at least be able to tell which ones are lying or hedging for some reason, and go from there...."

He went to the credenza and examined the casts of the tire prints Rhodes and Doug had brought in, touching them in several places with his fingers. They were made by a little foreign truck as Doug had pointed out. He squinted at a couple of worn places long and wide enough to identify the vehicle if they got lucky and found something to compare them with. A small rock was stuck in the tread of one of them. "Not much help, as many gravel roads as there were in this area."

He sat down and opened the flat file on the Davis case before reaching for the phone. He dialed the coroner's office.

After several rings he was surprised to hear Clint answer the call himself.

"We're a little short of help around here today," he explained.

"I know how that is. I don't mean to put the rush on you about this Davis case but we haven't got a thing to go on. Is there anything you can tell me yet? Anything that might at least give me something to work with?"

"I was looking at it when you called. Some notes. Hasn't been typed up yet, just some handwritten notes and a tape that will have to be transcribed. Hang on a second, will you?"

"Sure." Cas tried not to get his hopes up. He heard footsteps and the sound of papers being shuffled.

"Here we are. Time of death as close as we can figure was between ten and eleven o'clock. The murder weapon was driven in with such force we had to work on it to get it out and examine the area around it. Someone has written that here. You knew that, huh." Clint read to himself before continuing.

"No abnormalities. Well nourished female about fifteen, et cetera." He paused again. "She had eaten at some fast food place shortly before she died, the usual burger and fries."

"She hadn't been raped or molested, you said earlier. Were there any other wounds? Or maybe needle marks or anything like that? I don't really expect she might have been experimenting with drugs after talking with her mother. But sometimes the families and the ones who love them best are the last to know about such things."

"No, nothing like that. And nothing in the handwritten notes about anything in her system. She wasn't on drugs."

His voice rose a little. "Here's something. There weren't any other puncture wounds, but there was bruising around one of her ankles and the upper part of her foot."

"You mean she may have been tied up?"

"No. There would have been different marks if there had been a rope or chain or a restraint like that. I went down and looked at them when I first glanced over this. She wasn't tied up. It's more like a turned ankle, and it must have been extremely painful. It happened before the stabbing."

"Before the stabbing. You think she may have been trying to get away?"

"I don't know. I suppose it's possible, given what happened to her. That's all we found. The tape I've got here deals with organs, weights, and technical things that won't help you."

"You mean I wouldn't understand it?" Cas grinned into the phone.

"I didn't say that," Clint laughed. "But, what it boils down to, is there weren't any abnormalities and the stab wound to the heart is what killed her."

"There was nothing else then, but the bruised ankle."

Cas tried to think of something constructive to ask while he had Clint on the phone, but came up with nothing.

"Well, thanks for the Pine County translation. It looks like I'm going to have to keep leaning on everybody who knew her or had any connection with her family to get a start on this." He paused, discouraged. "They already hate to see me coming."

"There is one other thing," Clint hesitated. "Almost too trifling to bring up."

"Nothing is too trifling. Right now, I'd be grateful for anything. What is it?"

"The report hasn't been typed up yet as I said, but in the handwritten notes on one of the forms under Toxicology is written, 'trace of mild sedative'. There weren't any drugs, poisons or anything unusual except that. Trace means it was so little it wouldn't have had any effect. It was just noted because it was there. You said anything would help, so I'm telling you about it."

"You're trying awfully hard not to get my hopes up, aren't you? What was the sedative, do you know?"

"No idea. The notes, word for word, say 'trace of mild tranquilizer or sedative', guess it will be on the report when it's typed up, but it's nothing. It could be one of the sleeping pills they sell at most drugstores. But Cas, a trace wouldn't have any effect at all on a young, healthy, teenager."

"Hmm, just this 'trace of a mild sedative' is all."

"Right. And don't hang too much on that," Clint insisted. "The only thing unusual about it is the age of the victim. It probably wouldn't even be worth mentioning in someone say, sixty or more. Tranquilizers and pain killers are common in that age group. My mother takes a mild tranquilizer. She calls it her 'cope pill'. So the only thing unusual about it is the age factor and I'm sure it had no effect at all on the victim."

"All right, you've dampened down what little hope I'd built up. So all we've got besides the fatal stab wound is the mild, not even effective tranquilizer and the bruised ankle?"

"That's it. The bruised ankle and the top of the foot. Probably twisted it some way. Hadn't had time to swell much."

"Okay. Thanks for your help, and explaining the notes too. I'd have wondered at that last entry."

"You're welcome, sorry I couldn't help more. This will be typed up on a form soon as we can get somebody roped in to catch us up on our paperwork."

"Okay, thanks again."

Hanging up the phone, Cas went back to the skimpy file. He wrote down everything Clint had told him and added questions and some guesses of his own about the tranquilizer, none of which he felt would help. He drew a line and wrote, 'sleeping pill?' and 'cope pill?' after Clint's comments.

He still considered the possibility of a sleeping pill, remembering Muriel had thought Denise was asleep when she looked in on her the night before they knew she was missing.

Cas resolved to ask Muriel about the sleeping pill next time he talked to her. Maybe she did have something on her mind and couldn't sleep? He'd check that out. He was still holding the file, sifting possibilities, when Gladys came in.

"I know that was a long list, but I was glad to see Mrs. Davis wrote down everyone she could think of. And this gives me a list I can check off or tell who I've talked to twice," Cas said.

"Oh, it's not so long. I've still got some to check, but I knew you were wanting this so I brought this part. It's most of them. Since she wrote these first, they're probably the most important anyway."

Cas favored her with the skeptical look he always gave her when she tried to do his detecting for him. She ignored it as she always did and went to finish the list as the phone rang. Cas reached for the phone.

"Sheriff Larkin." Cas answered with one eye on the neat pages.

"I don't know whether this is the right way to report it or not," an irritated voice began. "But I'm missing two cows and a calf. And it's not the first time, either!"

That got his attention. Cas held the phone away from his ear. The voice rose as it continued and its anger showed. It was a loud male voice and full of barely suppressed indignation.

"Yes, sir," Cas said as soon as he got a chance. "Let me get your name and a few facts and there will be someone at your place this afternoon to take a full report. You say this is not the first time?"

"No," the voice sounded a little calmer. "This is the last straw, though. The calf was the last straw. I've been missing a head or two at a time for a little over a year now, and it's got to stop."

"Yes, sir, I certainly agree with you there. I wish you had called us sooner. Was there some reason why you didn't?"

"Well, ah," There was a pause.

"I think I recognize your voice. Is this Caleb Martin?"

"Yes," Caleb was pleased. "I didn't think you'd remember me."

"Your place is on the other side of Peaceful Ridge, isn't it?"

"Yes, you go on past the Peaceful Ridge Cemetery entrance. Then a bit farther on, you will see the gate to my place. Did you say you'll be out this afternoon?" Caleb wanted action as soon as possible.

"I've got something I have to do this afternoon regarding another case," Cas apologized. "But a deputy will be out there and take a report. We'll try to find out who's responsible for this and keep it from happening again. Be sure to tell the deputy everything you can remember that might be of help."

"I will, and thank you. I'll be expecting him then, this afternoon."

Cas replaced the receiver wondering why Caleb Martin hadn't reported the cattle thefts. Even losing a head at a time would have been an expensive loss and he had certainly sounded mad enough to report it.

He stepped over to his office door. "Gladys that was Caleb Martin on the phone. He said he's missing some cattle and it's not the first time. Someone needs to go over to his place and make a report on it. Send Rhodes as soon as he gets back. He's good at handling ruffled feelings and getting information while he's at it. He knows where Caleb Martin's place is."

Gladys looked at the wall clock. "Okay. He should be in any minute now. And here are the rest of the names and phone numbers you wanted."

"Thanks. I hope I'll be able to find out something from some of these friends. Looks like it's going to take a while to find a place to start on this." He went back into his office, reading the rest of the list.

Muriel had obviously given the list a lot of thought. There were more names than Cas was aware of in her and Missy's high school classes. Most of the family names sounded familiar to him. The children's names were not unless they had been in some kind of trouble, and there were very few of those. "Thank goodness!" He mumbled to himself, his eyes busy.

After reading it over Cas decided to show the list to Missy when he got home and get a peer's eye view of these friends.

Muriel Davis's number was not in the file. He looked it up and added it before dialing her number. Muriel answered at once.

"This is Sheriff Larkin. I'm sorry to bother you again so soon. I meant to ask you about something when I was out there this afternoon."

"That's all right. I tried to tell you everything I could remember of what Rhodes said you might need. What else is it you need to know?"

"Your sister, Margaret, said Denise had gone out the window once before. Do you remember that?"

"Yes," Muriel's voice had a smile in it. Cas was relieved it wasn't a bad memory he had brought up.

"As I remember, it was about a year ago. Maybe not quite that long. Denise had just started going out some. That is, with groups like the Latin Club, and with several friends to a game or a play. That particular time she wanted to go to the mall to shop and have a milkshake. That sounds innocent enough, but they wanted to stay until the mall closes about ten o'clock. There was no definite plan and no older ones to go with them, so it sounded like what they call 'hanging out' to me. I wouldn't let her go. She got mad at me. Pouted and went up to her room early."

Muriel's voice sounded soft and distant as she thought back. "Margaret and I both remember that night, all right. Denise went out the window while she was still mad at me, I guess. She evidently hadn't been gone long when I went up to see if she would like some hot chocolate. No one should go to sleep mad," Muriel explained. The affection in her voice was audible as Cas imagined her smiling into the phone.

Cas smiled too as he listened to Muriel's voice, not interrupting, picturing the teenage rebellion.

"My sister, Margaret, went to the mall and I waited at home in her room. Then in about an hour after we discovered she was gone here came Denise, over the carport and in the window. She sure was surprised to see me! She'd been gone about two hours. Must have been a real lark for her. She thought she was home free and got by with it. I sat her down and talked to her, not losing my temper. Since she was home and all right, it really was sort of a comic situation. But after talking to her, and impressing her about how worried I was about her, I grounded her for two weeks. There weren't any more trips out the window until this one." Muriel's voice had dropped, sounding hurt. Cas pricked up his ears.

"That's one reason I worried so much as soon as we found out she was gone. She knew how I would worry. I just, you know, I just had a bad feeling about it because I didn't think she would do it again. Not unless, oh, I don't know. I just didn't think she would slip out that window again after our talk and she understood how worried I was."

"You feel whatever she went out for was pretty important to her then?"

"Yes. I just don't know what it could have been. I've wondered and tried to think where she could have gone, but I don't know. I wish I could be more help," Muriel added sadly.

"Thank you. I appreciate your cooperation, trying to help. We're getting everything we can learn to try to put together what happened. We have to keep asking questions and talking to people. It takes an awful lot of time and investigation to get all the bits and pieces of information together. And there's a lot more of this ahead of us, so bear with us."

"I understand, it's all right."

"You feel," Cas pressed, "It must have been something important to her for her to go out that window again?"

Muriel took a deep breath. "Either important to her or something she didn't want to talk to me or Margaret about, though I can't imagine what that would be. As I told you before, there weren't any problems here at home or with any of her friends that I was aware of."

"All right, thank you. You have my card with the office and my home number on it, so call whenever you want to."

Cas broke the connection and sat eyeing the silent phone. "So, it was something important that called her out that window. Something or someone…?"

CHAPTER 5

A t home a few feet into the drive, Cas saw the light in the kitchen window and felt his lips curve up in an expectant smile. He wondered what Connie was fixing for dinner. Whatever nightmares the office held, his worries lifted when he turned into the driveway at home. They lived just far enough out of town for privacy and space, home was his seven acre sanctuary.

Missy heard his truck and leaned out her bedroom window upstairs to call and wave to him. "Hi, dad!"

Getting out, Cas beckoned to her to come down. He pointed at the kitchen door. "I need your expert opinion," he called back to her..

"You're pretty bad off, then!" Missy laughed, wrinkling her nose. "I'll be right down!"

He hoped she would have time to look at the list he brought home with him while Connie finished dinner. The door knob turned as he reached for it.

"Hi!" Connie opened the door and gave him a big hug. "Hope you had a good day, welcome home, and all that." She kissed his cheek and snuggled against him.

"Something smells good." He returned her hug and kissed her forehead. "You do, too," he murmured against her hair.

"I borrowed some of Missy's bubble bath. The other good smell is peach upside down cake. It's all that brown sugar and butter you're smelling. And it turned out just right." She gently turned him towards the counter.

Cas was admiring the swirl of peaches and brown sugar when Missy came in.

"Didn't that turn out great? Mom, you're an artist."

"Sure, some artist. It's really simple. All in the wrist. Next time if you're here and not too busy with homework you can try turning one out."

"Well, whatever you did must have been the thing to do," Cas let his admiration show. "Have I got time to show Missy this list of Denise's friends before dinner?"

"Uh-huh. It will be a little while. Go sit in the den and get comfortable. I'll set the table," she told Missy when she looked back.

In the den Cas handed Missy the list and turned on the lamp on the end table between them. "You look these over and I'll get some paper to make notes on." He came back with a legal pad and pencil.

Her eyes on the list, Missy scanned quickly. "I know all these people, dad. Or sort of know them. Do you want to know which ones were particular friends of Denise's or what?"

"Take them one at a time and tell me whatever you know about them. General description, anything out of the norm. Special friends of Denise's or anything you can think of, including what grade they're in. I don't know what to ask right now. I'm looking for any little hint that might start unraveling things that led up to what happened and why it happened. All I know for sure right now is I'm going to talk to all of them. And as many times as it takes."

"Okay." Missy took a deep breath. She got settled in her chair and started on the list.

"The first one is a sophomore like Denise was. She dated him once that I know of. I think it was a basketball game or something."

There were not many she pointed out as dates and the dates were occasions at school. Plays, games, school activities. They went through the list, Missy telling whatever she knew or thought relevant about each one; which she thought were particularly close friends or other things which came to mind.

"These names on the first page that start with D's were the ones I saw her with most often. I guess they are the ones her mother thought of first. They're the ones who were at the slumber party, dad. All I can tell you is the ones I saw her with at school and at games and things. We weren't very close."

"That's what I wanted you to do. Diane and Doris were about the closest friends you know of then?"

"Yes, and I guess mom told you, they were at the slumber party. Denise was invited too."

Missy looked up at her dad, her eyes haunted with guilt. "There we were, all of us having a good time. And somewhere out in the dark, Denise was getting killed! It's hard to believe that she's gone! I saw her last Friday at school, standing at her locker in the hall. I guess I'll always remember that's the last time I saw her. And now," she shook her head. "I'm glad you told us she didn't suffer, dad."

Cas nodded, confirming it. "No, she didn't suffer. It must have been too fast for her to feel much of anything, probably even fright, and it's over now. It's hard for all of us to believe. There's nothing we can do for her now except to find out what happened and keep it from happening to anybody else."

He gave her the second sheet of names. "These are some more names Mrs. Davis wrote down, said that Denise had mentioned them by name, or they had come once or twice to their house for some reason or occasion. It's the first six she thought to list I'll concentrate on most. The closest ones. I'm not sure about these yet."

Missy looked over the second sheet and shook her head. "No, I don't think any of these were with her very much that I can remember. But she always ate lunch with a big group in the lunch room, so it's kind of hard to tell."

"All right." Cas straightened the two sheets. "I wanted to learn what I could before talking to them." He replaced the list in his file and looked up. Missy had a worried look on her face.

"What is it? Is there something else you thought of?"

"Dad," Missy said slowly as if she was not sure she should point it out. "Darrell Spruce should be on this list. He dated her. I saw them at the school play. Denise was with Darrell and Doris and Diane and their dates sat with them not far from where Chuck and I were sitting."

"You're sure it was Darrell?"

"Oh, yes. The auditorium isn't that big. I noticed because I had seen them having their lunch together a couple of days before that."

Cas frowned. "I wonder why her mother left his name off the list? Do you know if they ever dated before, or just that once? Maybe it was only once and that's why she left it off." He recalled Muriel Davis's lovely, sad face patiently answering his questions.

The grim expression that followed denied that one date was a valid excuse to leave a name off the list as another reason crossed his mind.

"I hope she didn't leave Darrell's name off because he's Judge Spruce's son. Do you remember ever seeing them together before the lunch and the school play?"

"No. I was surprised too. That's why I remembered it. He's a senior and will be going to college next year. And even if he wasn't, he's always acting like he thinks he's better or smarter or something than the rest of us."

Cas pounced on it. "He's hateful? A bully?"

"No, it's not that. Just his superior attitude sometimes." Missy's grin widened. "I was surprised to see him with a lowly sophomore, that's all."

"I'll ask Mrs. Davis about it next time I talk to her. Thank you for your help."

"Dad?" Missy started then stopped, undecided.

"It's okay to tell me if it's something you're not sure about. It will be between us."

Missy still stood looking a little worried. Cas added ruefully, "You'd be surprised how much guess work there is in being a good detective. You have to explore all possibilities, no matter how far out they may seem at the time. Now, what is it?"

"There's some kind of group or club I've been hearing about for several months now. I've only heard rumors and snatches of conversations but Darrel has something to do with it, I think. I've seen him look daggers at whoever is talking about it, and they stop talking. Immediately!"

"Something secret, huh? Can you remember what it was you heard? Or who it was he looked daggers at? What about Denise, since you saw them together. Did he ever look daggers at Denise or actually threaten her or anyone else?"

"No," Missy shook her head. "I never have heard him threaten anyone. But once, in the crowd when we were waiting to go into the assembly hall at school I saw him look daggers at someone. Like he could, I don't know, just literally wring his neck! I don't remember who it was talking because I didn't pay any attention until I saw the look on Darrell's face. Whoever it was, was saying something about a goat." She shook her head. "It didn't make any sense to me."

"A goat? You're sure he said a goat, not something that just sounded like goat?"

"That's all I am sure about, dad. That he said something about a goat, I mean. I hadn't been paying any attention. We were waiting to go into assembly and there was a lot of talking and I heard this boy's voice say something about a goat. I turned around and saw Darrell look at him like that, like he'd gladly strangle him!"

"Do you know who he was looking at?"

"No. I just remember looking at Darrell, surprised at how mean he looked. Then the doors opened and the crowd started moving and I couldn't see him anymore."

"Did Darrell say anything at all when he looked like that, or did you hear anything else? From the other boy or anyone else?"

"No." Missy shook her head. "It was just the way Darrel looked. There wasn't anything else. The doors were opened then and everyone was moving forward, going in. But I remember when it was. It was not long after someone made that mess at the cemetery." Missy looked at him, "No one ever admitted to that did they?"

"No, the caretakers cleaned it up and let it drop. Not much real damage was done except the mess. Two of the older tombstones were pushed over and there was a lot of trash thrown around. Most of it from fast food places. There also was blood on one of the stones from a dead chicken we found."

He winked at Missy as he got up. "No one ever claimed the chicken, either."

Missy giggled.

After dinner Cas showed Connie the names Muriel Davis had given him. "This is the list of Denise's friends I showed Missy. Do you recognize any of them or know anything about any of them?"

She looked it over briefly. "No, not really. The only students I know are the friends who come home with Missy. And Chuck, of course. I see he's not on here."

"I'll start talking to some of them tomorrow at the school. I've got to cover every possible source of information. We haven't got a thing so far except everybody liked her. But popular or not, someone killed her. There's got to be a reason behind it." Cas's eyes were distant, his mind back in his office.

"That's tomorrow." Connie said firmly. "You put that away and rest. Get your mind off of it. Want another cup of coffee to wash down your dessert?"

With the Mom half of her brain she nodded at Missy who pointed upstairs and left.

"Sounds good, and that cake looks good." He looked up at her, "I guess you've got two more weeks to work in Fort Craig?"

"That's what I thought when I resigned. But Mr. Allen told me today I've got enough vacation and personal holidays to make tomorrow my last day if I want to. And I want to."

She flashed him a radiant smile. "I'm getting excited about staying home. Especially, since it won't be any great tragedy if I can't get any work here in Maryvale. And that's verified by the Head of the House, no less!"

Cas laughed, "I told you I'm glad of it. Take it easy for a while, you might like it." He grinned, happy because she was.

Connie poured him more coffee. "There may not be any choice, but we'll see. I'll get up bright and early the first day and call on some people and see how it goes."

The morning's mail brought Cas the autopsy report on Denise Davis. He pulled it out of the stack, anxious to see what it looked like in black and white on the proper form.

It took him a while to read it, impressed at how thorough it was. All the organ weights and things Clint told him about were there.

Cas took out a pen and paper to jot down the main points without having to wade through all that medical jargon again. He condensed the information in language he could understand to have it readily at hand and because he remembered his notes better after he'd written them down. The main points noted, he wrote a few more notes and questions of his own as he organized the file.

The bruised ankle and the top of the foot, the left one, he noted. It had happened just before she was killed so it was important to the sequence of events. Must be, if he could just figure out how to get at what led up to the attack. The knife went straight in, with a lot of force. Last meal was fast food, then there was the trace of mild sedative. He went back. Fast food? A young killer? He hurriedly went on.

Coming to the organ weights he smiled at how careful Clint had been to explain about that. He put his hand written notes on top where he could get to them first. He turned the autopsy form over to scan it again and saw something new. It was on the back and he hadn't noticed it. It was under Scars and Identifying Marks.

"A star. Done with ink. On her forehead, up under her bangs."

Cas wonderingly studied the notation like it was some new kind of bug.

"Now, what is that all about? Why would she have drawn a star on her forehead, and hidden it under her hair if she thought it was ornamental? Or maybe it was hidden on purpose? Kids get funny ideas!"

He shrugged and reached for the phone.

"Gladys, I'm going over to the high school and will be there a while if you need me. Yes, I'm going now." He closed the drawer with a curious look at the file, still wondering why Denise had the decoration.

He checked his watch as he parked in front of the school. It was two o'clock. He planned to look at the files on some of the list and perhaps be able to see the students scheduled for study hall or were free for some other reason to come to the office where he could talk to them.

At the school he almost bumped into Janice Cobb, who was coming out of the office. Janice was as valuable to the school as Gladys was to Cas. She had married and moved away after college. But when the marriage failed, she came home to work for the Maryvale school system. She was attractive and fortyish and on Cas's list classified as 'good people'. The school was fortunate to have her services.

"Hi, Cas. What can we do for you today?" Friendly and helpful were also on her list of virtues.

"I want to look at some files. It's in connection with the Davis case."

"Okay. Is it all right if I just show you where they are and leave you with it for about an hour? I got drafted to monitor a physical education class whose teacher isn't here. I'll be in the gym next door if you need me for anything. I'll be back in an hour." She smiled, "Less, if I can manage it."

"That's fine with me. I can take my time looking at the files. Where are they?"

"In the file cabinets along that wall are the students' files. Over there, faculty. There's an extension at the gym but I don't know whether or not I'd hear it. The number's three-oh-three if you want to try it. But I will definitely be back in an hour, hopefully less."

"Don't hurry on my account. I'll look and make any notes I need to. I won't need to call. Thank you."

Janice left and Cas closed the door behind her.

Having the place to himself was a lucky break and he used it. He could look up anything he wanted to without any interruptions or explanations. He looked at the students' files then while he had the chance, looked up something he had wondered about in the other bank of files.

Going to the faculty files he pulled Margaret Avery's first in case Janice came back for something. It held the usual statistics and qualifications he assumed most of the rest of the faculty had. A brief look was enough. He crossed back to the students' files.

Still wondering why his name had been left off the list Muriel gave him he pulled Darrell Spruce's file first, laying his list on the desk behind him.

He had finished looking at Darrell's and several files on his list and was rereading one of them when Janice got back.

"Did you find everything you wanted?" Janice was a little out of breath from hurrying.

"Yes, thank you, I did. I need another favor though."

He handed her the list of Denise's closest friends as he spoke. "Are any of these students perhaps in a study hall, or gym, or otherwise available to come to the office so I can talk to them? I should be able to talk to about three of them before the end of the school day, if there are that many available."

Janice studied the list. "Yes, this boy and these two girls can come now. If you come back tomorrow, the other three will be in a physical education class at three o'clock. You can see them then. Oh, wait." She frowned.

"What is it?" He took back the list and eyed the three she had indicated for today. "Is there a problem?"

"Not with the three for today. I'll get them for you. But, one of the boys left for tomorrow is not here. He's out sick. I can get his home phone number if you want it?"

"I want it. And get his address, too. I may go by and see him at home."

Janice wrote the phone number and address at the bottom of his list.

Cas noted the address was the same street as one on the list Gladys had typed for the file. "Thanks."

"I'll get the first three for you. Wait in the office there if you want to, I'm acting principal today."

"I'm impressed, that pay good?"

"Only in aggravation!" Janice grinned, "All I can handle. I won't be a minute."

Cas nodded, but waited where he was.

Entering the office, the two girls and the boy smiled nervously as Janice introduced them.

"Will you two wait here," Cas gestured. "I want to talk to each of you." He beckoned one of the girls into the principal's office.

Cas smiled as he sat down, trying to put her more at ease. "Won't you have a seat," he consulted his list, "Marilyn?"

"Yes, sir?"

"You knew Denise Davis and were in the same grade she was, isn't that right?"

"Yes, sir." Marilyn was a slender, polite, and typical looking sophomore and seemed cooperative as she settled in the chair. Cas asked a few more routine things before pressing her with more direct questions.

"Did you know of any sort of problem or disagreement Denise had with anyone? Anyone who might have been envious or any other kind of problem?"

Marilyn shook her head. "No sir, I can't think of anything at all. Everyone liked Denise."

Her expression was sad and bewildered at the same time. "I don't know of anyone who would want to—to—hurt her."

She was uncomfortable trying to express her feelings. She sat gazing at the desk. Wariness at bay for the moment, sorrow was the only emotion showing on her young face.

"Are you a member of the club?" Cas asked without warning.

He followed up quickly with, "What do you know about the meeting up on Peaceful Ridge?"

Marilyn paled. Her nervousness returned, worse than before. She shook her head without speaking. There was something different in her eyes now. She squirmed a little in her chair, glancing at the door as if she wanted to escape.

Cas wondered if it was fear about this secret club he saw and pressed on. "Where does this club meet, or does it meet different places? Who else do you know who are members of it?" He asked the questions in rapid succession, watching her closely. Marilyn clasped her hands and squirmed in her chair, nervously shifting her feet, seemingly unable to tear her eyes from his.

"I, ah, I don't know anything about it," she stammered.

Cas glanced away then turned a skeptical look on her. "Don't tell me you've never heard of it?"

His sarcasm stung, his disbelief obvious. Marilyn twisted her handkerchief, darting miserable glances at the closed door. She bowed her head, unable to look at him. "I don't know anything about it, Sheriff Larkin."

Cas didn't comment and after a few seconds of uncomfortable silence, she lifted her head to meet his eyes. "I liked Denise. I don't know anyone who didn't, or why anyone would want to hurt her. Please, may I go now?"

Cas knew this speech was the truth as surely as he knew the denial of knowing anything about the club was not. He reached for one of his cards. "Yes, you can leave, Marilyn. But I may have to talk to you again, either here or at your

home. If you want to talk to me, if you think of anything
that might shed some light on this, no matter how
unimportant you think it is, call me at the number on this
card."

Marilyn accepted the card he handed her.

"Anything you tell me will stay between us. So if you
think of something you feel would help clear up what
happened or might have any connection with it, call the
number on that card."

"Yes, sir." Marilyn made her escape.

He called Doris and Curtis next. Though he asked his
routine questions and followed up with some about the
club, he got the same negative results as with Marilyn.
None of them knew of anything negative about Denise's
relationships with her friends. As for the club, they didn't
admit knowing anything about it. But they were so nervous
hearing the questions it was obvious they either knew about
it or were members. They were just too frightened to talk
about it.

"Someone's done a good job of frightening them." Cas
frowned as they left quickly, not waiting to completely
close the door.

Janice stuck her head in, her pleasant face lightening the
gloom that was trying to settle over him. "I guess I'll see
you tomorrow at three?" She watched as he collected his
notes.

"Yes, I'll be here. Let's see. That's Marilyn, Doris, and
Curtis. Tomorrow I'll see Diane and Dennis. Casey is the
one that's at home sick."

"Right." Janice's dimples showed.

"Until tomorrow then. And thanks for your help, Janice, I
appreciate it. If anyone comes to you with anything or
wants to talk with me be sure to let me know. I'll leave a
few cards here on the desk, just in case. Thanks again."

His briefcase and notes he laid beside him on the car seat
as he left. Reading the address Janice had written out for
him he made a note to himself to get the few notes he'd
taken typed up when he got back if Gladys wasn't too busy.

Casey's home address he found with no difficulty and pulled up in front of it, wishing he'd thought to call first.

A woman he felt must be Casey's mother opened the door to him. Her face took on a puzzled expression when she saw him. She glanced out at his car at the curb.

"I'm sorry to bother you," Cas apologized. "I went by the school and talked to some of Denise Davis's friends and learned Casey was absent due to illness. May I talk to him, please? I won't be long, just some routine questions."

Casey's mother was hesitant and Cas added, "I'm talking to all of her friends in an effort to find anything that can shed some light on what happened to her or what led up to it." His voice hardened a little as he added, "Is Casey able to get up, or should I go in to see him?" The way he worded it and his expression made it clear he meant to question Casey.

"I guess it might be better if you come with me, he's in his bedroom." She opened the door for him and crossed the living room to enter a hallway. Cas followed.

Pausing in the hall, he heard her talking to someone in the bedroom before she beckoned to him.

"He's not really sick," Mrs. Taylor explained. "Just awfully sore. He will be able to go back to school in another day or so."

Cas went in and sat in a chair which had been placed near the bed. He started when he boy turned toward him.

Casey had a black eye, a messy looking cut above his eyebrow, and his lips were swollen and split. He seemed careful not to move any more than he had to. His expression and the rainbow hue of healing wounds told more about his pain than he would admit out loud.

"Casey," Cas asked in his no-nonsense tone. "Who did this to you?"

"Oh, it was only a misunderstanding. There aren't any hard feelings now. It's all been cleared up."

Cas didn't buy it. "Someone beat you up so bad you're too sore to get up. That doesn't sound like any mistake or minor disagreement to me. Now tell me. Who did this to you?"

"Would you believe it if I told you I don't know them?" Casey asked so hopefully it was comical.

"Would I be sheriff if I was that stupid?" Cas replied in the same tone.

"I guess not." Casey tried to grin, but his mouth was too sore.

They heard someone stifle a chuckle and Casey's mother came to sit on the end of the bed.

"Casey," she entreated her son. "I don't want to be afraid I'm never going to see you again when you go back to school. Tell the sheriff who it was who did this to you. Please?"

"I can't, mom." Casey spoke directly to his mother. "If it just drops now there'll be no more trouble, I promise. He only did this to punish me for something he thinks I did."

Punish. Punish? The word was somehow familiar, but eluded Cas. He couldn't place where he'd heard it, just that it was recently.

Aloud, Cas asked, "Who is it that wanted to punish you and what for? If I hurt as bad as I know you do I'd want to see whoever hurt me that much get what's coming to him."

"I can't tell you. I'm sorry," Casey added with an apologetic look at his mother.

"I think you're making a mistake. What if this person does this again? Or worse?" Cas eyed the bruises and split lip as he spoke.

"He won't." Casey seemed sure. "It'll be all right now. It's all over."

Cas sympathized with Casey's mother. "You can stay if you want to while I ask my questions. And if you find out any more about this," he gestured toward Casey. "Call and let me know." He gave her one of his cards. He noticed she was attractive, about Connie's age and dressed neatly and casually as Connie did.

"I will. Thank you." She tucked the card into a sweater pocket. "And I'd like to stay."

Cas asked all the questions he had asked the others with the same results. When he asked about the secret club,

Casey looked down and wouldn't meet his eyes.

"No, I don't know anything about it or of anyone who belongs to it, or might belong to it," Casey carefully told the sheet in front of him.

Cas knew without looking at his mother she was as concerned as he was about finding out who had given Casey those bruises. He left, hoping she could change his mind about naming them.

Back in his office unanswered questions about Denise and her killer, the secret club, and the beating someone gave Casey Taylor churned in Cas's mind.

An invisible killer, an invisible club. But their results were certainly visible. Cas clenched his fists. Denise was dead and someone or more likely, two someones, had worked Casey Taylor over good.

The two bursts of violence must be somehow connected but how eluded him as he pulled out the file and his writing pad. Putting the notes about Casey in a separate file he wrote down everything he'd heard, thought of, and some remote possibilities along with things to follow up on. He kept the two files together.

It was obvious the three students he had talked to were either members of this mysterious club no one wanted to talk about or knew who the members were. Casey was too, and he'd got a beating for some reason. Maybe he had told someone about the club and been punished for it.

Punished! It fell into place.

He remembered what Missy had said she overheard at the slumber party about somebody being punished. And by the devil? Yes, this is the work of some of the hooligans in that mysterious, anonymous club. He scowled at the double file and closed it, leaving any more organizing or questions for later.

Casey Taylor's bruised face haunted him as he drove home. He was a nice clean kid, Cas thought. He couldn't look him in the eye and tell a lie when he was asked about that club, even though he knew neither Cas nor his mother believed him. For some reason he thought he couldn't talk about it.

"Kids! I'd like to get hold of the low life that beat him up like that and give him, or them, a dose of their own medicine." Cas thought. His knuckles showed white on the steering wheel.

CHAPTER 6

"Today's the day!" Connie's heart danced.

Her excitement mounted as she hurriedly inspected the kitchen. All the debris from a hurried breakfast was cleaned up or in the dishwasher. She turned her attention to her own appearance. More nervous than she dreamed she would be, she examined her nail polish as she climbed the stairs.

She chose a light suit and the shoes she'd bought to work in. Moving quickly she concentrated on preparations to keep from worrying she wouldn't find any local business or professional office in need of her services. She scolded herself to get on with it as she walked resolutely out the door.

She laid her purse along with the envelope with the resume and Jed Allen's recommendation in it on the car seat beside her and backed the car around to head out the long driveway. On the way to her new career? She tried not to think about it. Being able to take her time, along with the conviction her decision was right, calmed her enough to let her enjoy her short trip to town.

Everything looked so pretty in the spring. If she didn't have any luck after the three calls she had scheduled she promised herself she would just come back and enjoy being home. For the first day, anyway.

She drove around the square admiring its quaint old-fashioned look as she always did. The courthouse that housed the city offices was almost exactly the same size as the old Nelson mansion across the street from it. The little park in the middle of the square made a pretty picture with its fountain and iron benches to sit on. The Nelson mansion was beautiful on its own. It had azaleas almost in bloom and other foliage thrusting through the wrought iron fence surrounding it.

Admiring the old mansion and the azaleas she was glad the city council had decided to keep the square the way it was when the city was incorporated. That it was so long ago was part of its charm. Pride swelled her heart and came out to form a smile on her lips as she drove.

The Nelson mansion housed a large and much enjoyed county library. The City Beautiful Commission saw to the gardening and upkeep of it and the rest of the town square. Connie drove slowly, enjoying her unaccustomed leisure.

She turned and drove past The Smithy. It hadn't changed very much either though it was now in the business of selling hearty stew and chili in the winter and sandwiches and ice cream in the summer. It still looked much as it had when shoeing horses and ironwork were its only functions. Half of it was the open blacksmith shop with a dirt floor, where in the summer there were tables set out to eat, visit, and people watch when the weather was warm. The other half was the actual restaurant part where the food was prepared and had seating for the winter months.

Two blocks down a side street Connie stopped at The Secretary's Necessary. The quaint name always brought out a giggle.

The place was well named. It had everything from paper clips on up. She wanted to get some copies of her resume and the recommendation from her job in Fort Craig.

Connie thanked the Lord for copy machines.

She looked critically at the papers. She had been hanging onto them like a drowning man clutching a log. There was a tiny ink stain on the resume but it didn't detract from the content and might not even show up on the copies since it was at the bottom.

These were all that stood between her pride and the embarrassment of being unemployed. The thought still scared her.

Glancing in the window as she parked she made a guess at what she would need. She decided on twenty copies of each so she wouldn't have to come back.

"If I haven't got any encouragement after making twenty calls I guess I'd better try something else whether I've been endorsed by the Head of the House or not!"

While she waited for her copies she bought a manila folder to put them in and two typewriter ribbons, resolving to keep her receipts just in case for her tax return.

With her copies and bolstered up determination the first office she visited was Dick Randolph's law office.

When she entered, a receptionist at a desk just inside the door looked up. Connie mentally crossed her fingers and asked, "May I see Mr. Randolph?"

"Do you have an appointment?" The question was softened by a friendly smile.

"No, I don't have an appointment. My name is Connie Larkin and I would like to talk to him about possibly doing some work for him. I don't mind waiting," she added hopefully. "If he can spare me a few minutes?"

A voice behind Connie spoke. "I'm Lisa Randolph, could I help you, Ms. Larkin?"

"Yes, thank you." Connie smiled as she turned. She knew Lisa acted as her husband's secretary.

"Please come in."

Connie entered the small office and took the chair indicated.

"I have been working in Fort Craig and am trying to find work here in Maryvale. I would like to do secretarial work. Typing; filing; correspondence; monthly statements, or whatever you have need of." Connie's fingers clung to the folder as she talked.

"I will be freelancing and will come in only when you need me. That would also save you paying for benefits on a full time employee." Connie smiled hopefully around dry teeth and her nervousness.

"You mean, if I understand you, not exactly part-time. Only when we need you?"

"Yes, that's right. I'm going to call on some more people here in Maryvale, too and hope to work for several places on an as needed basis. I don't want to work full time as I did in Fort Craig. So it would be as you said, only when you might need me."

"I see." Lisa was reading the resume and Jed Allen's recommendation which Connie had laid on her desk when she came in. She looked up.

"Have you decided on rates yet? And what if we only need you for half a day?"

"Yes, I would come in for half a day. I charge eighty dollars for nine to five o'clock and forty dollars for eight to twelve noon. I do my own taxes, so you won't have that to do. And I will bring my own typewriter to use."

Lisa laughed at that part of the offer. "You must have seen the monster when you came in."

"Monster? No, I didn't. I did see a quite impressive looking word processor near the front desk."

Lisa Randolph smiled. "We'd have to fight Jill for that word processor and I wouldn't give us any great odds on winning." Lisa pointed to something across the room. "That's the monster, over there."

Connie turned and saw an old model Underwood manual typewriter sitting on a low file cabinet.

"I use it sometimes when there is something I have to type. An extra envelope or something. It does pretty well, believe it or not."

"Oh, I believe it. I've typed on one like it, but it was a long time ago. The main thing is you have to hit the keys so hard, or it seems like it, after using an electric one for so long."

"What kind of typewriter is yours?"

"It's a Royal. A Swintek portable. And I supply my own ribbons. It's got the usual readout, memory, and it justifies."

"Justifies?"

"Yes. It lines up the right margin."

Lisa did not look enlightened.

"Look at my resume and the recommendation. See how the right side is even?"

"Oh, I see. Yes, that does look good. I wasn't sure what you meant by justifies. You've broadened my education," she smiled at Connie.

"I don't have any business cards yet. But I'm going to have some printed," Connie assured her, thinking she would like to work for her. "In the meantime, my name, address, and phone number is there on the resume. My husband is Casper Larkin, and we're listed in the phone book if you don't happen have the resume close at hand when you want to call."

"Oh, of course! Sheriff Larkin. I knew your name sounded familiar, I just hadn't connected it yet."

"If there is anything else you need in the way of records or references, I'll be glad to supply it." Connie pictured herself putting her bare foot on a huge ink pad for a footprint if that was needed. The thought let her relax a little and smile.

"No, this is fine, right here." Lisa looked at the clock. "I'm afraid Dick is going to be quite a while. He's working on a business merger of some kind. If it's all right with you, I'll keep these," she picked up the resume and recommendation. "And I'll tell him about your service. Or we can get Jill to set you up an appointment to talk to him another time if you would prefer to?"

Connie shook her head. "No. That won't be necessary. Thank you for taking time to talk to me. If there's anything else you want to ask or you need me, Please give me a call."

* * *

Connie's next stop was Pronto Prints. She ordered five hundred business cards. She handed the manager or the man behind the counter, all the information she wanted on them.

"I'll do my own talking, all I need is a way to get in touch with me," she explained.

The man nodded and scooted one of the large books over in front of her. "Here's some examples, these have proved to be the most popular ones."

Connie began looking through the card samples. "The two color ones are attractive," she sighed. "But I'm really at the black and white stage right now. I want them plain black print on white and easy to read."

She pointed to the one she liked, raising an eyebrow.

"You said five hundred?"

"Yes, five hundred. I may not even need those," she added. Her hands felt clammy at the immensity of five hundred.

"I asked because you can save by ordering a thousand at a time. They're cheaper that way. Are you starting a new business?" He read the card information.

Connie explained what she was trying to do. "I've only called on one office so far."

"Be sure to call on everyone, every business," the man advised her. "You never can tell. Even if the place you leave a card doesn't have anything for you, they may know someone who does. Word will get around," he encouraged her. "Getting cards out will be worth the effort."

"I hope so. I'm certainly going to try."

"I'll call you when these come in." He smiled, "Good luck."

"Thanks." Connie opened the door, already thinking about her next stop.

Getting a scary case of cold feet after ordering her cards she determined firmly to herself to make the three calls she had listed for that day and stick to her plans.

Passing near the square again she glanced at the clock on the dashboard. She promised herself if she got through with her calls before the flower shop closed she would stop by to see the Anderson sisters. She also wondered how Cas was doing with his list of student's names and was glad he didn't know what a wimp she was now that it was up to her to find some work for herself.

Cas opened the door to Judge Spruce's office and went in, speaking to a clerk as he went and waving to two others passing in the corridor. Past the clerk at the counter he could see a little alcove where Muriel Davis sat at her desk.

She saw him coming and smiled up at him as he took the chair beside her desk.

"You aren't going to scold me, too, are you? I felt I needed to come back. Judge Spruce has been so good, as has everyone else. But I needed to come back. To catch up on my work and keep my mind busy too," Muriel explained.

"I can understand that," Cas nodded. "It's best to keep busy. There's something I wanted to ask you about the list of Denise's friends you gave me."

"All right, if I can help."

"Judge Spruce has a son who is a senior at the high school. I was surprised to see his name wasn't on the list." He looked directly at her, watching her face.

Her reaction was mild surprise. "But the list was of Denise's friends. Not that they weren't friends," Muriel hurriedly explained, a little flustered. "I mean, they know each other and get along all right but they're in different grades, and not particular friends. That's what I meant to say." She returned his direct look.

He knew she was telling him the truth, or what she thought was the truth.

"They don't or didn't, have much contact then," Cas pursued. "They've never dated?"

"No. I don't think his name has ever come up at home but once."

"When was that, and what was it about?"

"I don't remember the exact date," Muriel said thoughtfully. "But it must have been around this time last year because it was about a picnic that was planned."

Cas listened and watched her as he did everyone he questioned. Eyes had sometimes told him more than lips as his Aunt Harriet always said. Aunt Harry was very wise. Muriel seemed cooperative and was trying to help.

"Denise and her friends, Doris and Diane, were going to a picnic some group at the school was sponsoring and Denise didn't have anyone to take with her. She said something about asking Darrell Spruce to go with her." She looked embarrassed and Cas waited for her to continue.

"I sat her down and talked to her. She hadn't ever mentioned him before, and I told her I would rather she would not ask him. I work for Judge Spruce and I feel if we don't mix very much we won't have any conflicts. It's sort of like not dating anyone who works for the same company, if you know what I mean?"

"Yes, I think it's probably a good policy. So they knew each other, but weren't close and have never dated?"

"That's right. That's why it never occurred to me to put his name on the list."

"All right, I just wondered about it when I remembered he was a senior. Thank you."

Outside, Cas looked toward the flower shop and saw Connie's car parked in front of it. He walked over to see if she'd had any luck finding something to do.

Approaching the new shop, he noticed how festive it looked with a bunch of ribbons lying carelessly in a window. A brightly colored sign leaned against the front waiting to be hung.

It said ANDERSON'S FLOWERS. Showy in petunia colors. Cas grinned as he admired the splash of pastels and went inside looking for his wife. It was obvious the shop was not yet open for business. Potted plants, balloons, and assorted decorating materials were strewn about.

"Cas," Connie's voice called. "I wondered if I might run into you. We're back here."

"You're just in time for coffee break," Miss Mayme Anderson informed him. Her sister, Miss Minnie Anderson, poured a cup for him.

The Anderson sisters had been Connie's favorite teachers. Miss Mayme taught English and art. Her ample figure fairly shouted it housed a good cook and her heart was as generous as her proportions. Miss Minnie taught math, was as thin as her sister was wide, did not suffer fools gladly but did her best to educate the ones depending on her for that. Her teaching math and her expectations resulted in her being called Miss Meanie by some of her less than brilliant and studious math students. "Miss Mayme and Miss Meanie," Connie thought to herself as she smiled at them both.

"What's all this hogwash I hear about you girls quitting the school system?" Cas teased them.

"You've got it all wrong," Miss Minnie explained. "They quit us. We got to something called retirement age and they gave us the jolly old ax, to make a long story short."

She raised her coffee cup. "Here's to good brains and good discipline, and good books, in that order."

Cas laughed. "Now, that was a dumb thing for them to do. It's the school's loss. So, now you're going into the flower business, are you?"

"It's something I've always wanted to do," Miss Mayme confided. "And Minnie needs something to do too. We managed to get this little cubby hole when the dress shop moved out, so here we are, 'Open and hopin!' Well, almost, give or take a few days and some cleaning."

"I think it's great," Connie exclaimed. "If I get a vote. It's the only florist shop in town. And Cas, don't you love their sign?"

"Yes, it's pretty. Eye catching. It's the colors I remember in my mother's petunia bed." He looked around at the frilly chaos of ribbon bolts and pastel decorations. He gestured at some shelves beside the door.

"Would you like me to move these shelves where you want them? They look pretty heavy."

"No, but thanks. We haven't decided what to do where yet." Miss Mayme chuckled, enjoying the disorder and excitement.

"Did you get to call on anyone?" Cas asked Connie.

"Sure did. I was just telling Miss Mayme and Miss Minnie about it, about my freelancing. I got to talk to Lisa Randolph and left my resume. I think she sounded interested and she's going to talk to her husband about my doing some work for them. She asked questions about my work and my rates, so that's a good sign. Then I went by and put in an order for some cards. I only ordered five hundred." She hesitated, wondering if Cas would approve. "They should be in about a week from now."

"Good idea. It may take some time for word to get around." He smiled at his wife, his confidence buoying her hopes. "You'll probably have all the work you want."

"Of course you will," Miss Minnie agreed.

"You've got your skills and the recommendation from Mr. Allen and you don't have warts on your nose." Miss Mayme was famous for being optimistic to the bone. Connie smiled at her pep talk, feeling encouraged.

"When you get your cards be sure to bring one by," Miss Minnie told her. "We're going to have a bulletin board."

"You are? Good! I will. I wish I already had them. I'm going to call on two more law offices before I go home. I was going to make my calls first, but my car just couldn't pass the square." She grinned at Cas.

"A likely story." He grinned back, getting up. "See you later then. Thanks for the coffee, ladies. Let me know if you need help getting settled in." Cas's mind was back on files and business before he got to the door.

He crossed the street and continued on to the back parking lot to get his truck. On a vague hunch, he drove through town and out toward Peaceful Ridge. He tried to remember the incident when the cemetery was vandalized. As he started up the hill in the cemetery he decided to hunt up the report when he got back.

There was a level place to park about halfway to the top. He got out and walked, looking around at some of the weather beaten tombstones.

"No telling how old some of these stones are. The place is well named, it's peaceful up here." He looked down at the graves around him. "No one up here but them and the mocking birds." He turned around and looked down the hill and around the surrounding countryside he could see from the ridge. The view from up there was beautiful. That was one thing besides the square that hadn't changed.

The place where the vandalism had occurred was up high where the tombstones were the oldest. Noticing a stone that leaned slightly, he walked over for a closer look at it.

This must have been one of the stones that were knocked down. Two or three were not exactly straight. He bent to examine the leaning stone, "This must have been one of the easiest to push over, the little devils. Wanted to look macho, no doubt."

He began reading the names and inscriptions on the stones around him. "Some of these are so old, there probably aren't any family members around here any more. The slanted one says, 'Charity Morris, Good Wife to Lemuel Morris, Mother to…?' I can't make out the rest of it, it's so eroded away."

The next stone was old too. It was bigger. Cas could tell it had been pushed over, but it had been righted and now stood fairly straight.

"Sarah Spruce," he read. "Wonder if there's any connection to the family living here now. It's easier to read than the last one, must be a better grade of stone."

He bent to examine the rest of the inscription. "What's this? 'Tried for witchcraft,' hanged April something. Can't make out the rest. But, witchcraft? And 'We hope she lyeth stille' under that."

Cas stood up, stretching his back muscles. Sorry for the poor woman, he realized every age seemed to have had its problems and conflicts. Down below he could see what must have been part of Caleb Martin's land. There was no one in sight. The cattle grazed peacefully. The scene looked like a landscape in an art gallery.

With a regretful glance back at the grave of the condemned witch he retraced his steps, his mind back on county business.

"I've got to get with Rhodes and see what he found out about the cattle Caleb Martin's been missing, and why he waited till now to report it."

He parked and on the way in and glanced across the street between the courthouse and the huge old magnolia tree. Connie's car was gone.

"Has Rhodes come in," Cas asked Gladys on his way to his office.

"No, but I told him about the missing cattle over the phone and he said he'd go out to the Martin place as soon as he could."

Cas nodded, going on into his office. He went directly to the files and pulled out the report about the vandalism at the cemetery.

There wasn't much there. "Just noted a lot of footprints, looked like dancing? Must have taken cassettes with them," Cas thought and read on. "Hmm. 'Found dead chicken, blood on toppled tombstone, goat tracks and claw marks that looked like they were made artificially, no droppings found.' Goat tracks and claw marks made artificially? Sounds like a Halloween party except for the time of year."

Cas smiled to himself picturing some of the young people he'd been talking to dancing in the cemetery.

He reread the brief report again before replacing the file and called to Gladys.

"Yes, sir?" Gladys peered around the door.

"Do you know of any recent reports we've had about animals being stolen?"

"Animals?" Gladys thought about it.

"Cows, horses, goats?" Cas raised his eyebrows.

"Goats rings a bell. There was one reported stolen about a year ago, I think. It was somewhere around the time of that vandalism at the cemetery and didn't get much attention if I remember right. Handled routinely, never did find it, or know who took it. Don't even remember who took the report."

"Would you find me the report, and while you're at it, look for any other animals reported stolen too."

Cas moved the Davis file over and picked up the phone to dial Judge Spruce's office. Muriel answered.

"This is Cas Larkin, I won't keep you but a minute. I keep running into things I need to ask you to put in the file. Was Denise on any kind of medication? Or did she take a sleeping pill once in a while, anything like that?"

"No, there weren't any health problems, and none of us have ever needed any help getting to sleep." Muriel sounded amused at the thought. "I've been known to go to sleep watching the news."

"Okay, that clears that up," Cas chuckled. "Another little piece in the routine information puzzle. Thanks."

Gladys had laid computer sheets on his desk as he talked to Muriel Davis. He pulled over the file notes to read them. There were three reports besides the goat there. "The goat belonged to Matthew Tinwhistle, I remember it now. Couple of weeks before the Peaceful Ridge to do I think it was."

He wrote the name of Matthew Tinwhistle and Sheriff Harlan Glover on a piece of paper and took it out to Gladys.

"I want a phone number and directions how to get to Tinwhistle's place when you can get around to it. And I want to talk to Harlan Glover any time at all as long is it's in the next ten minutes," he grinned at her.

"I can handle that." Gladys took the challenge.

Cas was still looking over the computer pages when his phone rang.

"Sheriff Glover's on the phone, sir," Gladys called.

"Great," he picked up the phone with a smile. "Hi, Cas here. Haven't seen you for a while, how are you Harlan?"

"I've been better, I've been worse," Harlan answered cautiously. "What are you buttering me up with small talk for?"

"I was looking at some animal thefts we've had in the past year and I noticed one you investigated."

"I remember it. It was cattle. Wasn't in my county, but close to the line, and I'd had two other incidents. That's why my name was on it. Never did find out who was doing the stealing though. We haven't had any more until about two weeks ago. But, this last was not exactly theft. The two cows were not stolen, they were mutilated."

"Mutilated?" Cas raised his eyebrows.

"Yeah. Had their udders, eyes, and horns cut out. They were longhorns. Somebody probably wanted those horns. We got a tire print, or part of one but haven't got much hope of finding out what it was done for or who did it, with nothing else to go on. I promised we'd try to patrol the roads more often. Wasn't much else I could do."

"The latest animal theft we've had reported in this county till now was a goat. It made me curious about what other animal thefts there have been in this area. The owner of the current one said he's been missing some cattle along this year, but he hadn't reported it for some reason. Would you send me printouts of all the reports you've had of cattle thefts for the last year and a half?" Cas grinned, "Keeping in mind of course, a goat is cattle too."

"I'll do it, a goat is a goat is a goat, horns and all," Harlan chuckled. "And if you get anywhere with it, I'd like to know about it."

CHAPTER 7

Connie pulled up in front of the building which according to the expensive looking sign, housed the Laurence Fields Law Office. She took note of the neat and lush commercial landscaping as she parked.

It was obvious Lawrence Fields was the established legal light in the area and 'famous for his courtroom successes,' as the paper usually said. She took a deep breath.

Connie held onto her purse and the folder holding her resume and recommendation to keep her hands from shaking. On her way in she patted her hair since there was a little breeze.

"I feel like I've been sent to the principal's office for shooting spit-balls!" She caught her lower lip in her teeth as she stopped in front of the reception desk to address the stern looking secretary.

"I don't have an appointment." She apologized, knowing at once that was a mistake. "I would like to speak to Mr. Fields if he can spare me a moment."

The effect this had was not exactly a frown, but too close to quibble about.

"Mr. Fields is in, but he is ready to leave."

"Connie Larkin!" a hearty and friendly voice boomed. "Come in."

When she turned, Laurence Fields stood in his office door smiling at her. He was about the same age as Cas but a little heavier. She remembered he had been a football player in college and turned down offers from professional teams to pursue his law career. Part of his charm was he was down to earth and friendly in spite of looking like the classic example of what a successful attorney should look like. And there was also in his favor the fact that Cas liked him. She put more faith in her husband's opinion than the things she had heard or read in the paper.

Connie smiled happily back at him. The pleasure of being welcomed by a handsome and busy man completely eclipsed the elderly watchdog behind the reception desk.

She practically skipped into his office and took the chair Fields indicated.

At ease now, she told him her plans and laid the folder on his desk. She was brief and to the point, grateful he had taken the time to talk to her.

Fields was pleasant and predicted she would probably get more work than she wanted, though he himself didn't promise anything.

"I need a collector more than a typist right now."

"A collector? I'm afraid I have no experience in that. Just in sending out the bills," Connie ruefully admitted.

Fields was pleasant but she didn't feel encouraged in spite of his keeping the recommendation and the resume with her phone number on it.

"I'm having some cards printed," she said with more verbally upbeat hope than she felt. "They should be ready in about a week. I would appreciate it if you would keep me in mind if you should hear of anyone who needs temporary help."

"I'll certainly do that, and good luck. You should do well. I don't know of anyone else here who offers this kind of service." He walked her to the office door, making her feel like someone important.

"Well, you can't win them all," Connie consoled herself as she left. "He's a charmer, all right, but that secretary of his looks to me like she could handle any collection problems they might have on break!" Connie shuddered at the thought.

Back in the car she consulted the clock again. She would have to hurry to catch Tim Carpenter in. He was the last of the three lawyers she had planned to call on today.

She parked close as possible to the courthouse and when she entered, met Tim Carpenter in the hall. Her heart sank. "He must be leaving for the day. Bad timing, Connie!"

Summoning up the ghost of the hopeful smile that died in Laurence Fields's office, she timidly touched his arm to get his attention, "Excuse me?"

"Yes ma'am?"

Connie aged twenty years at the 'ma'am', but got over it fast.

"If you can spare me a few minutes, I'd like to talk to you. Or just leave my name and number if you're interested in someone to help with office work? I'm doing typing and general office work. Freelancing."

She talked fast, wanting to present her service and qualifications. "Filing or correspondence you need to get out?"

"You're doing freelance typing?" Tim Carpenter's young face broke into a delighted smile. "I sure am interested. Come on into my broom closet." He held the door for her.

"Thank you. I, I don't have any cards yet. I've ordered some. But I use my own typewriter and ribbons and will work when you need me." Connie clutched her folder as he gestured her to a chair.

"My guardian angel must have sent you," Tim told her as they sat down opposite each other. "I've got correspondence backed up and I don't type. I was thinking of approaching the high school typing teacher to see if one of her students would be interested in doing some typing for me. I wasn't too happy about it, but the work is piling up."

"That's good news to me." Connie pounced on the opportunity.

"Can I afford you, though? How much do you charge? Or how do you charge, for that matter?" He was a little dubious and at a loss how to make arrangements.

"I charge eighty dollars for all day, that's nine to five o'clock. Or forty dollars for half a day, eight o'clock to twelve noon."

He hesitated, not sure how to relate the hours to the work he wanted done.

Connie anticipated his needs. Her experience as a secretary came in as handy as her willingness to bring her own equipment. She looked but didn't see any work on the desk or in a basket.

"If you'll show me what you've got to type up to give me some idea, I can make a guess about how long it will take me. But don't hold me to it like it's chiseled in stone," she warned with a grin. She felt from what he said they could get together.

"Good. I've got the things I need most written out." He opened a couple of drawers and brought out files and papers. He got together what he had prepared and pushed the pile of paper across the battered desk for Connie to look at.

There were letters, itemized bills, lists of some kind, and correspondence to other lawyers.

"I'm glad you're such a legible writer." Connie straightened the stack. "I believe I can get them done in half a day. But in case I'm flattering myself, why don't you look them over again and arrange them by priority so I'll be sure to get done what you have to have?"

"Good thinking. I've added some recent correspondence to the heap as things came in," Tim admitted. As he shuffled papers he glanced up. "You couldn't possibly come in and do this tomorrow, could you?"

"Yes, I can. I'll be here at eight o'clock. I'll bring my own typewriter to use. All I need is a plug and a place to work."

"You can? Tomorrow? And you'll bring your typewriter? I think I love you!" Tim was so pleased Connie laughed with him.

"I'm as glad to find work as you are to get some help. I'm trying to get started freelancing here in Maryvale. I've only called on three people so far and you're the first one who's given me some work."

"Couldn't have worked out better, then. I'll see you in the morning. I have to be in court at nine but I'll be here to let you in and get set up."

Connie floated out the door on an accomplishment high and smiled all the way home.

"Eeeyahooooooo!" She squealed, gripping the steering wheel. "The first day out! Oh, I can't wait to tell Cas!"

While she got out the things she wanted to fix for dinner at home Missy came in and the phone rang at the same time. She beckoned to Missy and picked up the phone.

"Larkin residence."

"Mrs. Larkin," the soft voice hesitated. "This is Muriel Davis."

"Oh, I'm sorry I didn't recognize your voice. Cas is not here yet, can I help you?"

"I'm sorry to bother him at home. I can call him at his office tomorrow."

"No, no, it's all right. Please, call any time Mrs. Davis. All of our hearts are with you. I'll tell Cas to call as soon as he gets here."

"That's all right. But, would you tell him I believe Denise must have been wearing a bracelet when, when…."

"A bracelet?" Connie wished she could somehow make this call easier for her. "She was wearing a bracelet. What kind of bracelet, or shall I just get Cas to call you back?"

"Well, if it's not too much trouble. She wore the bracelet all the time and I looked for it. It's not in her room. It was one of those little gold chains. It had a 'D' on it."

"Of course it's no trouble, I'll tell Cas about it as soon as he comes in. And please, call any time."

She said goodbye and hung up, realizing Missy was watching.

"Was that Denise's mom?"

"Yes. She said she thinks Denise must have been wearing a gold bracelet when she was attacked. It's not in her room and she wore it all the time. She said she'd called the office, but your father was already gone."

"I think I've seen Denise wearing the bracelet, mom. A plain gold chain?"

"That's what she said. We'll tell him when he comes in. What I wanted to tell you when the phone rang is I've got a half day's work. Tomorrow."

"Tomorrow! Wow!" Missy's face lit up at the news. "Mom, you got something the very first day, that's really great." Missy hugged her. "Who is the half day for?"

"For Tim Carpenter. He's the young lawyer who's using one of the little offices in the courthouse and has just been appointed Public Defender, probably pro tem or something. He doesn't even have a typewriter, and he really needs some work done."

"That's neat." Missy started setting the table.

"You don't need to do that yet."

"I thought I'd get it done so I can do some of my reading. I wonder what sadist makes up those required reading lists anyway?" Missy gave a water glass she was holding a disgusted grimace.

"Oh, you'll live. You might even enjoy some of it." Connie took a plate from her hand. "Scoot! I'll yell if I need you."

A little later Cas came in the back door. He sniffed appreciatively at the scent of pork chops simmering on low.

"Ah, Sanctuary," he breathed with his eyes closed. "I'm thinking of digging us a moat around the place."

"A moat? You mean with crocodiles and dragons and such? Has it been that bad?" Connie gave him an extra close hug.

The farmers and their rustled cattle, the lack of anything new on the Davis case, and the beating Casey Taylor had suffered ran through his mind in a kaleidoscope of unfinished business. His own personal and up-close dragons. He returned her hug and put all of them firmly out of his thoughts.

"Oh, I guess not. Anyway, I'm home now. What are you grinning about," he asked indignantly. "Don't you understand my problems?" He tickled her.

Connie got out, "Stop!" between giggles. "I've got good news for a change. Think you can stand the shock?"

"Try me."

"I called on all three of the lawyers on my list to contact today and I've got a half day's work for tomorrow!"

"That is good news. Who for?"

"Tim Carpenter. I'll tell you all about it after dinner. Also," her smile faded a bit. "Mrs. Davis called and left you a message."

"Mrs. Davis?" She had his full attention. "I'll call her now." He reached for the phone book. "Did she say what she wanted?"

"She said Denise was probably wearing a gold bracelet when she was attacked. She always wore it, and it's not in her room so she feels she must have had it on."

"You mean, one of those little gold chains?"

"Yes, Missy said she's seen her wearing it, too. Mrs. Davis said it had a gold initial 'D' on it. I offered to tell you to call her back, but she was afraid of it being too much trouble. I said I'd tell you."

"I'll call her anyway. It will make her feel better and she may have thought of something else."

The next day was a busy one for Cas. The first thing he did was tell Rhodes about the bracelet and send him and another deputy to the scene to search for it.

"You say it's one of those little gold chains with an initial 'D' on it?" Rhodes looked dubious as he started out.

"That's what Mrs. Davis said, and she's almost certain she was wearing it. It will be tough to spot out there, I know. If you don't find it at the scene, backtrack the way we went in."

Gladys came in with the mail. "Caleb Martin called but didn't leave his number. He wondered if there was anything new on the cattle thefts. Also, Matthew Tinwhistle called. Isn't he the one who had the goat stolen?"

"Yes," Cas made a pained grimace. "Don't tell me he's missing another one?"

"No." Gladys laughed. "The way he carried on, I'm sure that was the only one he had. But he said when you had time he wanted to tell you about losing a head or two of cattle. I think he must have been talking to Caleb Martin from the way he said it. He did leave his number." Gladys pointed, "It's on the top of the mail there."

"Okay, I'll call him as soon as I can get around to it." He laid the note aside and went through the mail, pulling out a large brown envelope. It turned out to be the printouts of the cattle thefts in Marble County Harlan Glover had promised to send. He laid it in front of him and took a brief look through the rest of the mail before opening it.

He was on the last page of the printouts, checking the dates and what was taken, when the phone rang. It was Deputy Doug Freeman. He didn't bother with amenities.

"I thought I'd best call and tell you since I know you questioned the Taylor boy in connection with the Davis case."

"What happened?" Cas snapped.

"It's not him, it's his mother. Her car ran off the road and went into a ditch out by the Green Thumb Nursery. She's not hurt, but the car is in pretty bad shape. It will have to be towed. It's an old car. She said it was her son's. She borrowed it to go get some plants at the nursery."

"Is she all right?"

"Yes, we're taking her home."

"Where are they towing the car to?"

"Howard's Garage. That's where she told them to take it."

"Okay, thanks for calling." He pushed the mail into a rough stack and reached for his hat, his face a grim mask.

"Gladys," he ordered without slowing down. "Be sure to send Rhodes out to Tinwhistle's to get a report on his missing cattle when he gets in if he hasn't already been out there. I'm going over to Howard's garage."

He saw Casey Taylor as soon as he got close enough to see inside the shop. Casey's taped places stood out as he turned to look at Cas. Again, Cas felt the anger he felt when he had first seen Casey's bruised face and the careful way he moved to keep from hurting any worse.

Cas nodded to Howard Giles and went to where Casey stood. He was looking up at the underside of his car. Cas was glad to see Casey looked ready to punch someone and knew he saw the same thing he did.

"I don't know what you're looking for, Sheriff Larkin. But I've seen all I need to. Someone cut the brake line. My mother is lucky she wasn't hurt or killed."

Cas nodded agreement. "Yes, that was the one good thing about it." He glanced at the faded paint. "You got any insurance on it?"

"Only liability. But I can afford to lose the car a lot easier than I can my mother. Would you still like to know where I got these bruises?"

"Yes, I would. Did you walk over here?"

Casey nodded. "That's why mom had the car brought here. It's close and this is where I come when I need something done to it."

"It's about lunch time. Call your mother so she'll know where you are. We'll go have lunch at the drive-in and talk."

The call didn't take long and they left in Cas's car. As they waited for their lunch orders, Casey told Cas about the club he had asked him about.

"When it first got organized, everyone thought the club was something different. A fun thing to do. Harmless and fun. But the one who got everyone interested and organized it turned out to be a real power freak. He had officers who 'punished' members who got out of line, or talked about the club."

'Punished' clicked again in Cas's memory. "Who organized it? Who is the one behind this so-called club?"

"Darrell Spruce."

"Was it the club that made the mess up on Peaceful Ridge?"

"Yes. He had us come up there for a meeting. He wanted us to think he has supernatural powers, if you can believe such a thing. He showed us the tombstone of a great aunt or something who was a witch. And you know," Casey turned unbelieving eyes on Cas. "Some of them were actually falling for that garbage!"

"Did he have his officers beat you up?"

"Yes, that's who it was." He gave Cas the names of two members of the football team who were both a lot bigger than Casey.

"Sounds a little rigged in their favor." Cas remembered the two from seeing them play.

"I got in a couple of good licks, but not much more. Only enough that it wasn't as much fun as they thought it was going to be." Casey finished with a lopsided grin.

"Good for you. Now, what is this crap about Darrell having supernatural powers?"

"He thinks he can hypnotize people. And the reason he had us go up on Peaceful Ridge was to show us that tombstone, like it was a résumé or something I guess. Then he had them kill a chicken on the tombstone and all that crazy stuff. I thought that was more voodoo than witchcraft. Then once, he got so wound up, I laughed out loud at him. He took it as a terrible insult. But it was so ridiculous, it seemed funny to me. Anyway, he put out the word that I would be 'punished'. I thought that would be all there was to it. When you came to my house, I thought it was all over. That this beating would be the end of it. But this is not funny any more. My mom could have been hurt, or even killed. It's got to stop."

"It will be stopped. Do you remember about how many meetings there have been and when they were?"

"Ah, probably, I'll have to think about it."

"You do that. Write the dates down and anything else you can remember about them as well. You have my card, and my home number is in the phone book. Where did they have these meetings? Or did you have them different places, like the one up on Peaceful Ridge?"

"We generally had them outside somewhere, but once we had one on a stormy night. The officers took us to it in vans. They blindfolded us and made several trips so I don't know where the place was."

"I know you couldn't see, being blindfolded. But did it seem far to you? What about unusual noises, or was it a rough road? Could you tell if it was uphill, or an unpaved road? Think back and see what you can remember."

"It did seem like a long way to me. But that may be because we must have got off on an unpaved road before we got there, and it was sort of rough. Then when we got out, somebody told us to stand still. We joined hands and went down some kind of an incline and waited till they said we could take the blindfolds off."

"What did you see when you took the blindfold off?"

"We were moving but slowly. Going into a dark place like a big hole. But when we got in I could see it must have been a house once, because it had stone walls. The stones felt damp and cold."

"What about the meeting? Who was there, the usual members and Darrell Spruce and his officers?"

"Yes, the usual members from school were there and Darrell said we could meet there when the weather was bad. I remember that. Then he introduced the man he said had given us the goat head."

"Goat head?"

"Yes, I should have told you about that first, I guess. The place had a thing rigged up like an altar with an upside down crucifix on it and there was a skeleton goat head hanging on the wall behind it. It looked like a place you'd see in a horror movie, with the candles and the stone walls and all that."

"Who was the man?"

"Darrell didn't tell us his name. Or if he did, I didn't hear it. Just that he had given us the goat head and some other things he said we could use. He had brought some other things in a box, but I didn't look at them."

"What did this stranger look like? Can you describe him to me?"

"He was, I'd guess, about twenty-eight or thirty. As tall as one of the officers, but skinnier. I don't think he weighed very much. He was about medium every other way, too, and had long dark hair. Or, sort of long hair, but not what mom would call 'fashionable long'. He just looked shaggy. Like he'd needed a haircut for a while."

"Did he say anything so you could hear his voice?"

"Yes, sir. He told us there were other groups and when we got better organized we could meet together and other things. Then after he left, Darrell told us we would have a real 'orgy' soon. That didn't go over as well as he was expecting it to, and he started telling us how great it was. Some of them got interested enough to satisfy him, I guess. He was real excited about the orgy as he kept calling it, and told us to be thinking about who we would bring. He said w'd have to be very careful and secretive to be able to 'enjoy our freedom'." Casey looked disgusted.

"The strange man left before Darrell started talking about the orgy, then?"

"Yes, he wasn't there very long."

"What did he sound like, this stranger? Rich man, poor man, beggar man, thief? Rocket scientist, third shift at the Dairy Queen?"

Casey laughed, "Definitely not rocket scientist. His voice was kind of low and his grammar wasn't very good. He seemed to want us to get more members and kept telling us to get organized. I hadn't seen him before and I had been to all the meetings but one. It didn't get silly until the last few meetings."

"Casey, I'm going to call on these two 'officers' of Darrell's and scare the pants off them. Would you be willing to prosecute these jokers if we need to?"

"I'd rather not. Mom and I don't have anyone to depend on but each other. I don't want any trouble." He looked up at Cas, "But if that's the only way to put a stop to this, I would. Yes."

CHAPTER 8

Cas pulled into the parking lot behind Rhodes.

He stopped to walk in with him, but waited until they got inside to talk.

"Hold the calls for a while, Gladys. Rhodes and I need to compare notes on a few things." Cas closed the office door.

Gladys nodded without looking up, busy typing something.

Cas put the notes he had taken under the edge of the file which was on the corner of his desk. He turned his attention to Rhodes who was going over some notes of his own.

"Did you get a chance to talk to Matthew Tinwhistle as well as Caleb Martin?"

"Yes, I talked to both of them." Rhodes thumbed through the notes he had separated with paper clips. He pulled out the ones he had taken at the Martin place first.

"From what Caleb said, he's lost a head or two of cattle since the first of the year."

"Does he know or can he estimate how many, or have any suspicions about who might be taking them?"

Rhodes shook his head slightly. "He's not sure about the times when he thought only one might be missing but he's going to try to remember as close as he can when he's sure two were taken. He said there were times he thought he was missing one or maybe two. But because they were so scattered, he wasn't sure about it. He wants to talk to a hand he has who comes to help when he needs him. He's a neighbor. I saw your ears prick up at that," Rhodes shook his head.

"Oh, not a suspect?"

"He's not under suspicion according to Caleb. They're going to get together and try to get as close a number as they can about how many they think were taken and when they realized they were missing."

Cas nodded as Rhodes shuffled and went on from his notes.

"He also told me some of them were not stolen, but killed and mutilated."

"I'm glad you got that. He brought it up, did he?"

"Yes, he looked kind of sheepish about it. He said that's the reason he didn't report these thefts before. His wife was really frightened about those mutilations. She didn't want any trouble, whether it's thieves or devil worshippers or what. Says they must be crazy, whoever they are, and liable to do anything. But this last time, Caleb put his foot down and called you about it."

"It was about time. He should have done it the first time he missed a head or two. This kind of thing isn't going to get better without some help."

"Yeah, that's about what he told her before he called."

"If he doesn't suspect the neighbor who comes to help, does he have any idea who might be doing it? Anything or anyone acting suspicious? Hanging around his place? Or were there tracks or anything else found after the cattle were stolen or mutilated?"

Rhodes looked up from his notes. "We may have got lucky there. There's a track. It's been there since one of the times when a cow was mutilated and he's checked with everyone who's had any reason to be out there. It wasn't made by any of them. I'm going out and make a cast of it."

"Good. Do it first thing in the morning. How does it happen it's still there? Was it, the mutilation, done recently?"

"No. It's older than the last time. It's in the edge of the stock pond. The water just got low enough for it to show. It's dried hard now and easy to see. It will be easy to get a good cast of it."

"Okay. I want to see it as soon as you get it. Keep me posted on anything else you find. I'm going to have a car swing by there more often. Tell him that when you get the cast. It's the best we can do right now. And tell him to report anything suspicious, anyone trespassing, a strange truck or other vehicle in that area. Anything."

"All right, I'm sure he will be around while I get the cast. I'll tell him."

"What about Tinwhistle?"

"I've got the report here for you to look at." Rhodes stood up and put it on Cas's desk. "It's short on anything definite. There's nothing new except what he told us before and it's short on numbers, too. He's going to think about it same as Caleb."

He turned at the door. "Oh, and the goat? Her name was Gertrude," Rhodes grinned. "The thing that made him the maddest wasn't losing a cow once in a while, it was stealing that goat." He chortled, "They got his goat in more ways than one!"

Gladys laughed too as Rhode left.

Promptly at five till eight o'clock the next morning Connie parked at the courthouse and opened the trunk of her car to get out her portable typewriter.

"Mrs. Larkin. Wait a minute. I'll get that for you."

She turned to see Tim Carpenter coming to meet her. "I've been watching for you."

He picked up the portable by its handle, appraising its lines. "This is a neat little machine. I guess I thought all of them would be as heavy as the antiques I've seen in some of the offices here."

"Uh-huh, I like my machine. That's why I decided to use it. I'm used to it and it's easy to take with me." She bit her lip to keep from adding that she could use a computer too if the county budget should ever spring for one for his office. Highly unlikely in the foreseeable future.

In the small office Tim set the machine on the typewriter shelf of the old desk. "Here's the plug," he unfolded the cord and plugged it in.

"This is the work in the box." Tim gestured. "And there's letterhead in the middle drawer, along with envelopes. But leave the envelopes till last. I can always manage those."

"All right. And this is in the order you want it?"

"Yes, by priority." He looked nervously around as if he must have forgotten something. Or maybe it was that he couldn't believe getting help and getting set up could be this easy.

"I've got to go to court. If I don't make it back by twelve, will you leave a note on my desk? I'll write you a check as soon as I get back if that's all right with you? But I'll probably make it all right." He smiled on the way out, "Judges like to eat too."

Connie got out a stack of letterhead to get started. The actual volume of work didn't look so bad and she was relieved to see all of them seemed easy to read.

"He's definitely in need of help with no secretary, so I'll more than likely be able to work for him quite a bit. He's nice, too," Connie smiled to herself, glad to be able to help him.

Cas looked up from his work as Gladys stopped in the office door. "Janice Cobb is out of the office but will be back soon. I left word for her to call you."

"Thanks, Gladys. I'm still talking to Denise's friends at school, whenever they're available."

"Whoever answered sounded young, like a student and said she would be back any minute. So you probably won't have long to wait."

Cas nodded, glancing over the several lists of names before him. He looked again too at the list of names Casey had given him of students he had seen at the club meetings.

* * *

Dana Green caught up with Missy on the way to history class and asked, "Did you see Casey Taylor?"

"Yes. But I saw him yesterday, when he first came back."

"He's sure got a lot of bruises. The ones by his eye are yellow and green and he has that cut on his lip." Dana laughed, "He told me to save any good jokes I know for a couple of weeks."

"I know, it's still easy to see why. When I saw him he started to grin, and put his fingers on his lip to keep it from hurting. But he must be about over it. My mom says those colors in the bruises mean they're nearly well."

Missy looked serious. "I'm sure sorry it happened, though."

"Me too, he's nice." Dana glanced sideways at Missy, "I think he kind of likes you, Missy."

"What makes you think so? We only have one class together. I don't run into him very often and he's never asked me to any of the games or anything at school."

"Just the same, I think he does. If it weren't for you going practically steady with Chuck he probably would. Ask you out, I mean."

"Well, in that case," Missy dumped her armload of books onto her desk with a frown. "He may get around to asking me out soon."

The buzzing of the bell drowned out Dana's next question, but she leaned closer to whisper quickly. "What do you mean, did you and Chuck break up?"

Missy turned away and sat down without answering and Dana went quickly to her own desk under the watchful eye of the history teacher who was waiting for quiet to settle.

"It's twelve-ten. I made it!"

Connie carefully replaced the handwritten material Tim Carpenter had given her in the envelope box he had put it in. She had all the priority work finished, laid out on his desk with the envelopes inserted with the letters. It looked nice. She was proud of it.

She turned with a smile as the door opened and Tim Carpenter hurried in.

"I got here as fast as I could." He looked pleased at the neat stack of typing as he went around his desk and took out his checkbook.

"We timed it just right. I was just putting things in order."

"It looks great, and you managed to get the envelopes done too." He cast a grateful look at her.

"It's a relief to get these things done. I really appreciate this." He handed her the check for forty dollars made out in his neat handwriting.

"Thank you, I was glad to have the work. You have my number, if you need anything else. And if you don't mind, would you tell anyone else you know that I'm looking for work? I'm getting some cards printed as I said, and I'll drop a couple of them by here when I get them."

"Good. I'll keep one right here by my phone and I certainly will recommend you."

Connie closed the cover on the typewriter.

"I'll take that out to your car for you." Tim reached for the handle, admiring the compact machine again.

"Thanks, call me soon as you have some more work I can help you with."

"I sure will. Thanks again, and drive safely!"

Amused at the 'drive safely', Connie thought he looked like he might take out a policy of some kind on her. She smiled after him as he hurried back to his office and looked around the parking lot.

The feeling of accomplishment was so good she wanted to tell someone about her first day's work in Maryvale. "I'll walk over and visit Miss Minnie and Miss Mayme at the flower shop a few minutes."

At the shop Miss Mayme was busily placing silk flowers in a large arrangement to display in the front window as Connie went in.

"How pretty," Connie admired the arrangement. "And I see Miss Minnie back there working on a big ledger of some kind. Both of you are doing your thing in this partnership."

"Yep." Miss Mayme nodded a greeting and held up ribbons in two shades of blue. "Which do you like best? Which will show up best in the window?"

Connie was giving the problem her careful consideration when Miss Minnie looked up and called from the office.

"Hallelujah! I'm in need of a coffee break. Connie, drag Mayme out of that pile of flowers and come in here."

"We'll be there in a minute," Miss Mayme promised. "What do you think, Connie?"

"I think the royal blue shade."

"Okay. I'll leave it here before Minnie has a stroke or something. It's coffee time."

The little office had a shelf with a microwave and other necessities behind a half wall beyond the credenza. There were more shelves yet to be installed.

"We're making progress as we go," Miss Minnie explained as Connie looked around. "We used up most of our 'fast' before we retired, on fast young'uns and slow red tape."

"I can understand that, all right. I didn't mean to take you away from your work. I was at the courthouse and wanted to tell someone about my first day's work here in Maryvale. I feel more encouraged about my prospects now."

"As you should. And we couldn't have gone much longer without a cup of coffee. We both need a break."

"Tell us about your work, Connie. I want to hear about something that doesn't have to be color coordinated." Miss Mayme pleaded, "It'll rest my ears."

She stirred an extra spoon of sugar into her coffee. "For energy," she quickly told Miss Minnie who rolled her eyes at such a flimsy justification.

"I worked half a day for Tim Carpenter. He's got a tiny little office over there at the courthouse, but no one to do his typing for him. It was good luck for both of us when we got together. He had correspondence and some other things piled up. I asked him to tell anyone he knew about me, that

I'm in the phone book and looking for work. I'll take him a couple of my cards when I get them."

Miss Minnie searched a bottom drawer beneath the coffee pot and brought out a box of graham crackers. "Mayme is trying to train me to eat these so she won't be tempted by doughnuts and Danish calories every time we have a break."

"Hmm," Mayme looked suspiciously at a graham cracker as she took it. "It may help and it may not. Sometimes I wonder." She bit into it, obviously wishing it was something gooey or at least had some frosting on it.

"These are good for snacks," Connie encouraged her. "We like these at home and the cinnamon ones too. Cas doesn't care for the messy things when he's trying to work, he likes to eat with his fingers too well."

"But the nice gooey ones are always so 'finger lickin' good!" Miss Mayme groaned.

"Don't forget when you take Tim some cards to bring one for our bulletin board," Miss Minnie reminded Connie and changed the subject.

"I will. And I do think it's a good idea to have the bulletin board."

"Minnie, I would like to go down to Lorenzo's Market and see what he's got on sale. I might get something to put in our crockpot."

"All right, it won't take long to go down there and see what he's got. Why don't you go with us, Connie? We can use the new sign we bought to show when we'll be back."

"Another first for today. We haven't used it before." Miss Mayme set down her cup. "I'll finish the windows when I get back."

"Why not?" Connie was definitely in favor of going. "Here I am with my first day's work done, and I don't have to rush home. But, what sale are you talking about? I haven't seen it in the paper."

"One of our customers told Mayme about it this morning. It's a one day sale on meat. To get people coming in. I guess that's the idea behind it."

"I like to get in on the sales and freeze things so I'll always have something to fix in the crockpot when I want to use it. It's a good way to cook something good without too much trouble," Miss Mayme explained. "You just put everything in there, vegetables too, when you want them. Then by the time they get to smelling really good, it's dinner time and all you have to do is take them up."

"I know what you mean and I can top that," Connie giggled. "I sometimes put in a lot so I can coast the next night on leftovers. It must have been rough before there were microwaves and crockpots. Let's go!"

"Grab the sign, Minnie." Miss Mayme headed for the door.

When Janice Cobb returned his call Cas asked her about the two boys he wanted to talk to. "And I'd like to speak to John, if he's not too busy."

"I see him coming down the hall now, if you can wait a second. While you talk I'll locate the boys you want to talk with."

John Squires, the high school principal, was tall and thin with a rather dry personality. But he was warm hearted and genuinely interested in the well-being and education of his children as he called his students.

Cas thanked him for the use of his office. "And I'm calling now to impose on you again. Janice is locating two students I want to talk to. I just wanted to thank you in person. "

"You're not imposing. You've got my permission to use my office to interview this afternoon or any other time you need to." John chuckled good naturedly. "I'm not in there any more than I can help anyway. If there's anything else I can do to help you, let me know."

Cas was not looking forward to the confrontation with the two self styled officers of Darrell's club. He hoped by interviewing them together he could either learn more than he had now or could tell by watching them how much of what they told him was true.

The two boys were waiting in the principal's office when Cas got to the school. The door was open and John Squires came to meet him.

"Sheriff Larkin," John said formally, "This is Todd Kelly." He pointed to the taller of the two. "And this is Sid Norton. I'll leave you to your talk, but Janice can find me. If you want me for anything, just step out and tell her." He sent a serious glance at the boys as he turned to go. Cas recognized that look as a not too subtle warning to the boys to behave themselves and appreciated the support.

"Thank you, sir." Cas went in and sat down behind the desk as Janice closed the office door. On the desk he laid out a file folder, writing pad, and some notes he had made. He didn't speak or look up until he had it all arranged to his satisfaction.

Todd and Sid squirmed uncomfortably in their straight chairs. Both of them looked rebellious and uncooperative. He thought what a satisfying feeling he would get out of going around the desk and just knocking their two hard heads together. Instead, he addressed the taller, fair-haired one.

"You're Todd Kelly?"

The boy nodded, his eyes watchful.

"And you're," Cas deliberately consulted the sheet in front of him, "Sid Norton."

Norton gave an impatient nod, looking like he resented being called in for this.

Norton was a couple of inches shorter than Kelly, but stout. He was dark, and had the beginnings of a dark shadow of beard.

"Looks like a mean one," Cas thought.

He addressed them both. "Are you members of this club I've heard about here at school? Before you answer, I have talked to other people and it will be a mark against you to lie about it."

Cas looked them in the eye, Todd, then Sid, letting his words sink in.

Todd returned the look Cas gave him for a few seconds. He seemed to want to look away, but couldn't.

"He's scared right down to his socks." Cas knew it. The boy dropped his eyes, not answering the question.

Cas looked at Sid. "And what about you?"

Sid seemed more worried about what Todd would say than what Cas might think. He watched him warily a few seconds before answering Cas. "I've ah, been to a couple of meetings," he admitted, his eyes going back to Todd.

"Todd?"

"I've been to a couple of meetings too." The answer was a little too quick.

"What kind of club is it? You say you've been to the meetings, tell me about it." Cas leaned back in the principal's swivel chair and waited.

"Nothin' to tell," Sid answered for them. "Some people getting together, friends having a good time."

Cas leaned forward, eyes nailing Sid. "You call trashing a cemetery and killing chickens a good time?" Cas was grim.

Sid was no longer so sure of himself, not certain how much Cas knew.

Todd spoke up. "It's only a club, I don't know why you want to ask about it, Sheriff." Todd's voice was a desperate whine.

"I'm asking about it because it came to my attention when I was looking into something else. Nobody ever paid for cleaning the cemetery up on Peaceful Ridge. It took some trouble to clean up the grounds and set up the tombstones that were turned over. Did you use that big flat one to kill the chicken on?" He shot the last question at Todd quickly, watching his reaction.

"Ch-ch-chicken?"

Sid quickly came to his defense. "We told you we went to a couple of meetings. That doesn't mean we went to any meeting at a cemetery or know anything about one, or no chicken either," Sid spat the words angrily.

"Okay, let's talk about the meetings you went to. Who was there? Who was in charge? And what did you do and talk about?"

"There wasn't anybody in charge. It was just friends getting together." Sid's flushed face dared Cas to prove otherwise.

"When I get around to the others on this list," Cas gestured at it. "I wonder if they'll be as reluctant as you to give me your names and tell me about your part in this club."

"It was Darrell! Darrell Spruce," Todd blurted out.

"Shut up, you nerd!" Sid glared at Cas, blaming him for Todd's lapse. He backed off a little, lowering his voice. "I think Darrell was there, but nobody was in charge. We were just there," Sid tried hard to sound convincing.

"Don't get in a lather. I already knew Darrell was in charge. You'd do well to tell me whatever you know that might help keep your own buns out of trouble," Cas pointed a finger at Sid.

"I'm not in any trouble!" Sid was vehement. "I haven't done anything to be in any trouble. I'm going to tell my folks about you coming down here and talking to me like this. You've got no right!"

The more Sid talked, the more excited he got. His voice rose to a shout.

Cas stood up, leaned across the desk and spoke to him. His face was mere inches away, his words coming out like a low growl between his teeth.

"You set your smart ass back down in that chair and speak with respect or we'll finish this little chat in my office. After which, we'll bring your parents down there to talk about it, too, if that's what you want."

Todd's mouth gaped open at this exchange. There was no doubt to anyone in that room that Cas was not impressed, much less intimidated, by these two roughnecks. The rest of the interview didn't net Cas much more in the way of information than he already had, but it ended on a more cooperative note, grudging or not.

Cas dismissed the boys and waited to thank John Squires before he left.

"The main thing I got out of this session was to put a fear in those two," he thought as he left." I wonder how much of this pressure is getting back to Darrell? I'm going to talk to everyone else before I tackle him, let him get good and worried."

CHAPTER 9

"**M**issy! Missy! Wait for me!"

Dana caught up with Missy after class. She tried to catch her breath and ask questions at the same time. It didn't work. She put her hand on Missy's arm to slow her down.

"Oh, I know what you're going to ask me. Yes, Chuck and I broke up. I don't want to talk about it." Missy pulled her arm free and hurried on.

Seated on the school bus, she gazed out the window, face averted from her schoolmates, seeing only the events of the day in her mind's eye.

"I guess I'll have to tell Dana. About me and Chuck. I hurt her feelings, and she means well. There's no way to explain how you feel seeing you've been mistaken about someone you thought you knew."

A wonderful aroma greeted Cas as he opened the kitchen door.

"Umm, something smells good, onions too." He moved toward the stove as if drawn by an irresistible force.

"Don't touch! It's about ready anyway. We're having steak smothered in onions and mashed potatoes to go with the good gravy," Connie told him as she set the table.

Cas stopped, looking into the hallway. "Where's Missy? Is the help on strike?"

"Upstairs. She seemed to have something on her mind, or maybe a lot of homework. So I went on and set the table myself. I'll call her if she's not down here by the time I get things on the table."

Cas went to wash his hands and met Missy as she came down the stairs. "Smells like a good dinner waiting for us in there, better go help your mother."

"Just in time," Connie greeted her without turning around. "Everything's ready. I'm taking things up now." She set the potatoes on the table as Cas came back in.

"Remind me not to fix anything with onions on Saturday," Connie told them.

"Why not?" Missy asked absently, placing kitchen ware beside the plates.

"You told me not to go so heavy on the onions when you're going out, remember? And you have a date with Chuck."

"Oh. Well, don't worry about it. He's not coming." She was facing away from Connie, still arranging things on the table.

"Not coming. Oh. Well," Connie swallowed the questions she knew would be labeled nosy. "That's one less worry about the menu. And onions, then."

Cas sat down and picked up his napkin, raising his eyebrows at Missy.

In the silence, Missy tilted her head, looking from her father's raised eyebrows to her mother's concerned but sealed lips.

"I just said I don't have a date with Chuck, Saturday. I didn't know it was going to be such a shock." She reached for a roll.

Connie laughed, realizing how overdrawn their reactions had been. "It's not really shocking. I only wondered what happened to make you cancel your date. And was trying not to ask any of those nosy questions I'm so famous for," she added.

"Thanks," Missy giggled. "I know that must have been a strain. Truth is, I didn't exactly cancel it. It was sort of a, ah, mutual cancellation. Then afterwards, I decided it was best anyway. I don't think I know him as well as I thought I did." She turned to Cas.

"And dad, I think where he wanted to go Saturday may be connected with Darrell Spruce's weird club and their wild and free meeting or whatever it is."

Cas put down his fork beside his plate. It's not every day your daughter gets invited to an orgy, or a meeting for planning one.

"You said any kind of information or talk might help, didn't you?"

"Don't tell me he wanted you to go to one of those meetings?" Cas's dark brows drew together darkening further an already stormy frown.

"From what he said, I think so. Anyway, we were talking between classes about our date for Saturday and he started talking about doing something different. That's what he called it, something different. He seemed excited about whatever it was. I still don't know for sure if that's what he was talking about. But he said this group he wanted to go somewhere with was doing a lot of fun things and they were soon going to have some kind of big party. With people from other counties coming to it too. Then he said something about Darrell Spruce being in the group."

Missy glanced at Connie, taking them both into her confidence. "You should have seen the look on his face! That's what made me see him as not too bright. You'd think he'd been invited to have lunch with the governor or something. I didn't say anything to that. I mean about Darrell coming. And he rattled on until I could see it must be one of those screwball meetings he wanted to go to. I was so disgusted with him! But by then he was so wound up about it I had to say something to make him understand what I thought of that. He was so excited it hadn't even dawned on him I wouldn't want to go. I told him I wouldn't go to one of those meetings if everything else in the county was closed."

"Good for you," came out in low growl between Cas's teeth.

Missy shrugged. "I guess we both sounded off. I said not to bother coming over Saturday, and that was that."

She tossed her head for emphasis and grinned at Connie. "I'm glad of it. So, bring on the onions!"

Cas resumed his dinner. "It sounds like Darrell Spruce is trying hard to impress everybody and set himself up as some kind of leader. Did Chuck tell you where the meeting is going to be?"

"From what he said they must be going up on Peaceful Ridge again. He told me they had met there before but this time, they're going to be careful not to leave any signs they've been there. He said there was plenty of room and privacy, no one around for miles, which sounds like the cemetery. You said they left trash and turned over some tombstones last time. So that must be where it's going to be since he mentioned it being so private, and cleaning up this time, don't you think?"

Cas nodded. "Yes. It's Peaceful Ridge, you can bet on it. That they're planning on cleaning up after themselves is a dead give-away, pardon the pun," he chuckled. "Thanks for the tip."

The smile quickly disappeared. "Missy, have you heard anything at all about Denise? Anyone hint there was anyone who didn't like her or jealous of her? Even a remote reason mentioned about why she was killed?"

"No, dad. I haven't heard anyone even mention her name. It's as if she's been forgotten in the excitement Darrell Spruce is stirring up with this club of his. Poor Denise," she added sadly.

"I know it must seem that way, but we've not forgotten her. Right now my office has more reports coming in about cattle thefts and related things than anything on the Davis case. There doesn't seem to be any place to start unraveling what happened to her." He noticed Connie's glum expression and helped himself to more meat.

"This good dinner deserves better conversation. This is good, Connie. I'm glad you're not driving to Fort Craig now, or is that selfish?"

"No, it's not." Connie perked up, "I'm glad too. I'd have missed this sale for one thing and we wouldn't be having this good dinner. Not to mention I enjoyed shopping with Miss Mayme and Miss Minnie."

At work, Cas jumped back into his jumble of unfinished cases and problems, following up on the reports of cattle thefts. He reached for the phone. When he got to feeling his problems were coming in bunches like bananas he called his fellow disciple of law and order, Harlan for a conference.

"Harlan," Cas said, pleased Harlan had answered the phone. "I've got those printouts you sent in front of me. There are several dates where these so-called supernatural doings and the suspected cattle thefts were either the same date or only one or two days apart. I noticed the goat, too. So Tinwhistle's wasn't the only goat stolen."

"Yeah, I remember that. And the farmer who owned it was just as mad as Matthew Tinwhistle, too. I don't have to tell you how much fun it is to have these farmers breathing down your neck when you don't know which way to turn or what to look for."

"I've not had any success on the Davis case either but I've got a chance to try something that might help. Will you do me a favor?"

"Anything I can do, what is it?"

"I've got hear-say information there's going to be one of those suspected devil worship meetings up on Peaceful Ridge tomorrow night. Have you got a man who could go and watch? He could report what's actually going on and maybe pick up something about the murder, since a lot of the school students will be there. I need someone who can pass for a high school student or someone close to their age, since they're trying to drum up members for their group."

"You need someone about eighteen with twenty years experience like all the other local employers?" Harlan laughed at his predicament. "Being that young he might need more experience than he's had a chance to get for going undercover. But it might work."

"Yeah, experience would be nice. But from what I hear these club members are doing, they're beating the bushes, trying to get everyone they can to come. So I don't think it will be dangerous unless he would stand out as way too old for this crowd and been in law enforcement long enough to look like a policeman. My youngest deputy is pushing the thirties, poor old guy."

Cas grinned into the phone, picturing Doug Freeman. "You got any young blood in Marble County?"

Harlan laughed again, "I've got just the man! He's new. My newest deputy. He's trying hard to fit in, in spite of being the rookie and teased, and called 'kid' by the others. He'd be perfect."

"Sounds like just what I'm looking for."

"I'll get hold of him and call you back. Just between us old folks, he'll be tickled to death to get this chance at something the others can't do. Let him get in a little teasing of his own. It'd be a bit of justice. Besides which, if the others let him live, I think he's going to be a good man. I'll get back with you soon as I can."

"Thanks. I'll be right here waiting for your call. We need a break of some kind, maybe this will be it."

Missy saw Casey out of the corner of her eye as she stood in front of her locker. He was coming down the hall toward her but walking slowly, as if he hadn't made up his mind whether to come and speak to her or not. She picked up two of the books she had put into the locker then replaced them, moving a bookmark in one of them. When he got closer, she looked around and smiled.

Casey smiled back, his lip was about healed.

"Hi," he said, stopping about three feet away from the locker door.

"Hi, yourself. I see your lip's almost healed now. And your yellow and green eye, too," Missy giggled.

She moved a little closer to look at it as she reached back to close the locker door.

"Yeah…." Casey grinned, touching the lip lightly. "It really stood out, didn't it? But I think I'm going to live, even if I can't play the grand piano."

"Oh well, I'm not all that hung up on piano music anyway," Missy dismissed that.

Encouraged by her grin he went on. "There's a new movie on at the theater in the Mall, or there will be Saturday. Would you like to go? I've got my car fixed so we'll have transportation," he added hopefully.

"Sure, I'd like to go. I heard about what happened to your car," she said carefully. "I'm glad your mom wasn't hurt." She gave him a serious look. "That's unofficial, off the record, and all that good stuff."

"Yeah, I understand that. Your dad's pretty sharp. You know, he got there almost as fast as I did to see what happened to the car."

Missy nodded. "I know. He doesn't usually talk about things at the office at home. But that made him so mad, for someone to do that. Your mom could have been hurt or even killed."

"That was the scary part, all right. The car's fixed now." He glanced at the closed locker. "I'll take you home if you're ready, unless you're going to ride with someone else?"

"No, this is one of the times I'd be riding the school bus. I'd be glad to have a ride home. Thanks."

Outside, "Someone's waving at you." Casey pointed. "Over there."

"Oh, it's Dana. Dana Green." Missy smiled and waved to Dana as they walked toward Casey's car. "I guess she can get off the panic button now."

"Hey! Take a number!" Connie called a halt to the chaos at the dinner table.

"I think," she decided, "Since your father is the Head of the House, he should go first. The floor is yours, Sheriff Larkin."

They had just sat down to dinner and all of them seemed to be bubbling over with news.

"Thank you, Judge Connie," Cas winked at her. "Listen up, troops. We may be on the verge of getting lucky. The meeting that's going to be held Saturday up on Peaceful Ridge, reported by Deputy Missy, here." He grinned.

Missy tossed her head as if it had grown two hat sizes and broke out in a pleased smile as he continued.

"The meeting will be attended by someone who will be listening and watching to find out what goes on at the meetings and anything else he can find out about the club or anything else of interest. Maybe someone will mention Denise, maybe not. We can hope. We'll at least have first hand information on their activities and any plans for further mischief they mention they're planning."

He tried to look like the FBI and CIA combined as he added officially: "Never mind, of course, about the ID, gender, or where the undercover officer will come from." He put on his Mission Impossible face, trying not to spoil it with a grin.

"That might be hard to figure out for someone who doesn't know you and Sheriff Harlan Glover are joined at the hip," Missy observed with altogether too much amusement.

"Lord!" Cas was floored. "When she gets a little older and heaven forbid, smarter, I'll either have to shoot her or hire her!"

He looked to Connie for advice. "Which do you think it should be?"

Connie cast a perplexed eye on her offspring. "How long have I got to think it over?"

"Mom!"

It was Cas's turn to laugh. "Come on back down to earth. I've questioned nearly everyone on that list Muriel Davis gave me, some of them twice, and haven't turned up a thing. All we've got right now is, she is known to have gone to some of those club meetings. This is not to be discussed, as you already know."

"I know, dad, and I hope you learn something that will help. I saw Mrs. Davis today and I felt so sorry for her."

"What was it you wanted to tell us?" Connie turned her attention to her daughter as she rose from the table.

"Onions are out again. I have a date for Saturday with Casey Taylor."

"Casey Taylor? That's fine. I talked to him when I was questioning students. I like that boy."

"I don't know him, but if your father has met him and likes him, that's good enough for me. He's coming here to get you, isn't he?"

"Yes, we're going to a movie in the Mall and he's coming to pick me up. You can meet him then," she reassured Connie.

"He got his car fixed, if you're worried about that." She told Cas.

"Fine. No regrets about Chuck?"

"Who?" Missy put on a blank expression.

"That's my girl!" Cas spared no further regrets on a young idiot who would invite his daughter out to worship the devil and turned to Connie. "Okay, it's your turn, Connie. What's your news?"

"It will sound downright dull after all that. Miss Mayme called me about another sale, so I went and got us these steaks we're having and a nice roast for the weekend, too. It's great to be able to stay home and go shopping when I want to."

"How are they doing at the flower shop?"

"They're always busy and it looks like they're doing pretty well to me, but Miss Minnie says they're not in black figures yet. It must have taken quite a bit to get started. I asked Tim Carpenter to put in a word for them too, whenever he gets a chance. He's got some friends who are being married soon, and I think they're going to have the Andersons do their flowers for them. So evidently, they're doing just fine."

"Have you heard any more from the lawyers or other offices about typing?"

"Yes! I nearly forgot to tell you in all this excitement. Lisa Randolph called and wants me to come in for one day on Monday. She wants to talk to me about something else, too, but didn't say what. Anyway, that's where I'll be Monday."

Cas patted his lips with his napkin and grinned at her and Missy. "Looks like a good week for the Larkin clan."

On Monday, Harlan Glover called Cas about the undercover assignment his deputy had handled for him.

"You were right about the meeting. My deputy, Joe Hebert, went up there early and hid his car far enough away that he could sidle off and get away without attracting any attention if he wanted to. Parked it on the other side of the hill in some trees. They started coming right after dark, some of them had met other places and came together in vans and cars. Joe melted into the crowd without any trouble. There's not much meat in the report except to substantiate that there is an organization; Darrell Spruce is in charge of it; and they're up to no good, all right. I'll fax you Joe's report then you can call and ask any questions you might have about it."

"Our machine is free now and I'm anxious to read it. Be sure to tell him how much I appreciate this. I'll tell him too. And I do want to talk to him when he comes in. Thanks again."

"One other thing, Cas."

"What's that?"

"There are three brothers here that have been in and out of trouble most of their young lives. I have a hunch they may be responsible for the missing cattle. I don't have anything concrete to go on, but none of them work what I'd call steady, and they've managed to get a new truck somehow. It's not brand new, but a late model used one. I'm going out there and see if there's anything else that looks like they're getting unexplained money from somewhere. This picture I've got of them is not all that good, but I'm sending it. It's good enough so you can tell if you've seen any of them around your county lately."

"Okay. I'll make copies and give them to my deputies in case they've been nosing around here. It wouldn't be a long drive since they've got new wheels. Crime must still be paying better than law enforcement."

"Yeah, tell me about it. Let me know if you find out anything new. We've had a couple incidents of cattle being mutilated and there were at least two in Crawford County too. They called me about it two months ago, if I remember right. Anyway, I'll get the report and the picture of these three 'no-counts' to you now."

"Thanks I'll keep you posted."

Cas stood over the fax machine waiting for the material to come through. There were seven pages counting the picture. The picture was a bit dark but he could see the faces well enough to know he hadn't seen them around Maryvale. He sat down to read the report.

"Hebert probably went by the book, since this was his first undercover assignment," Cas glanced at the text.

There was a description of the place where the meeting was held good enough to picture the cemetery setting and the people attending the meeting. They were mostly students and a few friends who had come with them. Someone had identified the leader to Hebert as Darrell Spruce and told him he was the judge's son. There were bits of conversations and things the deputy thought might be relevant. All of it was documented in a clear, legible hand with no embellishments or opinions added in.

Cas smiled, comparing it to Joe Friday's style on Dragnet. "'Just the facts, the way he witnessed it. Gives me a feeling of the eeriness of it, there among the grave stones. And if it looked that way to him, it must have had even more of an effect on those youngsters. That's what Darrell Spruce is after, trying to impress them and make them think he's more important and powerful than he is. Powerful!

Humpf," Cas grunted, slapping down that page on the desk to start on the next.

When he finished he scanned back to where he had noticed Todd Kelly and Sid Norton's names mentioned.

They had stood behind Darrell as he talked to the others. The deputy hadn't had to ask who they were either. One of the students pointed them out to him as the ones who did the punishing for the group.

"Some selling job this is. The student who told him about the 'punishing' said they were not doing anything wrong, 'but the older people wouldn't understand and the club has to be kept secret.' Yeah I'll bet."

Cas frowned, his hands crumpling the edges of the paper. "What's this? So, they really are planning to have an orgy. An orgy! I doubt if some of them can even spell it correctly." His lip curled in disgust. "Doesn't say when, just soon."

He scanned the rest of the report again carefully, noting the names the deputy had managed to get and write down. There was a boy named Chuck and a girl named Doris.

"So, Chuck found someone to go to the meeting with him," Cas mused. He was glad Chuck would not be darkening his door again, thanks to his daughter's good sense.

"There's no mention of Denise's name except when the deputy used it as an excuse for being there. That was a smart touch, to tell someone a girl named Denise told him about the meetings. Harlan's right, this boy will be good at his job. The student who asked him who told him about the meetings told him Denise had been a member of the club, but she had gone away and didn't come anymore."

Cas sighed. "Gone away…."

CHAPTER 10

Gladys put her hand over the phone's mouthpiece as Cas came into the office. "It's Tinwhistle," she mouthed silently.

Cas nodded, pointing to his door.

"Mr. Tinwhistle." Cas hugged his phone against his shoulder, pulling out his chair. "What can I do for you this morning?"

"I was just calling to see if you might have learned any more about who it is that's stealing cattle around here, and my goat too, of course."

"No, sir, but we're working on it and I do appreciate your cooperation. I've been routing patrols out your way as often as I can. Haven't had any more thefts, have you, or seen any suspicious people or activity?"

"No, and I saw the patrol car the other day. Thought they might be coming by more often. If you do find the one or ones responsible I'm sure going to prosecute. You don't have to worry about that!"

"Good for you. And you be sure to let me know if you see anyone suspicious, we don't have much to go on right now."

"I'll do it, Sheriff Larkin. Thank you."

He sounded like he'd been deputized. Cas smiled to himself. The phone rang as soon as he replaced it.

"Yes? This is Sheriff Larkin speaking." He looked up at the clock. Two calls as soon as he'd got in.

"It's me," Gladys told him. "Caleb Martin is on the phone. You're getting it with both barrels, aren't you?"

"I guess I'd feel the same in their shoes. Put him on, I can take it."

Caleb Martin's voice was more pleasant than Cas was braced for and had an edge of excitement in it.

"Sheriff Larkin, I wanted to call and see if you had learned anything else about who's stealing our cattle, and tell you there was another to do of some kind up on Peaceful Ridge. Up above my west pasture there. You said something about a bunch of kids being up there before, you know. Well, looks like there may have been another one."

"Yes, Caleb. There was some trouble up there before and there has been another gathering up there. In fact, we knew about this one and had someone up there observing what went on." He paused, letting the gravity of it sink in. "That's confidential, of course, Caleb."

"Yes, yes. Of course, I understand. Had someone up there, did you?"

"There wasn't anything unusual, just a large group of young people, and they were a lot more careful this time. I don't think they wanted anyone to know they were up there. There was no damage this time, and they didn't leave a mess of trash like they did before."

"Oh." Caleb's voice dropped, the excitement fading from it. "Well, I'm glad you knew about it. " Caleb managed to sound disappointed and relieved at the same time.

"Who were they? Was it just kids?"

"That's right. It was some high school students and some more of their friends they must have brought with them. There weren't many who don't live here."

"What were they up to? My wife has been afraid they were devil worshipers or a gang of some kind you know, that's why I didn't report the missing cattle sooner. Did you get the list of dates I sent you?"

"Yes, thank you. I got it. I've been comparing the dates you sent with some of the dates of the other things that have happened around here."

"You mean those kids and their carrying on?" Caleb sounded hesitant. "I can't believe kids would do that, would steal cattle, even if they do get strange ideas sometimes. They wouldn't have any use for the cattle or know what to do with them." Caleb was doubtful of any connection there.

"I don't know, Caleb. We're looking at it from every possible angle to try and figure out what's going on and find it if there is some kind of connection. Have you seen any strangers or noticed any strange trucks or other vehicles around your place recently?"

"No, not that I've seen. But I'll keep watching and let you know if I do."

"All right, Caleb, thanks for calling."

Gladys appeared in the door as he hung up. "Muriel Davis called while you were on the phone. She wouldn't leave a number, said not to bother you. She was just calling to see if there was anything new on her daughter's case or anything she could do." She paused, "I feel so sorry for her, she's such a nice person. Trying to hold her head up when I know how awful this is for her and her sister, too."

She looked at him wistfully with a half smile. "Nobody else seems to worry about bothering us."

"I wish I could tell her something encouraging. I'm about out of people to talk to and haven't turned up anything, even from those club members."

His jaw set like a vice, eyes hardening as he spoke. "There are some students I'm going to talk to again with regard to where they were that night. Those two hoodlums that beat up Casey Taylor are at the top of that list. I talked to them about this club of Darrell's, but I haven't really leaned on them yet as far as the Davis case goes, or asked where they were when Denise was killed. They put such a high priority on secrecy they could have thought she knew something they didn't want her to tell. That Norton boy looks mean enough to have done it."

Gladys nodded. "It would have to have been someone like that, someone mean. Everyone seems to have liked her and says Denise was a sweet girl. Shall I get Mrs. Davis's number for you?"

"No, it's here in the file." He reached for his phone. "I'll call her now."

Margaret Avery answered the phone.

"This is Cas Larkin, I'm returning Muriel's call."

Muriel Davis took the phone. "I'm sorry to have bothered you, I know how busy you are. I thought there might be something else I can do to help you."

"No, but I appreciate your asking. It's taking time to do all the investigating and talking to people that must be done. I wish I could tell you we're making better headway, but so far there is not one suspicious or negative thing we've run across. Denise was well liked. Do you know of anyone who might have resented her popularity or been jealous for any other reason?"

"No. There's no one I can think of. If anything," Muriel added sadly, "she and her friends got along too well. They were always thinking up things to do together. The only time I had to discipline her was the time I told you about, when she went out the window to join them at the Mall and I grounded her."

"I know how it is, I have a teenager myself. By the way, did the bracelet turn up? The gold chain?"

"No. No, it didn't," Muriel answered with a sigh. "She must have been wearing it as I thought."

"I sent deputies back to the scene to look for it, but they didn't find it. I've been meaning to ask you about it. And there is something you can do, if you will."

"Of course, what is it?"

"Give me a list of Denise's teachers. Sometimes things happen in school the child won't remember, but the teacher might. I don't believe I'd ever have the patience to teach," Cas admitted ruefully.

"I don't think I would either. Even Margaret has to rely on tranquilizers sometimes, and she has the patience of Job. Hold on a minute, will you?"

"All right." He made a mental note. "Margaret Avery relies on a tranquilizer sometimes. I wonder how many others do, and have teenagers around who can get at them?"

"Here we are. I had to find the name of the study hall teacher." She read the list slowly so Cas could write down each name.

"This will do it, thank you. Call if you remember anything or have anything you want to ask. We're in the phone book if you don't have the card with our home number on it at hand."

"I will. Thanks for returning my call."

Cas went out to the front desk. "Gladys, please type these names up and leave space in between for notes. They're Denise's teachers."

He dialed the high school's number and asked for John Squires. He was out but Janice Cobb offered her help.

"I want to make my usual visit about gym and study hall time."

"All right. Any time is fine with us."

"Thank you. Could I bring my list and talk to the ones that are available this afternoon?"

"Sure, no problem. I'll tell Mr. Squires when he gets back. Come on."

John Squires heard Cas arrive and came out of his office as the sheriff handed Janice his list.

"I was just keeping the seat warm," he smiled and gestured toward his office as he left.

"I'll get the first two," Janice said. "One of them can wait out here if you want him to."

"You're getting good at this," Cas teased her.

"Just you remember that, in case John turns hateful in his old age and decides to fire me!" She laughed as she started down the hall.

He brought them in together this time. One of them was Denise's friend, Doris. Knowing that Doris had been with Chuck at the last meeting he told her bluntly, "You were at that meeting Saturday night. The one up on Peaceful Ridge."

Doris paled. Both girls were frightened but neither would admit they were at the meeting.

The two boys he interviewed last took the attitude they didn't care if he knew they were there or not, and didn't volunteer any other information. They had risen from their seats to leave when Cas called them back. They turned bored, insolent faces to hear what he had to say.

Changing to interviewing two of them at once to play them against each other as he had Todd and Sid hadn't worked.

"There's something you two should know, and I'm sure your friend, Darrell, won't tell you. If those two goons he calls his 'punishers' accidentally kill someone, or they die as a result of a beating, you will be accessories to murder and will share their punishment. The law is a lot better at punishing than they are. You'd better keep that in mind."

He turned his back on them and returned to sit down at the desk to put away his notes. When he looked up, the two boys were still standing there. They looked shaken.

"What do you mean? They're not, I mean, we don't have anything to do with that."

"The law doesn't see it that way, boys." His notes in the folder, Cas got up and came to stand close to them, speaking softly but solemnly. "The smartest thing you can do at this point is stay away from those meetings and stay away from Darrell Spruce."

"But then," one of them panicked. "Darrell may send them to punish us!"

The other boy just nodded, as if this new peril had stolen his voice.

Cas said in a kinder tone. "These meetings are not actually against the law. Or at least, what they've done so far isn't, unless you count the mess in the cemetery they made once before. But beating someone up is." He paused for emphasis. "If you are threatened, or one of them hits you, you don't have to be afraid. All you have to do is tell me, and you can bet we'll nip that in the bud. Fast!"

He opened the door as he finished speaking. They shambled out. Quiet. Thinking about what Cas had said.

Cas waved and called a thank you to Janice Cobb as he left, feeling he had accomplished something good. He had, if he read their faces right, kept some of the members away from an influence which could only get worse.

He pictured Sid and Todd. He dreaded talking to those two thugs again, and he still hadn't talked to Darrell Spruce.

Cas tucked the unpleasant thought into the unfinished business section of his brain and looked around. "Guess I might as well give Missy a ride home if I can spot her in this crowd."

He smiled to himself when he saw her. He had missed his chance. She was standing near Casey Taylor's old car in the parking lot and Casey was holding the door for her to get in. Cas went on to his own car, trying not to feel so old.

He called Gladys from the car. "Looks like I'm not going to make it back before you leave. I'm at the school. Will you look up the Kelly's address for me? Todd Kelly's parents."

He jotted down the address and thanked Gladys. He drove slowly along the street in their neighborhood, checking the numbers until he saw the house.

A middle aged woman in a wide straw hat was weeding a flower bed on the front lawn and looked inquiringly up at him as she got to her feet to come to meet him.

"Mrs. Kelly?"

"Yes. You're Sheriff Larkin, aren't you?"

"Yes, ma'am. Is Todd home yet?"

"No, he's not here. He doesn't usually get in for another hour or so. Can I help you somehow, or would you like to wait?"

"If you can spare me a few minutes. Is Mr. Kelly here? I know he sells real estate," Cas eyed the two cars parked in the driveway.

"Yes, he's here. He's doing the paperwork on a couple of houses he's hoping to close on soon. Come in. I'll call him to talk to you."

Kelly wasn't long in coming into the living room and shook hands with Cas.

"He's got the good personality a salesman needs," Cas thought as they sat down. "They both look too good and honest to have an offspring who's trying to be a 'punisher' for Darrell Spruce."

Mrs. Kelly offered tea, which Cas declined. "I don't know whether or not Todd told you, but I talked to him in regard to the new club that seems to be growing at the school."

He watched their reactions. There was only a slight puzzled glance at each other.

"A club?" Mr. Kelly asked.

"Yes. It seems to be a secret thing. Nobody wants to talk about it. I talked to him and a friend of his named Sid Norton."

"No!" Mrs. Kelly's reaction to that was immediate and vehement. "I wouldn't consider Sid Norton a friend. I'd rather he didn't even go to the same school as Todd. Is Sid, or Todd, in some kind of trouble?"

"I don't think this club is one you would approve of, if you feel that way about Sid Norton," Cas said bluntly. "It's not anything I'd want my child involved in."

"What is it," Kelly asked. "We haven't heard Todd say anything about it."

"As I said, it's a secret thing nobody wants to talk about or admit they belong to. Remember when there was something that happened up on Peaceful Ridge? Some tombstones were turned over and trash thrown everywhere?"

"This is the group that did that?"

"And you say Todd and Sid Norton are members of it?" Mrs. Kelly looked worried.

"I'm sure the reason you haven't heard him say anything about it is they're trying to keep anyone from finding out about it. They have two so-called 'punishers' who enforce this code of silence. They beat up a boy pretty bad recently."

"Oh!" Mrs. Kelly was shocked.

Kelly chuckled nervously, "You make it sound like a junior mafia! An organized crime club. Punishers?"

"That's a pretty close description. They mean to get more powerful if they're not stopped, and stopped now. I mean to do that," Cas stated flatly.

"Well, thank heaven for that," Mrs. Kelly's hands twisted her wide brimmed hat.

"Is there something we can do to help? And who are these punishers you said they have?"

Cas gave it to them straight. "They're Sid Norton and your son, Todd."

The Kellys sat speechless. Dismayed. Before anyone spoke, they heard a noise in the room behind them. Todd had come in the back. He stuck his head in, saw Cas, and ran toward the back of the house.

"Todd," Kelly thundered, going in pursuit of his son.

Mrs. Kelly sat still as if stunned until Kelly came back holding Todd by the arm.

"Sit down," Kelly ordered.

Todd sat.

Cas leaned toward Todd. "Son, I want you to tell your parents about this club you've decided to join. About the beating you and your friend Sid Norton gave Casey Taylor. Get yourself straightened out."

"I don't have to talk to you!" Someone else's bravado came out of Todd's mouth. His lower lip trembled.

"Yes, you do. You will. I'm giving you a chance to get out of this mess before you get into any more serious trouble than you're in now. When I talked to Casey Taylor, he didn't want to tell me who beat him up, but there are other ways of finding out. You're lucky you're not in jail and being prosecuted for that beating. It's time to turn yourself around if you've got the stuff in you to do it."

Into the heavy silence Cas inserted with heavy emphasis. "There won't be any more chances."

It seemed an eternity Todd sat there, all their eyes on him. Then his eyes on his mother's, whose own eyes glistened with unshed tears, his shoulders sagged and tears welled up in his own. He dashed them away and got a grip on his emotions.

"Mother, I didn't want to do it." He looked at his dad. "It was no fun for me."

He studied the carpet between his feet, "But Sid, he enjoyed it! He likes to hurt people! You were right about him, Mom."

Cas spoke to Kelly. "As I said, Casey is not going to press charges against Todd, and what he told me can stay unofficial."

He turned to Todd. "You stay away from those meetings, and stay away from Darrell. If they threaten you or try to harm you in any way, call my office and we'll put a stop to that. You don't have to fear them."

"Thank you, sheriff." Kelly got up and extended his hand as Cas rose to go. "Todd will certainly not be at any more of those club meetings."

"One more thing. You knew Denise Davis, didn't you Todd? You were in some of the same classes."

"Yes, sir. I knew her. She came to some of the meetings. I think she was at the last one before she died. She came with Darrell. There were others around, but I think she was with him."

"Do you know of anyone who was mad at her or had anything against her? Would want to harm her?"

"No, sir. Everybody liked her. Even Darrell. I heard him say once she had one of the few good brains in the school." He added seriously, "I hope you find whoever killed her. I've heard other people talking about it, and nobody knows any reason anybody would do something like that."

"Where were you the night she was killed? Its a routine question," he explained for his parents' benefit as well as Todd's.

"I, we, Sid Norton and I went to a movie." A nervous smile appeared. "We ate so much buttered popcorn I think the girl behind the refreshment counter would remember us, she's in a couple of my classes, too."

"All right, thank you. I'll more than likely be talking to you again. Here's one of my cards, in case you should think of anything or hear anything that might help us find out what happened."

Cas headed home. "Sanctuary, I need you," he breathed as he pulled away from the curb. "I feel like I've taken a beating too, an emotional one. Maybe I should borrow one of Margaret Avery's tranquilizers myself!"

CHAPTER 11

Reluctant to move, Cas looked out the window at the blue sky. A slight breeze rustled the leaves of the old oak tree outside. It looked like a pleasant weekend weather-wise even if what was ahead of him wasn't.

He called and made an appointment to see Sid Norton's parents Sunday afternoon, wanting to talk to them and Sid at the same time. The rest of his time off he dedicated to catching up on yard work and other home chores he had let slide.

Connie cooked the roast she had bought at Lorenzo's market. Cas complimented it after the first couple of bites. "This the one you bought on sale?"

"Yes, it's good, isn't it?" Connie was pleased. "I told the Andersons to be sure and call me when Cortez Lorenzo puts out his signs from now on. He just sticks them up in the window and has the sale the next day."

"What happened to putting an ad in the paper? Does he just want to get people to watch his window? I'll bet that's it."

"I don't know. Miss Mayme might."

"It's not important. This is good, that's what's important. It's his business how he wants to advertise."

"Mom?"

"What is it?"

"I'm going to skip dessert. Casey will be here in half an hour and I'm going up to get dressed."

"All right, there will be apple crisp on the stove if you want it when you get home."

Cas's eyes followed Missy as she went out. "I can't believe our little girl is so grown-up. I'm not ready for her to be grown up." He looked so unhappy, Connie touched his hand.

"There, there," she patted his hand gently like a kindergartener with a problem. "You'll be all right. No parents are ever ready for their children to be grown-up. Think of the good points about it. There will be more time for just the two of us, and we will have a guest room, not that we need one," she smiled.

Cas grinned like an imp. "How much will you give me not to tell Harry we've got one?"

"Your Aunt Harriet's on the near side of seventy whether she admits it or not, and I won't deal with blackmail. Besides which, she's pretty good at finding out things for herself." Connie remembered Harry had informed her she had stopped counting when Connie had made the mistake of pointing out her age as an argument against something she wanted to do. An argument Connie had lost.

"I guess I get my detecting genes from that side of the family," Cas laughed.

"No, you didn't. Don't you remember her comments about inheriting genes? She always says nobody got anything from her, she's still got it all! Now, where was I?"

"Okay, okay. I know when I'm losing the debate. Besides, we aren't out of the woods yet. There's still college to get through. I hope Missy will go to a state school so she can be at home, at least on weekends."

"Might know you'd just go on to the next batch of problems. You're about the most dedicated worrier I know. Cut it out and enjoy life as it comes, why don't you?"

"Sure, I will, about the same time you retire from matchmaking."

Connie wrinkled her nose. "That was a low blow. I'd better get you some dessert to go with your coffee and sweeten you up."

Cas heard the doorbell when Casey arrived but stayed in the den, looking over some papers he had brought home with him. He heard voices coming toward the den. He laid aside the fax sheets Harlan had sent him and looked up.

"Dad, Casey's here!"

"Hi, son." Cas extended his hand and smiled. "You look a lot better than you did last time I saw you."

"Yes, sir. I feel a lot better, too," Casey grinned. "It's a pretty safe bet now I'm going to live."

Casey glanced at the papers. "I'll tell my mom she was right to vote for you, you even bring work home with you." He picked up the sheaf of papers.

"Now, how do you know that isn't classified, top secret and all that?" Cas stopped abruptly when he saw the expression change on Casey's face. "What is it?"

Casey stared at the fax of the three brothers from Marble County. "This is the man who came to the meeting I told you about. The one who gave us the goat head."

"Which one?" Cas took the paper.

"This one. It's a little dark but I'm sure that's the man. Is he in some kind of trouble?"

"He's in and out of trouble a lot, according to the Marble County Sheriff. He faxed me the picture along with some other information I needed from him. Are you positive that's the man?"

"I think so. If it's not, he sure did look an awful lot like him. But, I'm pretty sure that's him all right. Darrell didn't tell us his name. I don't know if anyone else heard what it was or not. Should I ask?"

"No. Don't do anything. Or say anything. I know who they are. Don't tell anyone anything about seeing this picture. We're on watch now in case any of them show up around here again."

"Okay." Casey looked toward the door of the den. "Missy's ready to go."

"Curfew is eleven or eleven-thirty at the latest."

"Good deal!" Casey grinned, "Missy's mom told us eleven o'clock."

"She did, hmm? Maybe I'd better just go with you!" Cas pretended to get up.

"Come on, Casey!" Missy took the hand Casey held out and ran with him to the front door, Cas's laughter following them.

Cas picked up the fax of the three brothers and studied the face of the generous citizen who had donated the club a goat's head. Somebody else's goat's head.

Earl Norton had grudgingly given Cas directions to find his way to their trailer. Cas left a little early to give himself time to look for it. Following the directions Norton gave him brought him to the eastern edge of town. It wasn't far from the box manufacturing plant where Earl Norton worked.

He found the trailer and was surprised to see it was neat and well cared for. Flowers bloomed around the foundation and the lawn was neatly cut. He'd had a different picture in mind after talking to Sid, and his brief phone conversation with Earl.

Mrs. Norton opened the door for him when he knocked.

As he came in, Earl stood up and nudged Sid who stood up too but slowly, as if to let Cas know it wasn't his idea to show any respect.

"Would you like some coffee, Sheriff Larkin?" Mrs. Norton asked him.

Cas smiled and refused, nodding to Earl.

Without speaking, Earl indicated a chair. They sat, waiting for Cas to tell them why he had come.

Cas explained he was questioning everyone who knew Denise Davis. He had a list of questions on a clipboard he laid on his lap as he spoke.

Sid answered his questions if not cheerfully, at least readily.

Earl Norton and his wife watched and listened.

"Where were you the night Denise Davis was killed?"

The question took Sid by surprise. He hesitated, giving Cas a dark look.

"You don't think he done that, do you?" Earl was hostile now, and Mrs. Norton was shocked.

"Who did it is a thing we haven't learned yet. This is one of the questions I'm asking everyone who knew her. Knew Denise," Cas explained.

"I was at the picture show. Me and Todd Kelly went. We didn't know nothin' about it till the next day."

"Anything," Mrs. Norton said absently correcting Sid.

"Todd Kelly told me the same thing, but I had to hear it from you for the record. Do you know of anyone who had any reason to do her any harm, or was mad at her for any reason, no matter how farfetched it seems?"

"No." Sid answered slowly, becoming wary as well as resentful.

"Are you still a member of that club that Darrell Spruce started?"

"Why do you want to know? It hasn't got anything to do with Denise."

"Denise went to some of the meetings. Do you remember seeing her there?"

Sid reluctantly nodded his head, wary eyes still on Cas. "Yeah, I saw her once or twice."

"And you and Todd are officers in that club."

"What difference does it make?"

"Just answer the question." Cas didn't smile.

"Yeah. Me and Todd went."

"And you are officers. They call you 'punishers'. Is that right?"

Earl Norton began to look suspiciously at Sid.

"Isn't that right?" Cas repeated.

"Yeah, I guess so," Sid muttered, studying the floor.

"And what is it you do? Why are you called 'punishers' by Darrell and the members?"

Sid seemed to shrink a little as he looked apprehensively at his father. Earl Norton was big enough to take him down a notch or two, and was beginning to look as if he might do it.

"What is all this punisher stuff," Earl Norton broke in. He directed the question to his son, demanding an answer.

Sid sat sullen and silent.

"Do you know, sheriff?" Mrs. Norton asked softly, as if hoping he didn't.

"They enforced the code of silence. Anyone who did anything Darrell didn't approve of, or if they spoke out of turn, Darrell had them punished for it."

"What did they do? I know there was something, for you to be here asking that." Earl turned his attention to Cas.

"They beat up one of the students. Pretty bad. He was out of school a couple of days because of it. He wouldn't tell me who did it, but in the course of the investigation we found out about it. Todd owned up to it. He's dropped out of the club and taken the chance he has to get himself back on the right track."

Cas looked at Sid until he met his eyes. "The boy you beat up is not pressing charges and I'm giving you the same chance I gave Todd to put this behind you and get out of trouble. You can take it, or you can get in worse trouble and wind up in jail. It's up to you." A deep silence followed.

"I think you better say something, boy!" Earl Norton leaned toward Sid.

"All right. I won't go to any more meetings." Sid shrugged, "I, I don't know what I'll tell Darrell though."

"You don't have to tell him anything." Mrs. Norton spoke up firmly.

"His dad's only a judge, not God," she informed him. "You don't have to tell him anything at all. You don't owe him any explanation."

Earl shot his wife an admiring glance. "Your ma's right. You don't have to tell him anything or explain anything.

And I don't want you going to any more of those meetings. You keep your word. You hear me?"

"Yes."

"Yes what?" His parents looked at him in stony silence, united and determined.

"Yes, sir. I won't go to any more of the meetings."

Sid was not happy, but Cas was sure he was in good hands. His mother and father would see that he stayed out of trouble. It was a relief that felt like a weight had been lifted from his shoulders as he got up to leave.

Earl Norton walked him to his car in a gesture that showed the gratitude he felt, but had trouble putting into words. Glad to have the chance to stop Sid from getting into deeper trouble.

Cas gave him one of his cards and thanked him for his cooperation, glad to have averted any further trouble with Sid.

"Hi," Lisa Randolph greeted Connie, Monday morning. "I'll help you get set up."

"Thanks, is that what you need on the desk there?"

"That's the correspondence. Here's a list of addresses for the box of envelopes. Let me know if you need more. The list is pretty long. And I want to talk to you before you get started."

"All right." Curious, Connie sat in the typing chair and turned around to face Lisa's desk.

Lisa indicated a machine on the other side of her desk. "Have you ever used one of these?"

"Yes," Connie examined the transcriber and the headset beside it.

"It's not the same as the one I used to use in Fort Craig, but most of them are pretty much alike."

"Before you get started on the correspondence, will you please try it out and see if you can manage it all right?"

Connie smiled confidently as she picked it up. "I'm sure there won't be that much difference."

Lisa plugged it in for her and showed her the controls. "There's a message on there for you to practice on. I'll be working here anyway, let me know when you finish."

Connie made all the adjustments and started the dictation, fingers poised to begin.

"This is a test," Dick Randolph's voice began the dictation. "I'm not too sure who it is who's being tested, you or me or the machine? This memo, hopefully, will let you get acquainted with the equipment and see if you can understand my dictation. There will also be statements from time to time, if you want to transcribe them. If you decide to take this on, as they say on Mission Impossible, I'll be grateful. I won't have to listen to Lisa and Jill gripe about doing statements any more. This is the end of the message. Thank you."

Smothering an amused chuckle, Connie turned and handed the typed memo to Lisa. "I'm sure it will be no problem."

Wondering at her expression, Lisa glanced at the memo. "That stinker!" She made a face at the paper she held, "We didn't gripe all that much."

She appealed to Connie. "We really don't have time to do the things."

"It takes a while to do them," Connie readily agreed. "That was the objection where I used to work, that and sometimes you couldn't hear them too well."

"At least we don't have that problem, it's just that you hate to start on them and have something else come up. And Jill out there could never get a whole sentence typed without some kind of interruption, you can imagine."

"I can. Meeting the public and answering the phone out there, it would be hard to concentrate on a statement."

"There just never seems to be a good time to do them. The bright side is the ones we've got from clients so far have been easy to hear, so that's not a problem. Perhaps coming in to do them and not having to take care of the every day interruptions will make the difference. Shall I tell him you'll come in and do the statements, then?" Lisa glanced again at the memo.

"Yes, I'll do them. The machine isn't all that different, I'll get used to it. And you say he knows they take a while to do, I don't want him to think I'm slow," Connie worried.

"Oh, he knows," Lisa smiled. "Jill and I have both told him that often enough, though I wouldn't have called it griping to point that out."

Missy saw Chuck and Doris walking together as she went to her locker between classes. Chuck went into a classroom and Doris came back when she saw Missy.

"Hi," Doris said a little uncertainly. "Chuck told me you and he broke up."

"I guess you might call it that," Missy stopped to talk. "But we were not going steady. We only dated quite a bit. We weren't all that serious."

"I've dated him since then, twice." Doris stopped, self-conscious.

"That's fine with me," Missy assured her. "I've been dating someone else too."

"Oh, good," Doris flashed a relieved smile. "I didn't want you to be mad at me. I wanted to make sure. There's the bell, bye!" Doris hurried away looking happy.

Missy wondered briefly about what Doris thought of Chuck and the club. She hadn't heard her or Diane mention Denise lately, and they had been her closest friends. Depressed at the thought, she hugged her books to her breast, feeling a chill.

"One day you've got a life and a future, and friends, then everything just moves on without you. Instant oblivion!"

Cas Larkn hadn't forgotten Denise. The only tangible clue he had to look for at the moment was the bracelet Muriel was certain she was wearing. Everywhere he turned he met either a wall of silence because of Darrell's club, or what he felt was genuine bewilderment that anyone would want to hurt Denise.

He hadn't been too surprised Rhodes couldn't find the bracelet when he sent him out to look for it. Such a tiny thing, like a needle in a haystack in that woodsy place. But if Denise was killed where her body was found, that bracelet should be there. Drumming his fingers on his desk thinking about the tiny thing in all that underbrush, he came to a decision and reached for the phone to dial Harlan Glover's number.

What are friends for? He smiled to himself already feeling better.

Harlan Glover was a couple of inches taller than Cas, a string bean like Rhodes Cromwell, and was about eight years older. He had a droll sense of humor, an easy going manner, and usually, a wad of tobacco in his jaw.

"Sheriff's Office. Harlan Glover speaking."

"I'm glad I caught you. I hate leaving messages when I'm in a hurry."

"Yeah, lucky you," was Harlan's dry comment. "What can I do for you?"

"I'll get to that. Remember the picture of the no 'count brothers you faxed me?"

"Yeah. Beauties, aren't they?"

"One of the high school students identified the youngest one as a man who came to one of their meetings. He said he gave them a goat's head. A skeleton head for their club to use at their meetings."

"It was him? The youngest one? He's sure?"

"Yes. At least ninety percent sure, to quote him. He said if it's not him, it was someone who looks just like him and that's good enough for me, I know the boy."

"Do you have those sheets with the dates on them there in front of you?"

"Them and the pictures too. I noticed the dates of the thefts and the few meetings I know about are around the same time, as I said before."

"There's been a little activity here too. Some cattle mutilations. I don't know of any more organizations yet. Do you suppose that's our connection, that these jerks are stealing cattle a few at a time under the cover of these kids and their nonsense? That would explain their generosity. Reckon they're trying to make people think it's this devil worship thing instead of plain out cattle rustling?"

"Sure points that way. Why else would one of them come to a meeting and give them a goat's head and all that nonsense? They don't strike me as being that interested in helping out a bunch of kids. As you pointed out, it would explain their generosity. They must think this devil worship thing will scare people enough to keep them from reporting the thefts right away. I know of one case where it worked. The first time Caleb Martin called me he said he'd been missing one or two head for about a year, but his wife didn't want any trouble. He finally got mad enough to call me anyway."

"I don't know. It's farfetched, but I wouldn't put anything past that bunch. I told you they've got a new truck. I went by there to look around after the last time we talked. In addition to the new truck, they've managed to get themselves a couple of beat up old horse trailers too. You'd think the dumb things could figure out having the horse trailers and no horses would generate some questions, wouldn't you?"

"Maybe they think they're safe. Have you talked to any of them?"

"Not officially. I saw one of them in town and asked him about that new truck. He told me it was in all of their names and they're all making the payments on it. He said they swapped in the two old trucks they had to get it. Pretty good deal if it's true. I'd have bet they couldn't sell them for junk, so I doubt it. They usually had to cannibalize parts off the others to get one of them in running condition."

"New truck and horse trailers, sounds like they're making plans to me. I'll watch for them around here. It was just luck I found out about this goat's head business. Listen, I've got a favor to ask."

"Okay," Harlan went along. "I think I still owe you a couple from before we stopped counting. Is it on the theft or the other?"

"The Davis case. Denise's mother says she was wearing a bracelet the night she was killed. We haven't been able to find it. I don't think she was killed where she was found, but if we find that bracelet, we'll know."

"You sure she was wearing it?" Harlan sounded doubtful, "This is a terrible thing, she may not remember exactly what the girl was wearing or not wearing."

"Yes, I think she was wearing it. Her mother says she always wore it, and it's not at home anywhere. She's sure she had it on. Missy's seen her wearing it too, at school. Didn't you tell me once you had one of those metal detectors?"

"Yeah, we've had it quite a while, but I can do better than that."

"Better than a metal detector? Like what?"

"I've got a nephew that's a rock hound. He's got a smaller one that detects gold."

"Gold? You're kidding. I didn't know there was such a thing."

"I wouldn't have either if he hadn't told me about it. But he's got one, I've seen it. In fact, I think he brought it home last time he came. He starts bringing home things he doesn't use very much to lighten the load coming home when the semester's over. You're welcome to the metal detector, of course, but I'll check on the one for gold if you want it."

"I want it. It would be exactly what we need if he'll lend it to me. How soon do you think I can get it? And Harlan," Cas promised hopefully, "I'll take care of it, use it myself and get it back to you as soon as we get through going over the scene with it."

CHAPTER 12

Miss Mayme answered the ringing phone with a smile in her voice.

"You sound so happy, business must be good." Connie smiled, too, as if happiness was contagious.

"I am. Can't imagine why I wasted all those years teaching school." Miss Mayme chuckled. "How's the typing business?"

"As well as I can honestly say I want it to be. I called to check on whether Lorenzo's got a sale sign up for today. I'm also going to call and check on whether my cards have come in. I thought I might get lucky on both counts."

"Haven't seen a sign today, at least so far. Better luck with the cards."

"They're probably in."

The tinkle of the bell on the flower shop door sounded. "Oh, I hear someone coming into the shop, I won't keep you. See you soon."

Connie thumbed through the phone book looking for Pronto Prints. Feeling sure it had been longer than the promised week she dialed the number.

"Pronto Prints," a woman said.

"My name is Connie Larkin. I'm calling to see if the cards I ordered have come in yet. It was for freelance typing, if that rings a bell."

"Why yes," the pleasant voice answered. "They're ready. I had your number here to call and let you know. You know they're a better buy in larger numbers," she said tentatively.

"I know. I'm just getting started in business now but I'll sure keep that in mind. I have some more errands to do so I'll come by and pick them up today. Thank you."

In his office, Cas was sitting over the phone like a mother hen waiting for Harlan's call. His mind had wandered and he jumped with a nervous start when the phone finally rang.

Gladys beat him to it and called, "It's Harlan Glover."

Cas picked up the phone. "Harlan?"

"Yeah. I checked on the metal detector as soon as I could, my sister's got her recorder on. My wife was out shopping somewhere, so it took me a while."

"Don't worry," Cas assured him with irritating camaraderie. "I won't tell anyone the sheriff of Marble County can't find his own wife!"

"Thank you, old buddy," came the sarcastic rejoinder. "Your luck is better than you deserve. She's already called me in case I was looking for her told me my nephew did bring the gold detector home. She told me they had laughed about whether he might need it at school or not. Soon as I can get my wife over there to get it, I can send one of my deputies to meet yours late this afternoon, if you need it that soon."

"I need it a week ago the way I'm getting along on this case. Needling you's been the only bright spot in my day."

"Still nothing to go on, huh? And the victim a youngster, too. I can understand you being on a low limb. But this gold detector will help, one way or another. You'd never be able to see something that small in a wooded area without it, so hang in there. Even if you don't find the bracelet, something's bound to turn up soon."

"Thanks. I'd bet my shirt the Davis girl wasn't killed where the body was found. As I said, it might convince me otherwise if that bracelet is there. But right now I'm not even sure that we're looking in the right place. It's just another one of those things we've got to do, find it if it's there. It could have been lost in the struggle, if there was one. There's no sign of any struggle either. It would take something concrete like finding that bracelet to convince me that's where she died."

"I remember you saying something about the position of the body."

"Yeah, it didn't look like she'd fallen. Not natural, more like she was dropped. There was no blood, no sign of a struggle and I can't see her going in there in the dark either if she was alive. Something's just not right."

"She was killed instantly. No chance to struggle maybe." Harlan helped him think of possibilities.

"There was some kind of action, for her to have the bruises on her ankle and foot. I don't know, it just doesn't add up for me. Anyway, there's so much underbrush around the scene. We'll go over all of it with that gold detector. If that bracelet's there, we'll find it this time."

"It's tough not to have any leads at all." Harlan's voice took on a positive tone, "But if your gut feeling is that she was killed somewhere else, she probably was."

"Since we'll have the detector we'll go over the pathway in as well as the scene. Cover all possibilities. Wherever it could have dropped off her arm that night."

"Keep pluggin' on it. Where do you want my deputy to meet yours? This side of the Roadhouse?"

"Yeah, that's fine. About five-thirty?"

"It'll be there. Good luck."

Connie was nervous as she parked her car outside Dick Randolph's law office. "I wonder if I was wise to take on those recorded statements. If they're hard to hear, and they aren't pleased with them they might not be pleased with the job I do. And I'm depending a lot on word of mouth recommendations right now, trying to get started. Since

I've told Lisa I would do them I'll just have to wait and see whether I've made a mistake or not."

When she entered the office Lisa Randolph came out to meet her before Jill had a chance to announce her.

"Hi, I was afraid you'd chicken out!" Lisa shot her a relieved smile as she opened the office door for her.

"Two of the statements are pretty long," she continued. "Do what you can on them now then come in tomorrow if you can. I put on the headphone and listened to parts of both of them and they sounded clear. They are usually audible, though. The two shorter ones are from an insurance company, routine statements on claims so I'm sure they will be all right."

"Ugh! Three of them," Connie cringed inwardly. She glanced toward them as she set down her typewriter.

"I'm glad you listened to them. I've tried to transcribe some really bad ones."

"I know, so have I. It seems like nothing is as frustrating as a bad statement. I had one once where the man who was doing the recording was taking the statement by phone and he had a rock program going in the background. That and another one where loud street noises drowned out the answers. Those were about the worst ones I've tried to do."

Connie nodded, plugging in both machines. "Makes you appreciate the good ones." She placed the paper supply Lisa had laid out within easy reach and settled herself in her chair.

Lisa looked around before closing the middle drawer of her desk. "I'll be working on some files. If there's anything you need pick up the phone and dial pound zero. I'll close the door on my way out so you won't be bothered with the noise out front."

Cas went out to Gladys's desk. "Is there, oh, I see Doug. I was looking for a deputy," he explained.

Doug Freeman heard him and stood waiting. "I'm available as they say in the ads, what is it?"

"I need someone to go and meet one of the Marble County deputies out the other side of the Roadhouse about

five-thirty. I want you to get there early so you won't miss
him or make him wait. They're doing us a favor. He's
bringing me a metal detector they're loaning us. It's not
county property, it belongs to Harlan's nephew."

"All right, sir. The other side of the Roadhouse?"

"Yeah, same place as when we sent him the copy paper.
You were the one who took it, weren't you?"

Doug nodded, "Yes, sir. That's a good place to meet, too.
You can see in all directions there. Is this metal detector to
help on the Davis case?"

"That's right. I'm hoping it will help us find the bracelet
Mrs. Davis told us about. I need the metal detector soon as
I can get it. And be careful with it when you put it in the
car. We're lucky to get it."

"Yes, sir, I'll be careful. I was just going back for coffee.
I'll have a cup and go on out there unless there's something
you want me to do here?" He looked up at the clock.

"No, go ahead. And take your time. It won't take long to
get out there."

Turning to go back into his office he spoke to Gladys.
"Soon as you hear from Rhodes or he comes in, I want to
talk to him."

"Yes, sir, should be soon."

About an hour later Rhodes knocked on the frame of the
open office door. "You looking for me?"

"Yes, I am. Come on in and close the door."

"Uh-oh," Rhodes said with mock gravity. "Am I fired?"

"You should get so lucky. I want to talk to you about the
Davis case."

"Have you found something?" Rhodes pushed a chair
closer to the desk.

"Not yet, but there's something that may help us." He
told Rhodes about the metal detector Harlan Glover was
sending them.

"If we can find that bracelet we'll know where the
struggle and the murder took place."

Rhodes studied the carpet, feeling guilty. "I looked the
best I could, especially where the body rested. I even

squinted from different directions, hoping the sun would pick it up if it was there."

"Don't feel bad about it. It would be next to impossible to find a thing that small in all that underbrush and weeds without a metal detector."

Cas leaned forward trying not to get too excited. "And this one I'm borrowing from Harlan detects gold!"

"Gold? That's a new one on me. I didn't know there were any that would do that."

"I didn't either. He says his nephew is a rock hound and interested in things like that and looking for old coins and buried treasure. I don't plan on ever being that hard up for something to do, but it's just what we need right now. The reason I wanted to talk to you is I want you to go with me to look for that bracelet. If it's there, we're going to find it this time."

"And, if it isn't?" Rhodes almost whispered, knowing Cas didn't think Denise was killed where the deputies had found her body.

"Then we'll at least know we were right and we need to be looking for where she was killed." He shook his head. "Don't ask me how we'll do that, I'm taking one thing at a time."

"Okay." Rhodes got up, unfolding his long frame to leave. "If there's nothing else you need me for I'll see you here first thing in the morning."

Connie was frying hamburgers when Cas opened the kitchen door.

"It's going to be burgers tonight but I'm making up for it with corn on the cob and a tossed salad with the blue cheese dressing you like."

"Nothing wrong with burgers,." Cas kissed the back of her neck. "If they were poison, I'd have been dead long before you came along and started cooking all these other good things for me."

He put his arms around her waist to give her a hug as he asked, "Have a good day or just busy?"

"I worked for Lisa Randolph today and worked a little longer than I planned. I'll have about the same amount to do tomorrow, then I'll be through with them. With the statements, I mean."

"I'm getting loud vibrations…." Cas put his forefingers to the sides of his head trying to look telepathic, "That you don't like statements?"

"No, I don't. But neither does anyone else. It's sort of job security right now, they're so unpopular. I'm sure I'll get more of them to do. If they're as good and audible as these first ones," Connie grinned, "I've got it made."

She laid down her spatula. "How about your day? Have you found anything new in the Davis case that might help?"

"Nothing I can count on yet. I'll tell you about it over dinner. I've got to get these boots off and get comfortable."

He left her looking after him, curiosity mingling with hope. The whole town was on edge with a murderer loose among them.

Rhodes's car was there when Cas parked his truck the next morning. He found him in his office examining the long handled metal detector Doug had leaned against the desk. He held it like a golf club, the head against the carpet.

"Some gizmo, isn't it?"

Cas nodded, "It looks brand new, too." Both of them looked closely at it.

"Probably an expensive toy, too. I promised him I'd take good care of it. Ever see one of these before?"

Rhodes studied it, running a finger around the head. "I've seen pictures. This looks like the advertisements I've seen except it has a smaller head, maybe because it detects gold? And it does look new."

Cas gave the thing a skeptical glance as he straightened up. "This is exactly what we need—if it works."

Rhodes raised an eyebrow at the gizmo, amused at Cas's lack of faith in it.

"Let's give it a try. No use going any further if it won't detect gold."

Cas took off his wedding ring and his watch. He placed them on opposite sides of the desk. The ring he covered with a file folder. He looked around the office.

"And we can use that trash can to make sure it will detect gold, and not just any metal." He set the trash can several feet away.

"Here's my tie clip I had in my pocket. It's supposed to be gold with an onyx set in it." Rhodes laid it a few feet the other side of the trash can.

Cas examined the controls and held the head above the watch at different heights, then the tie clip and the trash can. He went around the desk and tried it on the wedding ring under the file folder before he was satisfied.

"It passed! The smart little gizmo passed." Rhodes's gaunt features lit up in approval. "I guess we're in business."

"Yeah. Funny sound." The gold causes a high pitched continuous beep. "And this little red light blinks on and off."

Cas laughed, "Maybe for the hearing impaired sheriff? Sometimes I feel like I must have a lot of impairments."

"Anyway," he studied it, "since it didn't recognize the trash can at all, it does what Harlan said it would." Cas added, embarrassed, "Guess I'm faith impaired too." He reached for his watch and his ring.

Rhodes retrieved his tie clip. "I didn't believe it either," he admitted.

While Cas fastened his watch and put things back, Rhodes played with the detector, examining the head.

"We'll go in my car."

Rhodes nodded and followed him out holding the gold detector carefully.

Connie was pleased to find the last two statements she had been dreading were as good as the first ones. She would be able to finish them that day. She felt better, put her dislike behind her, and concentrated on getting them done.

Lisa came in as she took the last sheet out of her typewriter.

"All finished? How were they? I hope they were as good all the way through as they were in the places I happened to hear when I checked them."

"They were. I was getting them together with the tapes. Do you want me to make copies of them for you or address mailing envelopes?"

"No, getting them typed was the main thing. Jill and I can do the rest. If you've got a minute I'll write you a check now."

"Sure. I'd rather have it now than have it mailed to me. Who knows, I might pass a sale on the way home." Connie grinned happily, getting her typewriter ready to leave.

"You mean you could do that? Dick claims I can't pass one under any circumstances!" Lisa laughed as she opened the check book.

"You want this eighty dollars a day like a contract and you handle your own taxes, don't you?"

"Yes, that's right."

"A friend of Dick's does taxes and bookkeeping, if you ever need any help."

"I doubt I'll ever get that prosperous, but I'll keep it in mind. Oh, and I've got my cards, too." She got out two and handed them to Lisa.

"Good, I'll keep them here by my phone. I'll recommend you too."

She got up as Connie took her sweater off the back of the typing chair. "Thank you for coming. I'll call you as soon as we have anything else. And Dick told me to be sure and tell you how pleased we are with your work."

Driving home, Connie gave mental thanks to whoever it was who invented crockpots. The vegetables and roast she put in to cook on low that morning would be ready. Nothing else to do but open some rolls. She would have sweet rolls and coffee for dessert.

Finishing the dreaded statements had built up an appetite. Unconsciously, she drove a little faster going home.

"It looks like I'm going to have as much work as I want. I'm enjoying this freelancing. This hundred and sixty dollars burning a hole in my pocket feels good, too."

The sight of the high school as she passed it sobered her mood. She wondered if Cas had had any luck with the gold detector Harlan Glover loaned him. She thought of Missy's sad face when she said Denise had always worn the bracelet.

Arriving near the scene where Denise's body was found Cas and Rhodes parked and went immediately to the roped off area.

Rhodes watched as Cas carefully went over the place where the body had been lying. He slowly worked out from the center, the detector close to the ground.

When his arms tired, Rhodes took over continuing the pattern and going slowly and carefully. He overlapped the search areas a bit to make sure not one inch was missed in their search.

Taking turns resting their arms, their eyes took no break.

"It's such a small thing it would be easy to miss." Cas spoke without looking up, as if willing a glint of gold to make the red light appear.

"Right." Rhodes agreed without much enthusiasm. As Cas straightened up to rest his back, he reminded him, "We'll have to search the path while we're here. It could have dropped off on the way in here."

"Yes, we'll cover every possible place. Not much point in this unless we cover it all."

They finished the entire roped off area as well as a good bit of space around it. Then they went back to where the body had lain and worked their way back to where they had come in, still with not one peep from the 'educated gizmo' as Rhodes had dubbed it. Their backs hurt and they were thirsty.

"Why don't we go around to The Roadhouse for a barbecue and a gallon or two of iced tea? Then we can come back and go up another possible path in from the road where you found the tire prints." Rhodes suggested.

"Yeah, I had that in mind. We'll do it, and we'll also go on from where we found her to the water beyond. It's not all that far, and we don't want to overlook any possibility while we're here and have this detector to use no matter how far out it seems."

Rhodes nodded. "I wondered at the time we found her why he didn't go on to the water anyway. It looked to be where he was heading when he started in here. It seemed logical to put the body there if he wanted to hide it."

"He could have been scared off by something. Or maybe there was some reason he didn't have time to go any farther. That's one of the many things we've got to find out."

Rhodes took the detector as they started back. "Nothing about this case looks like it was planned."

"No. Not planned. The sudden death, the panic, the obvious lack of thought and the age of the victim. It all points to a kid. One of our teenagers."

Cas's face was a chiseled in stone sculpture of determination. "We've got to get to the bottom of this. Go as far as we can with anything we can get, but it's not a trip I want to take."

"Here's the car. Let's pour some tea and barbecue on the problem. Can't hurt."

Rhodes carefully laid the gizmo in the back seat as Cas got in.

The barbecue and tea at the Roadhouse helped their outlook as much as resting their back muscles. As they both lingered over a second huge glass of iced tea, Rhodes brightened. "I've got an idea."

"Like what? I'm open to anything you think might help."

"Let's go out in back—across from where we were and see if we turn up anything on this side of the water."

"He didn't get to the water," Cas reminded him. "But we're here, might as well practice with the detector. Why not?" Cas lightened up too, smiling at Rhodes. "We'll play with the educated gizmo a few minutes. Go on out and I'll get it."

He returned and handed the detector to Rhodes. "You detect and I'll eyeball." He got into the spirit of adventure.

Rhodes looked across the water, picturing where the murderer might have stood if he had come to the edge of the water on the other side. He held out the detector and started searching slowly and methodically, his ears alerted for a signal from the machine but not expecting one.

Neither of them spoke, intent on what they were doing.

Nothing turned up until Rhodes had searched almost to the water, close as he could get without getting into marshy ground. He swung the detector in a wide arc as far out as he could reach over some reeds growing down to the edge of the water.

Cas straightened his tired back, looking away from the detector, knowing they had covered the whole area. Then, midway through the arc, the machine beeped.

"What was that?" Cas came to Rhodes's side.

"I don't know, but the thing sure beeped."

Cas pictured the outline of the unknown murderer on the other side throwing the bracelet and shook his head.

"No, it would have been a senseless thing to do for him to throw it, even if a little thing like that would go this far. No matter how scared he was he'd have to know identity would not depend on a little thing like that."

Rhodes was swinging the detector again. He went more slowly this time and stopped where the detector beeped again.

"There's something there in the edge of the reeds."

Their eyes met, "And it's got to be gold."

He handed the detector to Cas. "Here, hold this a minute."

Rhodes was all business as he took off his boots and socks, glancing again at the edge of the water.

"You're courting pneumonia," Cas warned. "And you could hurt your feet, cut them on something without your boots."

"My foot'll heal up, my boots wouldn't." Rhodes set his boots neatly side by side and rolled up his pants.

Cas leaned forward and held the detector out as Rhodes waded carefully out to where the gold item had set off the signal. When they heard it again, instead of reaching down with his hands, Rhodes felt around with his toes in the soft, deep, silky mud.

As Cas watched, the thoughtful expression on his deputy's gaunt features was almost comically grave.

"You must be right on it. That's where the beep was the strongest," Cas encouraged him.

Cas pulled the detector back a little as Rhodes raised his left foot, his toes clenched on something. The detector beeped.

"That is it! You've got it, whatever it is."

Rhodes reached down and took the object in his hand. He waded out as Cas covered the area again to make sure.

"Yeah, that was it."

Rhodes went to a faucet at the back of The Roadhouse and washed the object. He handed it to Cas before turning back to wash the squishy black gumbo off his feet.

"Well, what about this?" Cas eyed the thing.

"I could tell it was some kind of ring when I got it in my toes." Rhodes came to look at the object.

"It is. It's a class ring. Look at the date on it."

"Nineteen forty-six! Been there all these years. Must be an interesting story behind this." He squinted at the date to make sure he was right.

"We've got enough problems on our hands right now." Cas put the ring in his shirt pocket.

"Yeah, back to the hunt. Hand me my other boot."

Returning to the other side of the water they went over the path into the trees searching as thoroughly as they had the place where they had found the body. They found nothing. They stretched aching muscles then searched from the roped area to the edge of the water, the knowledge growing in both of them that there was nothing to find.

"Tough," Rhodes sympathized. "If it was here, we'd have found it. I'm sure of that."

"Yeah, don't see how we could have missed it, if it was. That's why I wanted you to come with me. I know we've covered every inch where it could have fallen off. I had to be here myself to be sure. It's not here. Anyway, I can return this gizmo to Harlan. I was nervous about borrowing it, to tell the truth. Doug went and got it, will you take it back tomorrow? Same time, same place, as they say on the radio?"

Rhodes nodded. "I will. Sorry about the bracelet. It would have helped to know for sure where she was killed. I guess we're back to square one."

Cas shook his head with a grim look. "We haven't left square one on this case."

At dinner that night, Cas didn't have much to say, other than to answer Connie's questions about finding the bracelet.

He looked so depressed Connie didn't ask him anything else. She wished she could help him somehow. He had taken his coffee into the den when he heard Connie answer the phone.

"That was Miss Mayme," she came to tell him. "I've got to be careful and not get too successful to enjoy being home. She said Lorenzo put his sale sign in the window just before they closed the flower shop. I'll get there early tomorrow and get us another one of those good roasts and see what else he has this time."

"Sure," Cas grinned. "It would be a shame for mere typing to interfere with shopping and visiting." He laughed, feeling better, and picked up his paper again. Sanctuary always had a healing effect on his spirits.

CHAPTER 13

Cas mentally squared his shoulders, determined to beat the bushes until he could find some break. A starting point in finding out why Denise Davis was killed.

"Everyone else on this list of her acquaintances has been checked out, some several times. I guess Darrell has simmered long enough."

When he dialed the school Janice Cobb answered.

"This is Cas Larkin. You told me you have the schedules of the students in their folders, can you tell me what class Darrell Spruce is in or will be in at ten o'clock?"

"All right. It won't take long, but I can call you back if you'd rather."

"No, that's all right. I'll wait."

It was only a few minutes till Janice was back. "Okay, I've got it. Darrell's in Spanish class right now. At ten o'clock he goes to a study hall. He had it moved from the end of the day for some reason."

"Good. I was about due a little luck. Will you ask him to come to the office at ten? And if he isn't too tired of my using his office would you ask John if I can impose on him again?"

"I'm sure it's fine with him. I think he feels like it's the only way he can help. I'll tell him you'll be here. I'd better go on now so I won't miss Darrell. I'll notify his next class, too."

"Okay. Thanks."

Cas checked the clock as he replaced the receiver. He had been dreading talking to Darrell. This session would be at least as unpleasant and uncooperative as the one with Sid Norton was. Losing his club members wouldn't have improved his temper any either. Cas wondered briefly what they were telling him about not coming to the meetings any more. Maybe that the sheriff was leaning on them? Well, he was. And he was getting ready to lean on Darrell, too. He left, determined if not happy.

John Squires was outside looking over the shrubs along the driveway when Cas pulled up in front of the school.

"I'll not be long," Cas smiled. "Thanks for letting me use your office."

"Don't mention it. Anything I can do to help you, I'll be glad to do. I'd rather be out here in the sunshine anyway. You get to feeling cooped up working in an office all day."

He waved as he turned away, "Take your time." John Squires ambled toward the gym as if he were out for a stroll.

Inside, Cas noticed the door to the principal's office was closed and glanced at Janice.

"He's waiting for you," she said softly, making a sour face.

"Thanks." He nodded and Janice left the outer office on some other errand. From her look, Darrel had been less than thrilled at being called upon by the Pine County Sheriff. He braced himself for the unpleasantness he knew was in store and opened the door feeling any number of things besides grateful.

Darrel was sitting in a chair beside the desk and didn't bother to look around when he went in. Cas walked around Darrell and sat down at the desk, giving him a look more pleasant than he felt.

"Darrell, I'm Sheriff Larkin. I've been talking to everyone who knew Denise Davis hoping to shed some light on what happened to her."

Darrell listened, looking noncommittal. He didn't speak, and Cas continued. "There are the usual routine questions I have to ask but if you know of anything else that might help, please tell me."

Darrell nodded, a little suspicion showing in the eyes of his assumed blank mask.

"First of all, where were you the night this happened?"

"I was at home. I had some required reading to do so I did that and went to bed. I didn't go out that night." He looked at the calendar on the desk as he spoke, not at Cas.

"He's lying. I'd bet my shirt on it." Cas didn't let his expression change.

Darrell didn't volunteer anything further. He sat waiting with an air of complete disinterest for Cas to finish asking his questions.

"Were your mother and father at home too?"

"They were at home when I came in. I had a sandwich and started reading. They went to the club for a while, stopped by my room to tell me. I heard them when they came in. My mother opened the door and told me not to stay up too late, and I said goodnight to them."

"What time was that? When they came in?"

"I don't remember." Darrell looked out the window.

"I'm sure you can make a guess. Would you say eleven or twelve o'clock? Somewhere around there?"

"Earlier, around nine-thirty or ten. I went on with my reading and went to bed when I got sleepy."

"But you didn't look at the clock?"

"No." Darrell said it firmly, then turned to look at him.

Cas knew Darrell thought he was safe, his parents would back him up in whatever he said. Cas returned the steady look with one just as steady. Darrell obviously felt he was on safe ground.

"Had you or anyone you know of had any hard feelings toward Denise for any reason?"

"No," was Darrell's surprised answer. The surprise looked genuine.

"Then Denise was well liked, got along well with all her schoolmates and friends?"

"Yes, as far as I know, she did."

"Were you and she close friends?"

"No." Darrell's eyes were on the calendar again. After he answered, he looked up, meeting Cas's eyes. "Her mother works for my dad. She's the secretary there."

Cas recognized what Darrell was up to. He mused to himself, "He throws in a little honesty once in a while to try and stay convincing, to look truthful."

"What is this I hear about some kind of club you have organized?"

"Club?" Darrell stalled for time.

"Yes. Club. I've heard quite a bit about it and it sounds like you're the one in charge of the meetings. The organizer."

"It's only a group of friends getting together. Someone has to take charge once in a while. It's only a social thing."

"I don't call beating someone up social." Cas nailed him with his eyes and the blunt statement.

"I don't know what you're talking about." Darrell was insulted, color rising in his cheeks to the edge of his fair hair.

"You don't? That's certainly strange. The only reason the two boys who did it aren't in the county jail right now is the boy they beat up didn't press charges against them. And you say you don't know anything about it?"

"I didn't beat anybody up or hit anybody and you're not going to intimidate me into saying so!" Darrell's furious face full of hate made him look ready to put out a contract on Sheriff Cas Larkin.

"Simmer down and answer the questions. I know what I can and can't do. I also know a lot more about what you've been up to than you think I do. If there is anything else you can tell me about why Denise was killed, the time to say so is now. You've already lied to me at least once that I know of before we started talking about this club. You knew Denise better than you've admitted. You were seen with her at least twice at school activities. Is there something else you haven't told me? About her or about this club?"

"No. I don't know anything about it." Darrell was so miserable, Cas almost pitied him. Almost, but not quite. He hardened his heart by picturing Casey Taylor's bruised face.

"All right. I'll put down here what you told me. That you were at home doing some required reading the night Denise was killed." Cas made the entry and closed the manila folder.

"One last thing, Darrell. About this club and the things you've been up to. We know about the meeting you had when the tombstones were turned over and the mess that was left up on Peaceful Ridge. You were also seen having another meeting up there recently, though you did a better job of cleaning up after yourselves." Darrell didn't answer.

Cas leaned forward. "This sort of thing will not be tolerated. Do you understand me? The time to stop is right now, before you get into deeper trouble."

Darrell bent his dejected gaze on the door knob. "I ah, there aren't so many people interested in coming to the meetings any more." He frowned. "I don't know why." That was brief, his defiance returned, "We haven't done anything wrong."

Cas pointedly neither agreed nor disagreed with that statement, letting the silence hang between them a few seconds.

"I'm in the phone book, Darrell. The office and home number, too. Call me if you think of anything you've forgotten to mention. I'll probably be talking to you again before very long as I continue my investigation. When I need to ask you anything further, I'll let you know."

Connie stopped for a typewriter ribbon and a few other things before going to Anderson's flower shop. She wanted to show Miss Mayme the new purse she had bought and tell her the sale where she got it was still going on if she wanted to look around for herself.

At the shop, Miss Mayme was properly impressed with the new purse.

"I like all these compartments, Connie. There's one on the front to use for glasses." She frowned, "I hate digging around trying to find things."

"I remembered your telling me that. Me too. But having seen it had enough compartments, I bought it mostly for the colors." As she held the purse up she was distracted by a small plant in her line of vision.

"Say, that's a pretty little thing."

"It's some ivy I rooted before we fully decided to open our store. I'm using them for a sale item."

Miss Mayme put on her sly merchant's face, but couldn't help a little grin. "Could I interest you in one?"

"Yes, you could. I want two of them," Connie decided. "They're just right for my kitchen window. I'll pick them up later when we get back from the store."

At that point, Miss Minnie came out of the office, straightening her skirt. "I'm ready, what are you two so excited about?"

"I've made two sales while you were piddling around back there," Miss Mayme bragged.

"That's a step in the right direction." Miss Minnie declined to bicker. She put the sign on the door and shooed them out.

Making his way back to his office, his session with Darrell occupied almost all of Cas's mind except motor functions. He realized with a start the familiar looking car that had caught his attention was Connie's.

"She must be visiting the Andersons. I'll stop by and take my wife to lunch. I need something to put a better taste in my mouth after talking to Darrell."

Before he killed the ignition he saw the sign on the flower shop door. He smiled at it, recognizing it as the one Connie told him about. Remembering they were probably at Lorenzo's he pulled around into the alley in back of the store. He went in the back door, a mischievous grin on his face.

Entering quietly, he saw Connie at the meat counter. Miss Minnie and Miss Mayme were not far away. There was no one else in the store.

Raising his voice Cas said loudly, "So this is where all my hard earned money goes! Sales and such!" He winked at Lorenzo, who was packaging a cut of meat.

"Cas!" Connie was delighted. "I didn't see you come in."

"I parked in back." He smiled and waved to Miss Minnie and Miss Mayme. "Would you like to go to lunch, if you're through shopping?"

"Yes, but," Connie looked down at her basket.

"We can take your things over to the shop and put them into our refrigerator until you get back," Miss Mayme volunteered.

"That would solve my problem if you don't mind. Are you sure there's room enough?"

"No problem about room. Of course," Miss Mayme teased Cas, "Your roast may smell like gardenias."

"My garden nutty wife would probably like that," Cas rolled his eyes.

"I would! I definitely would, it sounds so chic and exotic. I'm going to be disappointed now if it doesn't." Connie laughed.

She wrote out a check for her meat and followed Cas out the back door to his car. He stopped with his hand on the car door.

"Just a minute." Cas walked to the back corner of the store building.

Settled in the car, Connie looked back to see what Cas was doing. He was setting up a trash can that had been turned over. "Probably dogs," she thought.

She used the mirror on back of the sun shade to apply a new coat of lipstick then turned to see what was keeping Cas.

"He's the one in a hurry and now that he's set the trash can up, he's across the alley looking at the ground for some reason!"

As Connie watched he checked to make sure his car wasn't blocking the alley then came to talk to her at the window.

"Going to arrest some dogs?" She raised an eyebrow and grinned.

"Never can tell," he didn't elaborate. "I'm going to use the phone and talk to Lorenzo a minute. It won't take long."

Connie nodded, watching him go. "Never a dull moment with Sheriff Cas Larkin. Now what was so interesting about that trash can? I guess he'll tell me when he gets through with his call." She wondered absently what he wanted to talk to Cortez Lorenzo about.

Reentering the store Cas signaled Lorenzo. He wanted to talk to him as soon as he finished with his customer and turned to use the phone.

Lorenzo sliced the ham he was working on faster, his eye on Cas who was talking to someone on the phone.

Gladys answered Cas's call.

"Is Rhodes by any chance there?"

"Just came in. I'll get him."

"I knew it was a bad idea to stop by here before lunch." Rhodes grumbled good naturedly when he picked up the phone.

"Yeah," Cas sympathized. "Your luck runs about like mine. But mine may have improved a little."

"You mean you've found something that will help on the Davis case?" Rhodes's heart beat faster.

"No, but maybe on the missing cattle. Remember the cast of the footprint we found at Caleb Martin's, the one in the edge of the stock pond? I've found one like it in back of Lorenzo's store. There's another one on the other side of the alley. I want you to get over here and make casts of both of them. Note where they were and see if there are any more in the alley. Look especially behind the jewelry store and the bank, but cover the whole alley."

"Okay, I'm on my way, are you going to be there?"

"No. I'll be back in about an hour. I'm going to tell Lorenzo you're coming. When you get here ask him if he's had anything missing out back, or had anyone trying to break in. Look at the locks on the back too. And be sure to note where each footprint is found. See you in a little while."

Cas told Lorenzo briefly about finding the footprints in the alley and his suspicions someone may have been trying to break into his store.

"Rhodes will be over here in a few minutes to make some casts of the footprints."

He left Lorenzo looking puzzled and concerned and returned to the car.

"What was that all about?" Connie wanted to know.

Cas explained as he started the car. "I found a footprint like the one we found at Caleb's. Rhodes is going to make a cast and check the store's locks."

Connie's eyes widened. "You think someone's been trying to break into Lorenzo's store?"

"I don't know. May have been nosing around to see what wasn't nailed down and easy to get. Then the jewelry store and the bank have back entrances on the alley too. Thought we'd better check it out. Rhodes is on his way over now. Let's go have our lunch."

CHAPTER 14

Cas beat Rhodes back to the office and was waiting as
he stopped to check with Gladys.

"Only one call that asked to be returned. Judge Spruce
called. He said to call him at his office when you came
back."

"He did, huh?" Cas studied Gladys's face. "I gather from
your tone, that was more of an order than a request?"

Gladys gave him an eloquent shrug and a sulky look, not
making any further comment.

Cas took the note with the judge's number, gestured to
Rhodes to wait and shut the door to his office.

"He's not too tickled about my talk with Darrell, as if
that's a surprise. Wonder what Darrell told him? Whatever
he said, I'm sure it had a definite slant to it." Cas put his
guesses aside and dialed the number before him.

A young voice answered, it wasn't Muriel Davis. He
recalled seeing a teenage clerk doing some filing in the
office the last time he had stopped by there.

"The judge is on another line. Would you like to leave
your number so he can call you back?"

"No, I'll hold a few minutes. This is Sheriff Larkin
returning his call."

It wasn't long before Judge Spruce picked up the phone. "I had a message to call you." Cas said and waited.

"Yes." The judge started slowly, as if he hadn't really wanted to talk to Cas. He cleared his throat.

"My son, Darrell, told me you came by the school today and asked him some questions about the girl who was killed."

"Denise Davis, yes. Muriel Davis's daughter." Cas didn't let him get away with putting any distance between the murder and his knowledge of it.

"I am well aware she's Muriel's daughter," the judge lashed out angrily. "I just don't see any reason for you to question Darrell about it."

"I've questioned everyone who knew her, some of them more than once. It's normal routine in a case of this kind, judge. Is there any reason you would object to my questioning Darrell? I may want to talk to him again in the course of my investigation."

"No, no reason. It's only that he doesn't know anything about it. I don't see any point in it. Questioning her close friends would seem to me to be more helpful," The judge tried a logical approach.

"I've done that. And some of them I've talked to several times. When I asked Darrell where he was at the time Denise was killed, he said he was at home that night studying. Is that right?"

"Yes, that's right."

"You and Mrs. Spruce went to the Country Club?"

"Yes, we went out there for a while. Darrell was still reading when we got back."

"And about what time was that? That you got back?"

"I don't know, about nine or ten o'clock would be my guess."

"About ten, maybe?"

"It was probably a little before ten, closer to nine-thirty. I don't remember exactly."

"He said he didn't remember what time you got back either. Judge, I told Darrell, and I would like to ask you too, if you think of anything or hear of anything you think might be of help in this, to let me know. Call me at home if you need to call after office hours or on the weekend. I would appreciate any help you can give me."

There was a small silence as the judge hesitated. "I will. I certainly will."

"Ashamed of his temper," Cas thought.

"I don't know of a thing right now that would help you but if there is anything I will call you, yes."

"Thank you. I expected Muriel to answer when I called, is she ill?"

"No, she's finalizing funeral arrangements. I offered to go with her, but her sister is going. This was a terrible thing."

The judge sounded so truly sympathetic and sorry for Muriel, Cas forgave him for being over protective of his son.

"Yes, it is," Cas answered. "Believe me, I'm doing everything I can to get to the bottom of it and find out what happened. There doesn't seem to have been any friction anywhere. Denise was well liked by everyone I have talked with."

"Yes, I'm sure she was. She was a lovely, sweet girl. Thank you for returning my call so promptly. If you need to ask Darrell anything else, to question him about anything as you said you might, let me know about it if you don't mind. He was upset about it and I would like to know."

"All right. I will. I can't see any harm in that."

As Cas hung up the phone Rhodes knocked and opened the office door a crack to look in.

"Come on in, Rhodes, and leave the door open. I brought you a barbecue." He gestured toward a sack on the desk.

Rhodes set a canned drink on the desk and reached for the sack as he sat down. "This is worth the wait for lunch. The Roadhouse makes the best barbecue in the county."

He took a bite and washed it down with the drink. "I got the casts of the footprints you found. They're out by Gladys's desk."

"Did you find any more?"

"No. The one you found by the trash can and the one on the other side of the alley is all we got. There were some partials on the other side too, but not enough or clear enough to make casts of."

"You looked all the way down the alley, didn't you? The whole block?"

"We did. Even moved some of the trash cans, since you found the first ones setting up Lorenzo's can. There weren't any more anywhere."

"So," Cas mused, "The only place they were interested in was Lorenzo's."

"Looks like." Rhodes finished his lunch. "Soon as I get the sauce washed off my hands I'll bring those casts in for you to see if you want them in here?"

"Yeah, I do."

Rhodes came back and Cas helped him bring in the two casts. They put them beside the tire prints and the footprint taken from Caleb Martin's stock pond.

"Like two peas in a pod. They're the same right down to the last scratch."

"Those holes look like he might have stepped on some barbed wire."

Rhodes carefully examined them, "Yeah, must have been what it was. There was a partial of the other foot, maybe I should have got it."

"No, this will be enough for identification if we get something to compare it with."

After Rhodes left, Cas again looked over the casts they had of the small vehicle tires and the footprints. He got out the file wishing his evidence was even half as strong as his suspicions and went over the little he had in the Davis case.

There had to be something, no murder was ever committed without some tell-tale evidence. There had to be some small, out of the ordinary thing that would start unraveling the sequence of events. He had nothing except the gut feeling Denise was not killed where her body was found. Plus the fact they had not found the bracelet her mother described.

"That bracelet bothers me. We've got to find that, then we'll know. Maybe the location would give us a direction to go if I can find where she died. You can't take a gut feeling to court. Either no one knows or is willing to point a finger at anything helpful. The reactions I've run into are shock and sorrow. A murder victim everybody likes? It's like dying in good health. I need help."

He closed his eyes in frustration, letting out a small groan. Elbows on his desk, he rested his head in his hands.

A few seconds later the phone on the desk rang. He picked it up, expecting to hear Gladys's voice. Instead, someone had dialed direct to his office.

He wondered if there had been another cattle theft and braced himself.

"Sheriff Larkin." A quiet, somehow comforting, feminine voice said without preamble, "I will help you."

Cas felt the hairs on the back of his neck stand up. He held his breath a second.

"Ma'am? This is Sheriff Larkin, may I be of help to you?" The voice had a strange effect on him. He shivered, not knowing why.

"My name is Hannah. Hannah McLaughlin. I don't really know if I can help you or not, but I will try."

The shiver had passed and Cas said curiously, "Help me with what?"

"With the murder case that's bothering you so." Hannah paused, "I heard you calling for help."

"You HEARD me calling for help?"

Cas began to wonder if she was pulling his leg. Some of Harlan Glover's past antics crossed his mind. But surely, even Harlan wouldn't resort to this. He rejected the idea.

"I don't know any Harlan Glover," the voice informed him as if she had heard the thought.

"What are you?" Cas demanded, his voice coming from somewhere between panic and anger. "Psychic or something?"

"Yes," the voice answered with infinite sadness.

Cas believed her. He didn't know why, and he didn't know what to say.

"I see things," Hannah tried to explain. "I don't want to. I wish there was some way to put a stop to it. But, there's nothing I can do about it. I can't tell you the solution to your case. But perhaps, if I went to the place where you found that poor girl, I might see something that would help you. I will try, if you want me to. The only thing is." She hesitated.

"What?" Cas found his tongue at last.

"I don't want anyone to know I helped you. Please, you must not tell anyone. I moved here not too long ago, and I don't want people here to know. Sometimes, when there are things people can't understand or explain, they can be cruel. You must not tell anyone."

"That's agreeable with me. In fact, I can understand it very well. I'll respect your wishes on that." He added hopefully, "Then, you think maybe you can help me?"

"I have before. If I do see something, I'll tell you what I see. You will be able to understand what I see better than I do, my not being familiar with the people involved."

"I do want your help. I'm about at my wits' end with nothing to go on. And I appreciate your offer to help. Do you, could you go to the scene with me now?"

"Yes. I can meet you on the parking lot behind the courthouse. I'd like to go now, so I can get back before too long. I have some things I need to do."

"How far away are you?"

"I can be there in about ten minutes."

"Fine. I'll be waiting for you."

The energy and motivation that had ebbed from him returned full force as Cas reached to break the connection and dialed, glancing up at the wall clock.

Harlan Glover answered on the first ring. "I was just on my way out, started to let someone else get the phone," Harlan said. "You lucky cuss, you."

"Yeah, I'm glad I caught you, I need to talk to you." Cas told him about the footprints and the casts he'd had made of them.

"I couldn't believe it when I saw that same print in back of Lorenzo's. It's the same as the one we found at Caleb's stock pond. There's no mistaking it, the marks are there where he must have stepped on some barbed wire. I'll fax you a copy, the machine will do it good enough to see the markings on it. Could you look around your suspects' place and see if you find any prints like it? But don't make casts or say anything to them. I'm betting this is a fit as good as Cinderella's glass slipper. I wouldn't want them to get rid of those shoes if one of your boys is our Prince of Thieves."

"The title's too good for any of them but send it. I'm leaving now, but I'll go looking for matches to the print first thing in the morning or later today if I get back in time. Have to check to make sure none of them are around. Hope we can nail them with something, I'd like to get these characters out of Marble County. I'll get out there soon's I can."

"Good 'nuff. Thanks."

Cas made the copy, faxed it and picked up his hat. As he left he slowed down by Gladys's desk. "I'm going to check on something, be back in an hour or so. I won't be where you can reach me, but I won't be out of touch long."

He closed the door behind him, looking forward to meeting Hannah McLaughlin.

CHAPTER 15

Cas knew it was foolish to put too much hope in this meeting. But he'd heard of psychics helping on cases like this and some had made big headlines in missing persons cases. He wondered what Hannah McLaughlin looked like. He gave himself a mental kick because he hadn't thought to ask, not that there would be many people out there on the parking lot.

Cas stood by his car in the lot knowing if she didn't know him by sight, she would recognize the car.

The promised ten minutes went by and stretched into fourteen by his watch. His state of mind made it seem much longer. He looked back at the courthouse, nervously shifting his weight to his other foot.

"She didn't tell me where she was coming from, maybe it's taking her longer to get here than she thought." He knew he was making up excuses. "And maybe I'm a complete idiot. Standing out here in the dust waiting for a psychic to come and solve my case for me."

Before he could mentally kick himself again a car pulled into the parking lot. There was a woman in it. She got out and walked toward him.

"Attractive," Cas thought. "About five-seven, slender, probably twenty-six or seven. I haven't met her, I'd have remembered that red hair."

She smiled as she neared him and held out her hand. Cas took it. "Hannah McLaughlin?"

"Yes, Sheriff Larkin. I'm sorry if I'm a few minutes late. I came from home and had to stop for gas on the way."

"No problem, it's only a few minutes." He came around and opened his car door for her. He noted she knew how to get in gracefully.

"I'll take you to the place where the body was found, it's the logical place to start."

"I hope I can help. But as I said, I don't know. It's not a thing I can control."

Cas nodded as he pulled out, watching traffic. "I understand, and I appreciate your offer to try. Did you say you moved here recently?"

"I've been here for three years now. I came from Fort Craig. I'm working in the library."

Cas smiled. "I guess that's why we haven't met, my wife and daughter are the readers in our family. I hope you like Maryvale."

"I do. I lived in Fort Craig all my life and was working at the library there. When I heard there was an opening at the library here I came and applied for the job. I got a higher classification and pay grade by taking the job here as Assistant and the housing here is less expensive. Besides, I've always liked Maryvale." Hannah paused, looking at the scenery along the highway.

"The place we're going to is a stand of woods off the highway near the junction of highway 220 and Harpers Road. Whoever killed Denise Davis either killed her there or took her there. He took her almost to the water beyond the woods but stopped about two-thirds of the way to it for some reason. He could have decided the body wouldn't be found for a while anyway there in the woods."

Hannah nodded, not commenting.

Cas parked where he and Doug had been when they found the tire prints and gestured toward the tree line.

"This is the way my men went in. We were answering a disturbance call and they were going toward the water to get to the back of the Roadhouse when they found her."

Hannah walked slowly beside him, looking around. They were into the first of the trees before she spoke.

"This isn't going to work," Cas thought. His hopes died a little more with each silent step.

"Here!" Hannah said suddenly. "This is where he came onto this path. He came in from a slightly different place, farther down the road than we did. But this is where he got on this path." Hannah gestured vaguely to her left and behind them. Her voice sounding positive.

Cas went a few steps in the direction she indicated, looking for signs of someone coming in that way. There was nothing except a few drooping weeds which could be the result of the weather and wind as easily as from someone's passing.

And no glint of gold either, Cas also noted, still looking for the bracelet.

"It was dark, he must have just made for this general direction," Cas thought aloud.

He looked at Hannah. She simply stood, her eyes didn't seem to be focused on any one thing. Cas waited for her to speak, wondering what she was sensing.

"He's so young," Hannah said. "Young and frightened."

"Is he, was he carrying her then? Or can you tell?"

Hannah's face was tired and miserable. "He's scared. There's a feeling of deep sorrow and guilt, almost as heavy as the fright."

"Heavy. You mean heavy emotions, the fright and guilt and sorrow. Was he carrying her? I had the feeling when we found her she was killed somewhere else."

Hannah took a few more steps forward. "His is the only presence I feel. So, yes. He must have been carrying her or I would feel her presence. I think the reason I feel him so strongly is the force of what he's feeling. So desperate."

"That's natural. There would be guilt and sorrow in a situation like this."

"There's something else." Hannah stopped again, her hands clasped over her heart. Her face was lined, stressed by the things she was feeling.

"We're assuming now, she's dead." Cas pinned her down. "He killed her somewhere else and he's carrying her at this point."

"Yes." Hannah nodded. "His is the only presence here. Let's walk on."

The path was easy to follow now. Cas walked a pace behind Hannah. She didn't speak until they were nearly upon the place where the body was found. She stumbled. Cas reached out to steady her, concerned by how she looked.

"Oh," Hannah's voice was anguished. She sank to the ground to rest. She leaned back against a tree, catching her breath.

"Take it easy, are you all right?" Cas patted her forehead with his handkerchief. "Rest and take your time. We're here anyway. This is where we found the body. Right there on the other side of this tree you're leaning against."

"I know. I saw them."

"You saw them?" Cas felt his heart leap. "Could you identify him?"

Hannah shook her head. "I don't think so. It was so dark. But he was carrying her like you thought. He stopped because he just couldn't go any farther. There's something wrong with him, he's almost unconscious himself."

Cas shrugged. "It's what he was doing. What he had done, probably just realizing the consequences of it."

"No," Hannah insisted. "It's something more."

Cas dismissed her concern. "What he did was an awful thing. He was out here in the dark, trying to hide his victim. And on top of what he had done, he had the fear of being caught. You said he was young and you saw them. Tell me what you saw. How big is he? Was his hair light or dark? Tell me anything you saw that would help identify him."

"I'll try." She held out her hand.

Cas helped her up, relieved that her color was better.

"He's about half a head shorter than you," Hannah continued. "No, he would be an inch or two taller than that, he was bent over by the weight."

Cas took off his hat, "About four inches shorter than I am?"

Hannah nodded, "About three or four, yes. And he's sturdy, but not overweight. Muscular, I guess you'd call it. And his hair is light."

"Light. Blond?"

"Yes, it caught what little light there was when he straightened up."

"Tell me what you saw beginning with when you saw him bent over, carrying her."

"He was bent over, coming into the path where I told you and struggling under the weight as if she was a burden to carry so far. He heard the water and was going that way but he was about at the end of his endurance when he stopped here. He struggled to hold onto her," Hannah's face contorted with the emotions she was feeling. "He doesn't want to drop her." Hannah's eyes held the misery of what she was feeling. Cas hardly breathed, listening and watching her face.

Hannah looked at him with a strange expression. "Her arm flops out, and he can't hold onto her. He's trying to ease her down so she won't be hurt."

"Won't be hurt?"

"That's right. I can only tell you what he's feeling. Tired and desperate as he was, he tried to ease her down the best he could instead of just letting go of her, but he couldn't hold onto her."

"Dropped the body, just like I thought."

Hannah looked puzzled and asked again hopefully. "Maybe he didn't do it, is there a chance he didn't?"

"No." Cas said it firmly. "The things you felt, the sorrow and guilt and desperation. The fright too. They're exactly the feelings he would have after doing something like this."

To remove any doubt from her mind he asked, "Why else would he be carrying her out here to hide her? There was no one else here. Only him, you said so yourself. No, he killed her, all right. Hannah, could you see any of his face at all?"

"His head was turned as he bent down. I saw the side of his forehead. There was just enough moonlight for an instant to see that his hair was light."

"Let's walk on toward the water, that's where we figured he was going."

Hannah walked with him. "I feel like we're leaving them," she said after a few steps.

"From what you saw, back there where we found the body was as far as he went, for whatever reason. We only looked on farther because it seemed to be where he was headed." He pointed across the water. "My deputies were trying to get to the back of the Roadhouse when they found her."

"No, he didn't come on this far. I don't feel anything here. Only back there where the body was and where he came into the pathway, so scared and hurting."

"Yes, it must have been bad, but it was worse for her." Cas spoke through grim lips. He reserved his sympathy for the victim not the criminals he had to deal with.

Returning to the courthouse, Cas thanked Hannah for her help as he walked her to her car.

"You've cleared up one important thing that worried me. We know for a fact now that she was killed somewhere else. I could tell what a strain it was on you. I appreciate your trying to help me."

Hannah nodded. "It's a gift I'd rather not have. But if I can help someone that makes me feel better about it. That at least there's some good in it."

"Would you, if we get anything else to work on consider helping us again? Or if you 'see' or think of anything else that might shed some light on this case I'd appreciate hearing from you."

"I'd be glad to help any way I can. But I don't want anyone to know about it. I know I'm repeating myself, but I don't want anyone to find out about this. I don't want people to think I'm a witch or something." Hannah smiled self-consciously at her apprehension, but her eyes held a serious plea.

"Don't worry about that," Cas assured her. "I won't even write your name in the file. Now that I'm sure that was not the death scene, I'm going to make an all out effort to find it."

CHAPTER 16

Cas picked up the phone on the first ring, alert and all business.

"Sheriff Larkin."

"This is Sheriff Glover," Harlan aped the seriousness in Cas's voice. "I'm glad I caught you in. I'm about thirty minutes late to where I'm supposed to be right now."

"Not that that's unusual, but don't let me hold you up." Cas grinned, "What is it?"

"Remember you wanted me to go out and nose around the Crow's place?"

Cas hesitated.

"Those three brothers I faxed you the picture of."

"Oh, yeah. I had my brain in another file, but the faces sure stick in my mind."

"Name might not have been on it, but it's Crow. Their names are Jake, John, and Jeremiah Crow. Jeremiah is the youngest one, they call him Jerry. Anyway, I went out there and since there was no sign of them I looked around the place while I had the chance. There was the hide of a goat in the shed and I found some prints of the shoe you told me about. Had the holes from stepping on a strand of barbed wire like the copy you faxed me. They must be Jerry's prints. It looks just like the one you got at Caleb Martin's place and the one you found in the alley. Of course he's not the only one around here who wears those shoes and could have stepped on a strand of barbed wire. But it's sure a good point in that direction."

"Good. I figured you'd find something, knowing as much as you already do about them. I've got a note in front of me to remind myself to talk to Cortez Lorenzo. He hasn't had any attempted break-ins that he knows about but I'm going to show him the pictures you sent in case he's noticed any of them hanging around there. There's a jewelry store a couple of doors down from him with a door on that alley and there's also a bank that faces the other street."

"Looks like they might be trying to graduate into a higher paying kind of thievery. Good thing you came upon those prints when you did."

"How come it's luck when I find something and it's good detective work when you do?"

"That's the breaks," Harlan laughed. "Let me know if you get lucky again."

"Yeah. Luck or not, I'll let you know if and when I get any more solid evidence. I want to be sure of my case when I charge them. Don't want them getting off for lack of evidence. They might decide to stop bugging you and move over here." Cas chuckled at the thought. "I'll be in touch." He hung up without giving Harlan a chance to answer.

Cas took the Davis file home with him that weekend along with the one on the cattle thefts. He wanted to look at the notes he had made and the list of things to do next week where he could think and not be interrupted by the phone.

At home he floated in the kitchen door on the aroma of smothered steak.

"Hi, we're having steak smothered in mushrooms." Connie gave him the menu and the news in the same breath. "Missy has a date with Casey and I'm supposed to remember onions are out for date nights."

Dinner was uneventful since the cook was so well trained.

After reminding Missy and Casey to be in by eleven-thirty, plus all the other instructions Missy could now recite blindfolded and backwards Cas settled back in his den to look at the files.

"Sanctuary," he sighed from the depths of his recliner. "It's another world."

Quiet or not, he wasn't making much progress. He had read the notes in both the files so many times he could tell which ones they were from looking at the back of the paper and still hadn't come up with any new ideas to follow up. He kept hammering at the few facts until his eyes hurt, trying to come up with something. Anything.

Leaning his head back against the chair, the ghost of a smile played around his lips. He wished he was as lucky as Harlan thought he was.

Sunday afternoon Harlan Glover called him. He took the phone from Connie, raising his eyebrows. "Must have something to be calling on Sunday."

Connie held up her crossed fingers by way of encouragement and left him to talk.

"Harlan? You got something?"

"Yeah. I watched for the Crow boys to start their whoopee Saturday night since I know most of their bad habits now, and got lucky. You know where the Starlight Bar is here?"

"Yes. I don't think I'd swap you the Roadhouse for it, either."

"Shucks!" Harlan voiced his disappointment at that. "What I did, I took my truck and parked out there. Waited for nature to take its course. To make a long story short, I picked up two of the brothers for drunk driving. John and Jerry."

"Drunk driving." Cas repeated the charge. He wasn't too impressed.

"Like shooting fish in a barrel. We took them in and put them in uniforms to sleep it off in the jail. We got a good cast of that shoe of Jerry's before brother Jake could come down and get them out. It's tagged and identified as Jerry's.

I've been afraid he'd buy new ones and discard it before we could use it for evidence."

"That's great, I'm proud of you. It's the best thing we've got so far. I'll let you know what I find out when I talk to Lorenzo tomorrow."

"I almost hate to ask, have you got anything else on the Davis case?"

"Only that we're sure now she wasn't killed where we found the body. Nothing yet to point to where it did happen. I'm ninety percent sure who did it, but have no way to tie him to it yet. I've got some things to check out about where he was at the time she was killed and one or two things that don't add up right to look into the first of the week. Maybe they will lead to something."

"Yeah, your gut feeling is usually right. Keep digging. And let me know if you get anything else on this flock of Crows."

"I'll do it."

As Cas hung up he heard the doorbell, then Casey's voice. He went to meet him.

"Casey, there's something I keep forgetting to ask you about."

Casey and Missy stopped. They were on their way to the swing in the backyard. "What is it?"

"This club of Darrell's, did he have you put signs on yourselves? Like a star or something like that?"

"Yes, he did. I'd forgot about it. I thought it was silly. They were just ink that washes off. Some of the members did and some didn't."

Casey stood still, thinking back. "It was supposed to be in a hidden place, like the sole of your foot or up under your hair where it wouldn't show. One boy I know of had a little star on the under side of his wrist and I suppose some of them put the signs other places. I don't know. All I know is I didn't."

Casey stopped short of asking questions, but shot Cas a puzzled look.

"Denise had a little ink star on her forehead. Up under her bangs," Cas explained. "I thought it probably had some connection with that club. That's not to be discussed."

"No, sir, I won't. But, if she had one, that's what she put it there for. Darrell told us to do it."

"Has he said any more about this 'orgy' as he called it? The big to-do with people from another county coming in?"

"I haven't heard any more about it, since I don't go to the meetings. In fact, I don't know if they're even having the meetings any more. I know that Todd and Sid don't go to them now. News about that got around fast." He grinned. "And of course, I haven't heard anything from Darrell, so I don't know."

"Maybe they've come to their senses then. I talked to some of them. Let's hope it did some good. I thought I'd ask about the star while you were here and I was thinking about it."

Casey and Missy went on out to the swing and Cas sat picturing what Hannah had told him she saw.

Age, height, blond hair, the description fit. And the star Denise had put on her forehead was his idea. Darrell Spruce. Everything about the club and the people close to Denise came back to involve him.

"He's the one I'm after, he killed her. But, why? It wasn't a sex crime. Todd said he thought she was smart, 'one of the good brains in the school.' So, what was the motive?"

Monday morning saw Cas trying to get everything lined up to get out and call on Cortez Lorenzo. The morning routine and the phone made such inroads into the time available he wasn't able to get out until almost eleven o'clock.

On impulse, Cas swung by the high school. He didn't have much but hunches to go on. But something in one of the school's files he'd helped himself to while Janice monitored the gym class had left a question in his mind.

Janice saw him coming in and waved to him. "Hi, can we help you with something?"

"Thought I'd stop by and ask Darrell Spruce something I forgot to ask him last time I talked to him. Is he available?"

"He's not here. He got excused from school Friday to go somewhere with his parents and won't be back until Wednesday. I think it was a family funeral in another state. I'll try to find out for you if you want me to?"

"No, it's nothing that won't keep. By the way, I saw Margaret Avery's file has her middle initial as D. Was Denise named for her?"

"No," some of the natural brightness went out of Janice's face as she remembered the popular young student. "I don't know what her middle name is. The D is for Margaret Avery's maiden name."

"Oh well, just a thought. Don't say anything to Darrell. I'll contact him when I need to. You say he will be gone until Wednesday?"

"That's right."

"Okay. Thanks."

Cas looked at his watch as he got back into his car. "I hope Lorenzo is not one of those who locks himself up during his lunch hour, or leaves."

Again, Cas parked at the back of Lorenzo's store, not wanting to take up his customer parking space out front. He glanced down to the end of the building where he'd seen the Crow boy's footprints as he picked up the picture.

Over his customer's shoulder, Lorenzo saw Cas coming in the back door. He finished as soon as he could and came to talk to him.

Trying to hide the mischief in his eyes, Lorenzo smiled ruefully. "Always, I am gladder to see Connie. She is the good customer," he eyed Cas. "And she is prettier, too."

Cas was affronted. "I can claim credit for that good customer compliment. It's my healthy appetite that sends her in here, just you keep that in mind."

"Oh. Then, I keep you healthy and happy," Lorenzo's smile wrinkles deepened. "What can do for you today?"

Cas got serious again. "I want to show you some pictures to see if you've seen any of these men, or all of them maybe, hanging around here."

Cas unrolled the paper. "I think it was one of them who made those prints we found back there in the alley."

Lorenzo reached into his apron pocket for his reading glasses and took the fax sheet. He peered closely at the three pictures a few seconds.

"Madre de Dios! Los hombres?"

"Lorenzo, I can't understand you. Have you seen them?"

Lorenzo nodded, looking unhappy. He beckoned Cas back behind the meat counter. They sat on a rude bench behind the butcher's block where Lorenzo cut his meat.

"These men you look for. They are criminals?" Lorenzo asked, studying Cas's face.

"Yes. They're always in some kind of trouble," Cas confirmed it. "That's why we checked all the windows and the door locks here when I saw those prints out back."

Lorenzo looked sorrowfully at the picture once more before handing it back to Cas. "I see them, yes."

"You have seen them? When was that?"

"I see them when they come here." Lorenzo shrugged, still looking unhappy. "They are the meat men."

"Meat men? I hope you don't mean? Did they come here and sell you some meat? Is that why you called them the meat men?"

"Yes." Lorenzo nodded. "Three, no, I think four times now. They go to the Prime Cut Packing Plant to sell, they tell me. And if they don't take all the meat, they come back to other places and sell the meat they have left. I buy meat from them three or four times now. The meat is always good. I sell it to my customers at a low price and they like it, so I buy from them when they come."

Lorenzo's big brown eyes looked intently at Cas. "Meat was stolen? I am in trouble?"

"I'm not sure it was stolen, Lorenzo, but it looks that way. As for your being in trouble you didn't know it was stolen, and I need your help."

"How I can help?"

"When do you expect them, the meat men, to come back?"

Lorenzo frowned. "I never know they are coming. They come here late in the afternoon and I put a sale sign in the window. The senoras come the next day and buy all of it at the good price."

Lorenzo smiled, thinking of his customers. "They are happy to get it."

"You mean these men show up here with no warning at all that they'll be here?"

"They call. This one," Lorenzo pointed to the youngest one. "He told me they call from the junction of the highways to see if I want the meat. If I do not want it they will go the other road and sell it to someone else. I don't know who else, but the times they call, I take the meat myself. Three times now, I am sure of, they come."

"Lorenzo, you can't buy any more meat from them. I'm more than ninety percent sure it's stolen. What I want you to do is when they call you again, say you will take the meat then call me. No matter what time it is, call me. Will you do that?"

"Si. I call when I hear from them." Lorenzo sighed, "It was the good meat...." His voice trailed off, remembering the meat sales he'd had, the enthusiasm his meat sales had met.

"Yes, it certainly was good meat. My stomach agrees, and grieves with you!" Cas made a comic face. "But we've got to catch these men and stop them from stealing cattle."

"They have stolen from the farmers here?"

"Here and neighboring counties as well. They steal a little at a time, maybe one or two head from each farmer, hoping they won't get caught. Caleb Martin has had some of his cattle stolen. Others here and in Marble County have been missing cattle too."

"Senora Martin, she is my customer." Lorenzo's eyes widened, "I may have sold to her some of this meat these men have stolen!" He bowed his head, looking miserable.

"We'll get them. We'll catch them and put a stop to the stealing. You call me as soon as you hear from them."

"I will. I will call, si."

Cas started out but stopped and turned back before he got to the door. "Lorenzo?"

"Si?" Lorenzo's worry wrinkles deepened again, fearing there was something else wrong.

"I'm not going to have time to stop anywhere to eat, will you make me a sandwich?"

Cas reached into his pocket in search of money. "Say, about two dollars worth?" He felt around in both his pockets for money for his lunch.

"Oh, I make you one, no charge." Lorenzo was relieved at having a problem he could handle so easily. He looked into the meat case and grinned with all his strong white teeth showing. "Beef?"

Cas cracked up, shaking with laughter at his expression. "Better make it ham, I guess, and here's the money for it." He laid the bills he'd found and change for tax on top of the counter. "We've got to stay honest."

Cas drove slowly, eating his sandwich, a drink in the holder on the floor. He stopped at the edge of the woods where he and Hannah had gone in to look at the scene where Denise's body was found. He went in from the angle Hannah said the murderer had, finishing his sandwich as he watched for any tell tale signs. There was nothing but a few broken places in the brush like the ones he'd been looking at from the other direction. He squatted down to look closer and was rewarded with what seemed to be part of a footprint where the weeds had been ground into the mud.

"Not plain enough to do us any good, but it's a track, and it's deep. He was carrying her just as Hannah said. She was heavy, so heavy he didn't make it when he tried to ease her down. I believed her, but this clinches it. I'll figure out how to get him."

He went back to his car, pausing to glance at the place they had got the casts of the small truck's tire prints. He peered down the empty road. "The print would have been made by someone who came from that direction and pulled off, and the Spruce's cabin is out that way. It's all pointing to Darrell. That print, the description of fair coloring and blond hair, muscular build. It all fits. And he's certainly been up to no good with that so-called club of his."

His features twisted into a disgusted mask, "Trying to con his friends into thinking he's got some kind of power."

He eyed the faded tracks. He had seen Darrell driving a little utility truck the judge had bought. "Haven't seen it around town but once or twice. They must keep it out there at the cabin. But it would make a track like that."

Cas started driving out the road before his plans were set on anything definite. Curiosity about the little utility truck and instinct guided him.

"I'm sure the judge took his family to the funeral in the Lincoln, might as well look around out there and if that truck is there, look at the tires on it. If it's got some kind of tread that couldn't fit that track, I won't have to upset the judge's blood pressure by asking about it. He's got a mighty low boiling point when it comes to my questioning Darrell."

Pulling off the road, Cas checked in. "Gladys, is anyone looking for me? Obscene, upset, or otherwise?"

Gladys laughed. "No, it's been a quiet day here."

"Is Doug or Rhodes around there?"

"Doug is here. He's got some paperwork he's catching up on. Do you want to talk to him?"

"No, I was just wondering. I'm out the highway past where we found the Davis girl. I wanted to know if one of them was there in case I want someone to come out and make another cast of a track or something. But I probably won't get that lucky. Don't bother him now. I'll let you know if I need him."

Cas felt he was getting closer to Darrell Spruce all the time, even if most of the corroboration of his theory was not useable in a court of law.

"Arrogant as he is, I still hate to think he's capable of murder. On the other hand it hurts to think that Denise Davis is dead, her young life ended in such a way. It's bad any way you look at it." He stifled every emotion but dutiful determination as he turned in toward the cabin.

The Spruce's cabin was large and comfortable looking. Cas admired the stone chimney, thinking the place must have been awfully expensive to build.

He went around it, checking windows and doors as he went. Everything was clean, neat, and well kept, including the grounds around it. There was a cleared area for extra parking. When he got to the back he gave a low whistle, his hand on a locked gate to the back area. There was a patio with expensive cook-out equipment and lawn furniture around an Olympic sized pool.

"Good thing he keeps the gate locked, with all that left out there." Looking away, he saw an old barn not far away and walked up the slight hill toward it.

Though the old wooden building didn't look too sturdy, the little utility truck was parked inside it. One of the weather beaten old doors was pushed closed, the other gaping with no way to fasten it.

"Looks like someone might have had the idea of hiding the truck. As if that would help if we were looking for it. That's immature thinking for you. Backed it in." Cas smiled to himself. "Ready for a quick get-away? Comic book mentality."

He bent down in front of the little truck. The tracks were recent, easy to see. Cas squinted at the tracks where the little truck had been backed into the old barn. He hoped Doug was still at the office.

In the truck he sat down to rest while he called in. Gladys affirmed Doug was still there.

"Ask him if he knows where the judge's cabin is. I need him to come out here and make a cast of some tire tracks."

Doug took the phone. "Yes, sir, I know where it is, I can leave now. I'd rather do that than paperwork anyway." He laughed.

"All right," Cas mentally agreed with him. "Don't stop to play marbles. You'll need good light to get the cast made. I'll wait here."

"Yes, sir. I'm coming."

CHAPTER 17

Cas began pacing as he waited, looking around the area surrounding the old barn to pass the time. He could see some ruins beyond it on the other side of the hill and went to investigate. He looked down on the remains of an old house.

"Must have been the original old home place, he thought. Not much left of it now."

He decided to investigate and went down a sharp decline at what must have been the back of the house, holding onto branches and outcroppings of rock on his way down. He stood at the bottom wiping his hands on his handkerchief and noticed a path he couldn't see from where he had looked down.

"I'm glad there's no one here to see how dumb I am. I could have gone a little farther up there and come down that path."

He turned his attention to the ruins of the old house. What was left was very little of the first floor and a cellar built before the rest of what must have been a large house. He went on down carefully, looking at the natural drain outside the native stone wall.

It took both hands and muscle power to open the old warped door. Discouraged at the first try he noticed marks in the earth where it had been opened recently and gave it another try.

This time it moved but made a loud protest. It creaked on its rusty hinges, groaning like a soul in torment. It opened on almost total darkness which repelled him for some reason.

He stepped back. "Guess I'm still sort of afraid of the dark." He hurriedly got out his flashlight.

The light played across a stone floor. Not very well set, he noticed. But native stone none the less.

"Must be awfully old," he said. "And look at the size of this thing! It must be as big as the house above it was."

He turned back before going farther and decided he didn't need to prop the door open. He used the flashlight before using his feet, flashing it around the dark interior. The place was bigger than it appeared from the outside.

There were benches and a few crates to sit on around the wall and some in the middle of the space. His flashlight could only show him small areas as he moved it around.

"Crude looking things. Looks like someone put them back together to make them usable. That board and a couple of others look like new additions, raw wood for legs. What's that?"

The light fell upon a table about seven by three feet standing a few feet from the wall he was facing.

"Looks like an old door. A discard from a second hand store. Humpf. Painting it black sure didn't help the looks of it."

There were several candles in odds and ends of holders grouped on each end of the table. There was something on the wall above it that caught his peripheral vision as he turned away. He looked again, flashing the light upward.

"A goat's head! A skeleton goat's head. Probably smells. That's why I had the weird feeling when I opened the door. I smelled death." He shivered and squinted, going closer to examine the goat's head in the light.

"The horns look like they've been polished with something to make them shine. Looks like I've found one of the club's meeting places and somebody's missing goat, too."

Cas continued around the wall with the light until he had covered the cellar.

"This is the meeting place Casey told me about right down to the cold, damp stones. Just the way he described them. And that awful looking goat's head." He examined it a few seconds in the beam of his flashlight.

Moving the light downward, he bent to look at the floor. There were many prints in the moist silt. Most of them were only partials, as if the place had been full of feet milling around. He shook his head.

"No chance of getting any identifiable prints from these old stones, even if they weren't so mixed up."

Finishing his inspection Cas stood in the door flashing the light on the cobbled floor and the walls again. Both were stone, and just as Casey had described them. It had to be the place where Darrell and his officers took the club members for their meeting on the 'dark and stormy nights'.

"Looks like a good place to tell the group about an upcoming orgy." Cas snorted in disgust. "Must have really sounded impressive, to be planning to meet with other groups in other counties."

Casting the light around for a last look at the old black painted table and the sinister looking goat's head, Cas turned off the flashlight and emerged again into the light of late afternoon.

Unconsciously, he breathed a deep sigh of relief getting out of the place. He carefully shut the noisy warped door before going to the path he'd sighted which led back up to the old barn. As he followed it back up he examined the ground and brush along the way.

"Partial tracks here and there like the ones in the cellar but even the ones that would have been plain are obliterated or partially obliterated by so many others there are none we can use. It looks like most of the upper classmen must have been here and a lot of others too. Darrell caught their interest all right but couldn't keep it. And my taking out his officers had its effect. He must have wanted to put some kind of a hex on me!"

Cas laughed to himself, picturing Darrell trying to put a hex on him. Just then he heard the sound of a car approaching.

Doug pulled his car up close to the barn and got out. Cas went to meet him.

"I'm sorry to spring this on you so late in the day." Cas greeted him. "I found this and thought we'd better get a cast while we have the opportunity and can see."

"Yes, sir."

Doug was looking at the tracks where the truck had been backed into the barn. "I see where he turned around out there to back it in." He nodded, "These are good prints."

"They are. They look to me to be the same size as the ones we found on the shoulder of the road. If it turns out to be a wrong idea, we don't have to tell anybody," Cas pointed out with a confidential grin.

"Oh, are the Spruces gone?"

Cas nodded, "Till Wednesday."

"Good. I stopped on the way out and looked at the casts we have. These are the same size."

"Wish I'd done that. What do you think?"

"See that thing in the tread there?"

"Yes, looks like a little piece of gravel to me."

Doug nodded. "I was looking at where it is. There's one about the same size in the same place in the cast we have. Of course, that's not much to go on, as many gravel roads as we have around here."

"The same size and the same place is promising, what are the odds on that? Let's get on with this. We can look closer when we've got it next to the other one. The main thing is where the prints were and the truck being here where Darrell could have used it. I'm going to have to talk to Darrell Spruce again as soon as they get back. As sure as God made little green apples, the judge is not going to be happy about that. I want to be dead sure about these tracks. Right now we don't have much else."

They worked quickly and silently then went to sit in the car while the casts dried.

"You think it looks bad for the Spruce boy, then?"

"It does. The trouble with that is I don't have anything concrete I can hold up as proof. There's this so-called club of his. The fact that Muriel didn't put his name on the list of Denise's friends, in spite of his being seen with her at least twice, and a gut feeling. But there's no tangible evidence at all to point to him or anyone else. His so-called alibi is he was at home at the time she was killed. And of course the Judge and his mother will back him up."

"Depending on his influence to save his son,." Doug's expression disapproved.

Cas nodded. "The judge went through the roof about my asking Darrell questions the first time. He wanted me to let him know if I talked to him again."

"Are you going to tell him?"

"Yes. I said I'd probably need to talk to him again and that I would let him know."

Doug didn't offer an opinion. He sat trying to remember anything he could about Darrell. "I think I'd recognize him when I see him but that's about all. Blond kid, stout looking?"

"Yeah, that's him. Looks like he should be playing football instead of thinking up mischief like this."

Cas frowned. "He also had Todd Kelly and Sid Norton beat up Casey Taylor. We could have nailed him on that if there hadn't been so many other things to consider. May have to use it yet. Darrell looks like the bad apple in the barrel to me."

"What about that trouble with Casey Taylor's car?"

"The brake line was cut and we know who did that, but proving it would be something else. Casey doesn't want him and his mother involved unless it's a have to case."

"I didn't know you were sure about the beating the Casey boy got. But the brake line on the car, that could have got someone killed. And they and Darrell are responsible for that, too, could be two people dead." Doug's face held no compassion for Darrell Spruce nor was there any in his voice.

"We have no proof about the brakes. And though I've talked to Todd Kelly and Sid Norton and their parents there were no charges brought against them. The brake line incident is the reason Casey finally told me the truth about who beat him up. He said he would bring charges if it was the only way to stop them but the club has about breathed its last now. It's dead. But so is Denise Davis. Who is responsible for that is what we've got find out about and prove. If we can."

"We'll find something. Something will turn up. He won't get by with this. Are you sure about this, one hundred percent sure he killed her?" Doug's eyes met his. "It will be hard to get a conviction with his dad running interference for him, even objecting to your talking to him."

"I know that. But one of his weak spots is his alibi for the night Denise was killed. Judge's son or not, that's his weak spot right now. I'm going to look into that and talk to some people. And I'm going to talk to him again as soon as they get back to town."

"I know I ask a lot of questions," Doug said self-consciously.

"It takes every member of the team, that's why it's so important to have a team you can depend on." Cas reminded him.

Doug glanced toward the barn. "I'll go check on the casts, I want to ask you something else, too."

"They ready?" Cas asked as he joined him.

"Just a couple more minutes. What I wanted to ask you is if you've had a chance to look at the applications we've got in to replace Raines when he retires? My cousin applied…is why I'm asking."

"Your cousin?" Cas was interested. "It would sure help to know the person I'm hiring. Or as much about him as possible. We've got a good group who works well and gets along well together. I want to keep it that way. What's his name?"

"Ah, no, not his name. Her name. Her name is Shirley Dalton."

"You've caught me," Cas admitted. "I piled the aps up in a stack as Gladys brought them in to me and haven't taken the time to look through them. Your cousin. You say she wants to be a deputy?"

"She's got her heart set on it, all right. In fact she's taking post graduate courses now that will help her. She can get night classes if she does get the job."

Doug smiled proudly. "She's already looked into that just in case she might get on."

"Tell her to come in to see me sometime next week and I'll make time to look at all those applications between now and then."

"Thanks. I'll tell her."

"Think we can handle these casts now?"

"Should be able to."

The casts were good ones. They put them in Doug's trunk and left.

Back in the office Cas reached for the file as Doug tagged the casts and stood looking at them.

"They're the same even to the little chunk of gravel I noticed. Size and tread's the same. Wear pattern too," Doug said over his shoulder.

Cas went to look. "Yeah, they're the same, no denying that. The truck was there where someone took Denise's body into the woods, that's established. Now, all we've got to do is prove the tracks were made when he killed her and took the body into the woods."

"We'll do it," Doug said confidently.

Turning into his driveway always relaxed Cas no matter what kind of day he had.

Sanctuary. Cas was home. He turned the wheel to enter the driveway.

The scent of cinnamon greeted Cas as he opened the kitchen door. He closed his eyes and pretended to drift toward the stove and the wonderful aroma.

"You'll get a blister if you kiss that stove," the Keeper of the Goodies informed him. "Besides, I'm the one who made the pie!"

"Oh." Cas opened his eyes. "Well, in that case," he put his arms around her. "Here's your kiss then, and a bonus." He gave her another peck on the cheek. "I'll go wash the county off me."

Over dinner, Cas brought up the subject of possibly hiring Doug Freeman's cousin as a deputy to take Raines's place when he retired. He glanced at Connie. "We'll have us a female deputy if I do."

"Daddy! That's neat!" Missy promptly held up both hands. "I vote yes for that. Twice!"

"Don't get too excited yet. I haven't even looked at her application, not to mention the others I've got. And there's a stack of them. I told Doug to tell her to come in some time next week so I've got to get on the ball and look at all those things between now and then."

"If you do hire her," Connie advised him seriously, "See that you don't try to make a secretary out of her. Let her work the same as the other deputies."

"I know we'll have some things to consider that we didn't have to worry about before." His concern showed in his face.

"Just treat her like the other deputies, I'm sure that's the reason she wants the job. Just let her do it. Is her name Freeman?"

"No. Her name is Shirley Dalton. I'll be able to tell a lot more about whether she'll fit in or not after I've talked to her. I'm going to make time to look at the applications I've got before she comes in, in case we've lucked up on a street smart Dudley Do-right or some other kind of genius. So we'll see."

He went back to serious at a look from Missy. "All the people who turned in applications deserve to have them read and considered. I've got to read and evaluate them all."

He couldn't help but add with feeling. "I'd rather be shot out of a cannon!"

Connie laughed even though she sympathized with him. "I'd already figured out replacement isn't your favorite thing. How old is she?"

"Just out of college. And I know you're going to point out that's good." He anticipated her and Missy's feelings.

"Remember, dad, having a female deputy will give you a different angle to see things. She might think of things that wouldn't occur to a man."

"I'll keep that in mind, that and your two votes for a lady deputy." He reached for a roll. "If my conscience would let me I'd hire her just to get out of looking at all those other applications."

True to his word, the next morning Cas pulled the stack of applications toward him on his desk. Before he started reading them he took a number from his billfold that Hannah McLaughlin had given him and dialed it.

There was no answer. He glanced up at the clock. "Must be the library's number. They don't open till nine o'clock. I'll look at a couple of these applications and try again."

He read carefully through the top two applications. The first was from a handicapped youngster about to graduate from a business school.

"As near as I can tell from this, he's applying for Gladys's job, wants Rhodes's salary, and doesn't have the necessary qualifications for either one. But then, when it comes to Gladys's job anybody would be handicapped just not being Gladys." He smiled and put it aside.

The next one was a female applicant. It was an impressive resume, but not for law enforcement.

He decided she'd be more useful at home or in a personnel department somewhere. He tossed it aside.

The next time he looked up it was after nine. He called the library again and someone answered on the second ring. It wasn't Hannah.

"Nelson Mansion, County Library," a bright young voice informed him.

"May I speak to Ms. McLaughin?"

"Of course, may I tell her who is calling?"

"Certainly." Cas searched his imagination for a name. "Tell her it's her Cousin Horace."

"Just a moment, please." Cas decided the young voice must belong to one of the students who worked at the library part-time.

After the promised moment, Hannah's voice said a little uncertainly, "Hello?"

"Hannah, it's me. Cas Larkin."

"Oh, how nice to hear from you, Horace." Cas could almost swear she was smiling.

He pictured the young helper listening and continued in a low voice he hoped only Hannah could hear.

"I know you don't want anyone to know you're helping me but I've found another location that I'd like for you to see as soon as you can find the time."

"Would it take more than an hour?"

Cas gave it a second's thought. "It might, counting traveling time. And I don't want to have to hurry."

They talked, Hannah choosing her words carefully, and got together on the time to meet feeling like undercover FBI agents.

"Fine. Just as you said," Hannah chirped into the phone. "I'll see you then."

"Thanks, I appreciate your help." He felt a twinge of guilt, remembering how distressed Hannah had looked before.

"That's all right, I'm glad to." Hannah couldn't stifle a laugh, "And do give Cousin Alice a big hug for me!"

Gladys came in with the mail as Cas replaced the receiver and wondered what he had to laugh about so early in the morning.

Cas glanced again at the clock. Plans for the rest of the day were beginning to gel.

A quick look through the mail revealed nothing that couldn't wait a while and Cas went back to his applications. He pulled Shirley Dalton's toward him to read last.

The stack was a long, dull, waste of time for the most part.

"It's beginning to look like if she has the normal number of arms and legs and the proper attitude, she'll be a shoo-in." Reading applications would never be on his list of fun things to do and he hated turnover anyway.

Gladys came in and set a cup of coffee on his desk. "I'm going over to The Smithy to get some of their good stew. I see you're in the middle of all those applications, would you like me to bring you some stew or a sandwich?"

"Some of that stew would hit the spot." He took out bills and handed them to her. "And a couple of rolls. I didn't realize what time it is."

"There's no one out front. I'll put the answer phone on till I can get back."

"No problem. I can hear it with the door open, in case there's an emergency of some kind." He grimaced at the applications he had left out to reread. "These things might look better on a full stomach."

He dialed Harlan Glover's number before continuing but he was out. He left a call and went back to his work.

When he finished, there were only two aps which interested him besides Shirley Dalton's. "The only thing against these two, is they're too young. Both right out of school. I'll go on and interview them. Keep them in mind if we grow and are authorized to hire more or if, heaven forbid, we need to replace anybody again soon."

He pushed the applications aside and dialed Harlan's number again. "I'll try again in case he's come in and planning to call me in the middle of my bowl of stew."

A Marble County Deputy answered. "Yes, sir. He's just coming in now. This is Sheriff Larkin, isn't it?"

"Yes, I called earlier. Tell him if he's in some kind of rush, he can call me back."

"He's headed this way."

"Cas!" Harlan's voice boomed as if he were still outdoors. "I had a call from you, got a handful of them here, I just got in. Have you got some news?"

"Yes, I have. Do you know where the Prime Cut plant is?"

"Yes, it's up in the northern part of the state. Big place, best I can remember. Next county above you on the state map. Don't tell me they're involved in this cattle rustling?"

"No. I don't think they are. Not directly, anyway. It looks like that's where our flock of Crows took the cattle they stole to have the meat cut up."

"Have you talked to them at the plant?"

"No, I've just found out about it. It seems the Crow boys go up there and get the meat cut then come back and sell it on the way home. They've sold some here in Maryvale. Remember the tracks I found in the alley? We thought they were casing the jewelry store, or maybe the bank?"

"Yeah?"

"Well, that wasn't it. They made them when they were unloading meat at the grocery store. I took that picture you sent over there and showed it to Cortez Lorenzo and he identified them as 'the meat men'. They told him they were selling what the plant didn't take from them."

"I don't think the plant does that." Harlan said doubtfully. "They go to the sales barns and buy their own, I think."

"I didn't think so. But that is where they got the meat cut up, or that's what they told Lorenzo."

"Lorenzo's cooperating with you?"

"Yes. He's to call me next time he hears from them. We'll be waiting for them."

"Let me know when it goes down. As soon as you call me I'm going out to their place and pick up some things I know are there. Those hides I saw, for one thing. They've got the brands on them."

"Okay, I'll call you."

* * *

Cas cleared off his desk about mid afternoon, putting away the three applications and making a note on his desk calendar to set up the interviews.

"Gladys," he slowed down passing her desk. "I'll be out a couple of hours, I'll call in."

He drove to the country club and explained to the man at the gate he wanted to talk with the dining room manager, not sure if that's who he needed to see or not.

The security man must have phoned ahead. The manager, maître d'hôtelor whatever he called himself came to meet him when he entered the dining room. He didn't look too happy to see Cas.

"Is there something I can do for you, Sheriff Larkin?"

"Yes. I would like to speak to the waiter or waitress who waited on Judge Spruce and his wife the last time they had dinner here."

"I'm not sure when that might have been."

Cas didn't buy that 'know nothing' smirk and gave him the date of Denise Davis's death. "It was a Friday," he added.

The manager had got the message in Cas's eyes and tone of voice and said smoothly, "I'm not sure if he or she is here. Shall I ask and check into it for you?"

"Please."

Cas frowned at his back. "That must be an art, making everything you do sound like a tip required service." He decided he'd talk with someone even if he had to go into the kitchen himself and ask around.

The maître d'returned with a woman a little past middle age, plain but honest looking. She wore no makeup, had on a skirt that came well below her knees and wore sensible shoes. She stood quietly as she was introduced to Cas as Mable Morris. The maître d' stood beside her as if he'd taken root.

Cas put on one of the painfully insincere smiles he had developed to deal with people who had an above-the-rules attitude like the maître d's. "Will you excuse us, please?"

Storm clouds gathered on the maître d's face. He stood a

moment staring into eyes as determined as his own before turning without a word and walking away. The waitress looked down at her shoes as if she had done something wrong.

"I'm not going to say anything X-rated," Cas smiled at the woman. "Or challenge you to arm wrestle either."

The woman laughed a little at that. "No, sir. I didn't think you were."

"Has the maître d' said something to you about the night the judge and his wife had dinner here?"

The only answer was an uncomfortable expression tinged pink by embarrassment.

"All I want to ask you is if you remember what time they left. Do you remember?"

Mable Morris nodded slowly. Reluctantly.

"You do, but, you would rather not say? Or you have been told not to say?"

A slight glimmer of hope appeared in the pale blue eyes.

"It's all right. I notice your name is Morris. Are you related to Chad Morris?"

"Yes, sir. He's my cousin."

"And you are Amish?"

"Yes, sir."

He smiled. "I didn't see any wagon out there by the BMW's and golf carts."

"My husband and boy bring me to work," Mable confided, feeling a little more at ease.

"Let me see how I can put this and keep us both out of trouble." Cas worked on it. "Do you remember about when the judge and his wife came in?"

"Yes, sir. It was a bit after seven forty-five. One of the other waitresses came back from her break then and they were just being seated."

"I see. Do you remember what they had for dinner or about how long they were here in the dining room?"

Mable's brows drew together. "It was a night we had oriental food and I believe they ordered pepper steak as an entree with other things. Egg rolls for one. I remembered because," she looked away as she explained. "The judge is sometimes a little impatient and pepper steak takes a long time to prepare."

"So they were here quite a while then?"

Instead of a definite yes she answered, "They had some drinks from the bar first and some appetizers."

"Would you say they were here an hour or more like two hours?"

"I guess if I had to say, they were in the dining room about two hours."

"That would make it about a quarter of ten or ten o'clock when they left."

"Left?" Mable's face was strained, as if she might be trying to translate words in a foreign language.

"There's something about the time they left," Cas thought studying her face.

"That's when the judge and his wife left the dining room?"

"Yes! Yes, they left the dining room."

She had pounced on it eagerly. Cas caught on. "They left the dining room but they went into the bar?"

Mable's smile said it all.

"Thank you, Mrs. Morris. I would never ask you to choose between your job and what you know is right. But, if I have to ask you when the Spruces left the dining room, may I count on you to testify?"

"I would rather not, sir."

"I know. And I probably won't need to ask you."

"Yes, sir. If I had to say."

"Thank you."

As they talked, Cas had heard the sound of a piano and a horn. He followed his ears to the bar.

The man holding a saxophone came to meet him and held out his hand. "Jon Gibson," he grinned. "Is my music that bad?" He eyed Cas's badge.

Cas laughed, openly admiring the horn. "If it was, I probably couldn't tell. I want to ask you some questions if you don't mind."

"No, I don't mind. I can use a break." The man playing the piano played softer, glancing their way.

"You play here regularly?"

"No, just passing through. We'll be here a couple more days."

Cas pulled out a newspaper with a picture showing the judge at a charity fund raising dinner. "I want to ask you if you remember this man…remember seeing him here at a certain time."

Cas gave him the date of Denise's death. "It was a weekend, Friday night. He was here with his wife. Do you remember seeing them?"

"Yes, I do." Jon Gibson's smile lit up his eyes. "A cool dude. He liked our music."

"Cool dude?"

"He got around the floor good for an old guy and he was definitely a good tipper. Isn't that right, Joe?" He raised his voice a little, turning toward the pianist. Joe gave that a thumbs up.

"What I want to know is how late was he here? Do you know or can you make a guess?"

"Oh, I know, all right. It was about midnight because that's when we quit playing. The guy was a pretty good dancer and tipped Joe good to play the old standards he liked. I know it was about midnight because I didn't want to make him mad. But he got himself in gear and left about five minutes before Goodnight Sweetheart, which is, I guess what he'd have wanted." He grinned again remembering that Friday night.

"And you and your band will be gone in a few days? Just passing through, you said?"

"Yes, we're already booked, gotta move."

"Do you mind if I record this? Get the answers to the questions I asked recorded and get a statement from you? About the date and the time they were here and left?"

"No, it's okay by me."

Cas pulled his small recorder out, identified himself, Gibson, and the time and place. He then repeated the questions he had asked. It was firmly established the judge and his wife had left about five minutes till midnight on the night in question.

"Come by my office tomorrow or the next day and sign the statement I'll have typed out for you."

"I'll be there. That all you need?"

"Yes. Thank you for your cooperation."

CHAPTER 18

The morning he was supposed to meet Hannah, Cas waited in the parking lot hoping she would be on time this time.

Hannah arrived five minutes early. She parked her car and came to him where he stood beside his car.

She smiled as if she'd seen him checking his watch a few minutes ago. The thought that maybe she did spooked him a little.

"I made sure there was nothing to stop for this time."

Cas returned her friendly smile mentally kicking himself for being spooked.

"Have you? Is the reason you called me you've found the place where the Davis girl was killed?"

"I'm not sure but I found a place that's a good possibility. If it isn't, at least you can tell me what you feel about the place. But I am sure it's where at least one meeting was held by the club I've been investigating. Denise went to several of their meetings. I want you to tell me what you can about the place even if it doesn't turn out to be the scene of the crime."

Cas paused after he got seated, his hand still on the door. "It might be very unpleasant for you if this is the place where it happened."

"I know," Hannah nodded. "Feeling what that boy felt wasn't pleasant either. But if it will help I'll at least know it was worth the unpleasantness."

As they drove Hannah told him about some of the things she had seen. "It's not a thing that can be controlled, as I told you. You see what you see or you don't see anything. I don't understand it any more than anyone else does. When I was growing up, I didn't know other people didn't see things too— that it was something different."

Cas was puzzled. "I'm not sure what you're trying to tell me."

"I didn't know that other people didn't see what was happening or had happened, or even would happen to people they were close to. Or people they knew. I didn't know that seeing things was unusual. I didn't give it much thought until one day when I was in high school. Someone I didn't know very well lost her mother's credit card. She was in one of my classes but I didn't know about her losing the card. Right after it happened when I passed close to her in the hall, I saw this bearded man. He was giving a clerk a credit card with her family name on it to pay for something. I told a friend about it and it got back to the girl and her family. Someone really had used the card and bought things with it. They wanted to know how I knew and I couldn't tell them. I learned the lesson fast and well from that, not to say anything to anybody about what I saw."

"I can sure understand that." Cas was sympathetic. "So you were cured of talking about it if not of seeing the visions? What do you call them?"

"I don't know. 'Seeing'. I guess."

"But that cured you of talking about it."

"You'd think so." Hannah's face was grim. "But it was hard to do. Two or three times after that I saw people in danger and tried to warn them. It did no good. They wouldn't listen to me. I couldn't help them. All it did was make people think I'm a little strange, or trying to be a witch or something. It took a long time to get over people's fear and aversion, or whatever it was. Some that remember me still think I'm weird or must be evil somehow. I finished the two year college in our area, married, and moved away while my husband was in service. When he was killed I sold the small house we'd bought in Fort Craig. Then I moved here as soon as there was an opening I could qualify for at the library. I don't want anyone here in Maryvale to know anything about my being able to see things that have happened or are going to happen. If I can be of help to you, I'm glad. But I don't want anyone else to know."

"I won't betray your confidence, Hannah. As I told you I didn't write your name down in the notes in my file. There is no need to write down your home phone number either since it's in the book. And I'll call you at the library when I need to talk to you."

"It's all right to call me at home if you need to but I'm at the library every day."

"I won't call at all unless there's an emergency of some kind."

"Thank you, Cousin Horace," Hannah smiled.

Cas grinned, then said more seriously. "We're almost there. I'm afraid this is where Denise was attacked. We'll soon know."

At the judge's place he parked by the old barn and led Connie down to the ruin by way of the path he had found. They walked slowly. Cas knew she could feel the presence of those who had come this way to the meeting place.

"So many young people," was her only comment until they arrived at the door with the rusty hinges.

Cas opened the door wide and propped it open with a rock he found nearby.

"Would it help for you to go just inside the place in the dark first? Or will my flashlight make any difference in whether you see anything or not?"

She shook her head. "No, I don't think it will."

Cas stepped inside first. "Wait just a minute. I came prepared this time."

He reached into his pocket for matches and lit all the candles on the table before turning on his flashlight.

"All right, Hannah. This must be a place they met more than once, from a description one of the students gave me. Tell me what you see or if you see anything?"

Hannah turned slowly looking around, not making any comment.

Cas began to have doubts. He'd had no experience with psychic phenomena and didn't know what to expect. He devoutly wished he could do something to help or take some of the burden from her.

Having lit all the candles, Cas stood still. He was behind the table with the candles on it, almost directly under where the goat's head was hung. As he watched, Hannah went back to the door and started walking around the area. She went slowly around the wall and talked about her feelings as she moved.

"The room is full, crowded with young people. Some of them are scared. Some of them are excited. They think they may learn something that will give them power, or prestige. A few are skeptical, but it affects them in different ways. Some are curious about what is going on. One or two are resolving not to come again."

She neared the table to Cas's left. "Here is one who is mean. He's enjoying being back there on the back side of the table set aside from the others. He feels he is more important than they are."

Cas moved a little to give her more room, not interrupting.

"There is someone else here on the other side. He's uncomfortable. He does not want to be here, but he's afraid. Not afraid of supernatural things, but the person standing between them. Here behind the table."

"How many are back here behind the table, Hannah? These three or more?"

"Three. The mean one, the uncomfortable one, and the one in the middle who's evidently the leader."

"Can you see them?"

"Not clearly, though all the candles are lit like you have them now. I can see them dimly, and their outlines in the candlelight."

"Can you tell me what this leader is feeling?"

"I can feel what he is feeling. He thinks the people gathered here are like sheep. He feels power, and he likes it."

Cas watched as she went on past the table and stopped at the first bench against the wall.

"Oh! They're here!"

Hannah's face was so contorted Cas felt goose pimples prick up on his arms. He held his breath.

"She, the girl named Denise, she's enjoying herself. This is another time, not the meeting. There is no one here but her and a boy. He's the one who was at the table. The leader. Denise has an empty take-out drink cup in her hand. She tosses it away. She feels a bit drowsy, but pleasantly so. She seems amused about something he is saying to her."

"Who? If you know it's Denise, can you see them well enough to know who he is?"

"Yes, I know he's the leader I saw. The one who was standing behind the table at the meeting. She's laughing. He's turning his head now, not pleased at her amusement. I see the forehead and the side of his face and his hair. He's the one who carried her into the woods."

Cas didn't dare move or make a sound. He waited while Hannah rested a few seconds, then continued.

"He's asking her something. She laughs a little and gets up, as if to end the conversation. He gets up too, growing angry at her reaction to whatever he said. She starts laughing again. He picks up a knife from the table and makes a threatening gesture with it. He's angry, embarrassed. He brandishes the knife. She is not afraid of him. She is still laughing heartily as she turns to face him."

Hannah draws a rasping breath. "Suddenly there is pain, sharp and bad, her ankle, and her foot. Oh! It hurts, she stumbles. Tries to stand on it, but it hurts so!"

Cas's lips parted. He stood frozen, his eyes on Hannah.

Hannah covered her face with her hands. "Oh! Oh!" She cried, sobs wracking her as she stood there, tears running between her fingers, near hysteria.

Cas covered the short distance between them. He didn't try to talk to her, he simply put his arms around her. He stood holding her, comforting her until she quieted and stopped shaking.

"I'm sorry. I'm so sorry for putting you through this. But it's all over, Hannah. There's no more pain now, it's gone now."

Hannah straightened up and took the handkerchief he handed her. She took a deep breath. "You were right. This is where it happened. Right here." She dabbed at her eyes. "I—the ankle, the knife!" She shivered.

"Come over here and rest a minute on this other bench. I've got to know all of it. Tell me the rest of what you saw. Is that when he stabbed her with the knife?"

"Yes. It pierced the heart. I don't think there was even time for her to feel any more pain. It was so quick, the only pain she felt was to her ankle when she turned."

"And you saw them clearly enough to know it was the leader of the meeting? That he is the one who did it?"

"Yes."

"Would you recognize a picture if I show you one?"

"Yes, I would." Hannah raised her eyes to his. "But I can't testify, I can't. And nobody would believe me anyway. I told you that. It would do no good."

"I understand that. I won't ask you to testify. All I want you to do is tell me who it was you saw. To identify him for me. Will you do that?"

"Yes. If you have a picture to show me I'll tell you if he is the one."

Cas looked at the bench across the stone floor. "He must have taken her from here to the path through the woods and left her there. Is that what happened?"

Hannah rose and walked slowly back across the room. "It was all over so quickly. He can't believe she's dead. That life could be taken so quickly. He's repulsed by it. Repulsed by her for some reason."

A frown crossed Hannah's face. "His heart is pounding, he's so scared."

Cas listened, feeling helpless but excited to know exactly what had happened. His hands clenched into fists in his pockets. His eyes never left Hannah's face.

"He must hide her somewhere...." Hannah went on, chronicling the killer's thoughts. "His mind is in a turmoil. He's ashamed, sorry, frightened at life being so fragile and so quickly lost. But most of all now, he's frightened of someone finding out about this. Yes, he took her to hide her somewhere. That's uppermost in his thoughts now. He thinks of the river behind the picnic area on the way to their cabin. She's heavy. He struggles, knowing he has to take her and hide her."

Hannah knelt down, her fingers brushing at the grime between the stones. She rose and turned to Cas, holding something out to him.

"She lost this when she fell."

Cas held the small gold chain in his hand. "It's the bracelet her mother said she was wearing that night."

Hannah simply nodded. Spent, glad the ordeal was over.

Cas pocketed the bracelet, satisfied now about what had happened and where.

"All right. This is what I needed to know and we've been looking for this bracelet. We can go now."

Hannah moved toward the door as Cas blew out the candles.

As he pushed the noisy warped door into place Hannah waited, not looking back.

Leaving the judge's property, Cas asked, "Will you do one more thing for me while we're out in this direction?"

"Yes, I have plenty of time, I think. What is it?"

"I want to go by Peaceful Ridge. There's a poor lady who's buried up there that they were so sure was a witch, they've written it on her tombstone. It has no bearing on the Davis case whether she's a witch or not, I'm just curious."

A wan smile appeared. "It will be good to get my mind on something else before I have to go home and get ready to go to work. But you know, I may not be able to tell you anything," she warned. "Because I'm not a witch, regardless of what anybody thinks." She laughed nervously and Cas laughed with her.

They arrived at the cemetery and climbed the hill to where Sarah Spruce's tombstone had been set back up. Hannah read the inscription and knelt, laying her hands on it.

She knelt there silently a few minutes then said with certainty, "She's at peace, Cas."

"They hanged her for being a witch. See that inscription they put on there hoping she won't come back?"

Hannah shook her head. "I don't feel any evil here. But this date, it was a long time ago. Why are you so curious about it now?"

"This self-styled leader you saw at the meeting and with Denise caught my attention. His name is Darrell Spruce. He tried to claim he was descended from people who had supernatural powers. He worked hard trying to get his club members to believe that."

Hannah regarded the tombstone sadly. "This poor lady was probably less of a witch than he was if he was trying to convince people of that. But I don't sense any evil here."

"So they could have saved all that stone chiseling? She can't come back?"

Hannah smiled at the childish question from the Sheriff of Pine County. "I don't know. But it looks to me like she probably has no reason to want to."

"All right. As I said, I was just curious."

At the office Cas pulled out the past year's high school yearbook and showed Hannah a picture of Darrell Spruce as a junior.

"Yes. That's the one I saw. At the meeting and with Denise Davis. The one who was carrying her through the woods. I'm sure of it."

"All right. Thank you. There's no one in now except Gladys, so there will be no one to ask you why you were here." Cas grinned, "And I doubt Gladys would even give anybody our mailing address without my okay."

After Hannah left, Cas sat looking thoughtfully at the picture of Darrell in the yearbook. "This is one place where being right is a mixed blessing. But at least I'm sure now."

He dialed the school's number to talk to Janice Cobb.

"When did that note in Darrell's file say the Spruces would be back?"

"Wednesday. Darrell is supposed to be back in class Thursday." She waited, wondering if there were others he might want to talk to.

"All right. I just wanted to make sure. Thanks."

Cas walked over to the corner of the room and gazed down at the two casts of truck tracks. They were identical down to the rock in the tread. He had one statement and another possible witness regarding Darrell's alibi; and Hannah had recognized him. It was Darrell's hand that held the knife, and he was the one who carried Denise into the woods.

"Now all I have to do is prove it to the rest of the world."

A couple of loud growls from his stomach interrupted his thoughts. "Haven't had time to think about lunch. Guess that muffin and jelly are all used up, the way it sounds in there. Maybe I can kill two birds with one stone." He reached for the phone again and dialed the school's number.

"Janice?"

"Yes, sir? Think of something else?" Janice's smile could be heard in her voice.

"Uh-huh, I did. I hate to bother you again, but does Margaret Avery by any chance have any spare time this afternoon?"

"In about fifteen minutes she will be keeping the study hall for two hours. If I can't find someone to con into it, I could stand in for her. If you want to talk to her I'll get her to call you as soon as the class bell rings."

"Good luck on the conning, but I do need to talk to her. Go, girl!" Cas laughed with Janice as he hung up.

It wasn't long before Margaret Avery returned his call. Her voice was apprehensive as she identified herself, obviously wondering why he had called her.

"Have you learned something new, Sheriff Larkin? I really think that Muriel is the one you need to tell."

"No, I haven't learned anything concrete to tell. And I don't want to talk to Muriel right at this point. I want to talk to you. If you will let me come by and get you, I'll get you back by the time the two hour study period is up. I need to talk to you."

He left her no choice but a pointblank refusal, and that would take some tall explaining.

"All right." Margaret agreed but she didn't sound happy about it. "Are you coming now?"

"Yes. I'll be there in a few minutes."

Margaret Avery was standing in front of the school when he pulled up to the curb. He leaned over and opened the door for her instead of going around the car. She got in quickly, wanting to get away as soon as possible from the school and anyone who might be watching.

"I haven't had time for lunch, Ms. Avery."

"Please, call me Margaret." She made an effort to be polite and cooperative even though she couldn't imagine any reason for Cas to want to talk to her instead of Muriel.

"All right, Margaret," Cas smiled. "I'm going out and have a barbecue while we talk, if you don't mind. The Roadhouse has very good barbecue or about anything else you would like and the service is usually fast."

"No, I don't mind," Margaret said a bit slowly. "But I don't go there very often unless it's with one of our school groups who especially want to go since they started selling beer out there."

"There won't be many people in there this time of day. It's late for lunch," Cas assured her. "And it will be a quiet place to talk and not be overheard."

Margaret didn't comment, still reluctant but agreeable. Her silence spoke louder than words. She was apprehensive about what he wanted to tell her that shouldn't be overheard. And why speak to her and not Muriel?

That worried her. It showed. Cas stole a glance at her from the corner of his eye. "Good," he thought. "I want some answers. Let her stew until we get there."

Neither of them spoke again until they arrived at the Roadhouse.

"I understand why you would only come here with a group," Cas conceded as they approached The Roadhouse door. "I don't come unless I'm called at night. But it's pretty tame in the daytime." He lead the way to open the door for her.

Margaret still was not too happy about the place or his wanting to talk to her but tried to be pleasant as they went in and got seated.

Cas knew what the menu had to offer. "I'll have the large sandwich with cole slaw and all the trimmings and iced tea to go with it. Margaret?" Cas handed the waitress his menu back.

Margaret Avery smiled, a little more at ease. "I'll probably gain five pounds just watching you eat that." She handed back her menu. "I'll have some potato salad and a diet Coke."

Cas knew his time was limited and got right to the point as soon as the waitress left them.

"Margaret, I looked at some of the files in the school office while I was waiting to talk to some of the students on the list I had of Denise's friends. While I was looking at the files of everyone connected with the case I looked at yours. It was filed under Avery, Margaret D."

Margaret nodded her head seeing nothing remarkable about that. Depressed, she wondered if he had brought her out there for some trivial thing and hadn't actually learned anything of value.

"I asked Janice Cobb if the D is for Denise, if Denise was named after you. She told me no. The D is for your maiden name?"

His eyes met Margaret's and held them. When she didn't answer, he asked, "Would that be Davis, like your sister's?"

He stopped, waiting for her to speak. To tell him what he felt he already knew.

Margaret's face told him she knew where this line of questioning was going. Her voice when she spoke was resigned. "Yes, Davis was my maiden name. Muriel had her child out of wedlock and gave Denise our family name. I don't know why that interested you. And I would, of course, ask that you not repeat that."

"I won't," Cas assured her. "What I want to ask you about will be strictly off the record. I'm not even going to note it in the file. However, what I do want to know is who is Denise's father? Was she Judge Spruce's child?"

Margaret had turned pale and looked trapped. "How? I mean, who? What makes you ask a thing like that?"

"You're hedging, Margaret, and I mean to know. There are other ways to find out. But most of them would be a lot more public than my just asking someone who knows the truth about it."

"I can see no reason at all why you would need to know that."

"You'll have to take my word for it at present that I do need to know. I've told you that it will go no farther. Are you so fond of the man you would protect him at the cost of solving this case?" Cas raised his eyebrows.

"Fond of him!" The very idea left Margaret appalled and shaken. Aghast at herself for raising her voice, Margaret looked hurriedly around. No one seemed to have noticed her outburst.

She went on quietly. "Fond of him, indeed! I hated him." She almost hissed the words at Cas, her voice and her face expressing the loathing she felt for Spruce.

"Because of his leaving your sister with a child to care for alone?"

"Yes, of course. Who wouldn't? Poor, gullible Muriel. He told her he was going to get a divorce and marry her. But then he got a chance to better himself in another town. All of us lived on the other side of the state then and he told her he thought it best that they not to see each other again. That his wife had a heart condition."

Margaret scowled. "Oh, you wouldn't believe the hearts and flowers and embroidery on his plausible excuses. He sent her his high school class ring in a note saying if she ever needed him, he would help her."

Margaret paused. "Muriel hadn't told him, but I wondered then if he wanted to get away from her because he suspected she was pregnant."

"He put his class ring in the note?"

"Yes! Can you imagine?" Margaret could hardly contain her disgust at the idea. "Just like an old knight in medieval times. A pledge of his affection and protection. But, I'm getting ahead of myself. I knew Muriel had been seeing someone, but I didn't know it was Troy Spruce. The first I knew of it was when she told me she was in trouble and the man she had been seeing was married. I was just floored, and so sorry for her. I was in the middle of moving at that time." She glanced around the room, there were only two or three people seated at a distance.

"I'd just got this teaching job I'd been trying to get here in Maryvale. I bundled up everything she wanted to move and took it with me. She worked as long as she could, on the job she had. Then after she had the baby she came here to live with me."

Margaret's eyes roamed the dining room as if she could see ghosts of the past.

"It's strange you brought me out here to ask me about it. We, Muriel and I, came out here right after she came to Maryvale. She had some résumés typed up and was going to try to get a job that would pay as much as possible. We came out here on my lunch hour from school and I looked at the résumés. Then she showed me the note and the class ring and asked if maybe she shouldn't ask him to help her find a job. He had come here to Maryvale when he left her."

Her eyes held a wild horror the rest of the faculty had never seen. "It was like a continuing nightmare." She shook her head, the pain of the memory showed on her face as she remembered the scene with her sister.

"Well, that sure was a blow. To know he was here too. Not that I didn't think Muriel had learned her lesson. It wasn't that. But, the thought of Muriel asking him for help? That was too much! We were sitting on the patio in back. That was before this place changed hands and they rearranged everything and started selling beer. Anyway, I took that class ring and threw it in the river right then. That's what I thought of him and his 'help'. After that, Muriel saw him somewhere, I don't know the details. Didn't ask. Anyway, she told me she had seen him and he was going to help her find a job."

"Did she tell him about the baby, that he had a daughter?"

"Yes. I asked her about that. She did tell him. And within the week, he called her to do secretarial work for him at a much more generous salary than she was hoping to get."

Margaret's face was grim. "But, I kept my eye on him."

"I'll bet you did," Cas said with feeling. "I would have too. But, Margaret, there's not a thing." Cas paused, not wanting to offend her. "There's never been the slightest breath of anything I mean."

"I know," Margaret admitted. "He's been a perfect gentleman and helped her out a lot as well. Then when they hired a couple more people he promoted her to Office Manager with a nice raise. He has been good to her." Margaret was grudging but honest about it.

"And Mrs. Spruce, did she know about the affair?"

"No. She never knew. She's a very sweet person. There was no reason to hurt her by telling her. And she does have a heart condition. That much of what he said was true. And as I said, he gave Muriel a good job and has always been a perfect gentleman," Margaret ended.

"Did Denise know? That Judge Spruce was her father?"

"Yes. She knew. Muriel told her. But she also knew she was never to let him know she knew, or tell anyone else. The tale was that her father was dead and Muriel was a widow, like me."

Cas checked the time on the clock over the cash register. "I guess we'd better get you back to the school. I appreciate your honesty, Margaret. It does help and it will go no farther, I promise you."

"You won't say anything to Muriel either?"

"No, not Muriel either. Are you ready to go?"

"Yes, I'm ready. And you know now. It's a relief really, to tell someone about it, after all this time."

CHAPTER 19

"This is some nest of snakes. It's going to take a while to untangle it and find anything strong enough to support my case. Makes me feel like I'm building a house from the roof down, from what I know to be true to proving it."

Having been accused by everyone who worked closely with him of making indecipherable notes, Cas smiled to himself as he updated the file. He referred to Hannah as M and Margaret as D.

He read his notes over making sure he hadn't left anything out of the sequence of events from reading Margaret's file at the school up to their talk at the Roadhouse. He could almost recite his handwritten notes word for word by the time he'd finished. He promised himself he would take them home and burn them in the fireplace when this was over.

Before continuing his work on the brief file he kept in his desk he carefully placed his confidential notes in the office safe where he had put Denise's bracelet. The tangible things he had were in plain sight across the room. The collection of casts on his two cases was beginning to look like museum artifacts.

The casts of the little truck tires made him shake his head in wonder that anyone could think he'd get away with murder by simply hiding the truck he used. The statement he had from the band leader at the country club effectively did away with Darrell's alibi. He had that in a signed statement as well as on tape. The club's meeting place being on Judge Spruce's property was another point, but it was still not enough to guarantee a conviction. Not when you're opposed by a county judge and his influence.

Cas frowned, concentrating on the problem. He noted that the interview with the leader of the combo playing at the country club also included their agent's address in case he needed it. Knowing that statement not only knocked Darrell's alibi in the sand but proved the judge a liar lifted his spirits. He pictured Spruce's face and his reaction if he had to use it. He hoped he wouldn't have to. That he could come up with something so incriminating there would be no defense possible. His mind worried at the problem like a dog with a flea he couldn't reach.

There was a lot more he'd uncovered with bad connotations attached whether it was tangible evidence or not. The old door painted black and used for an altar or table; the goat's head that looked like a cheap horror show prop; and the club Darrell had organized were not things that would help the boy's credibility any whether they were concrete evidence or not.

The beating his two officers gave Casey Taylor and having Howard Giles as a witness that the brake line on Casey's' car was cut after that beating would be damaging if it could be tied in with the murder. But he couldn't without bringing Casey in to testify. And he didn't want to do that.

"I've got to get Darrell wrapped up tight enough there won't be any harmful fall-out on other people who might be hurt."

He felt better remembering Casey identifying the Crow boy from the fax Harlan sent.

"At least we'll get the Crows red-handed with Lorenzo helping us. I've got my work cut out for me with Darrell and the judge."

He gathered everything up and cleared his desk, looking at his calendar.

"The other judge hasn't got here for a formal inquest yet," Cas thought. "Judge Spruce excusing himself because of his closeness to the victim and her mother has already caused a pretty big delay. Not that it hasn't come in handy. If I could just find a way to get Darrell to admit what he's done, what happened, before the inquest, oh, Lord." He held his head full of plans and groaned.

A few days later Harlan Glover called and reported he'd had two more head of cattle stolen in Marble County.

"Have you heard anything from the Crow brothers yet?"

"Not a peep. They haven't made contact with Lorenzo. I'm depending on his help to nail them. Maybe they'll try to sell those last two head they got over there in Marble County. What do you think?"

"It's possible. Looks like the way they've been working, keeping close to home. I've been keeping a close watch on their place and there were fresh tracks. I saw cattle tracks out there a little before this last report came in. Maybe they've got three or four head this time. If they do, you'll be getting some action soon."

"The tracks you saw and two more stolen? From your description of the place," Cas mused thoughtfully. "they haven't got a place to keep any more. It could be tomorrow. I'll let you know."

"Thanks. Good luck, and take care."

Time drug by. Cas rearranged and cleaned out some old files, a job he had been putting off. He stayed close to the office, expecting he wouldn't have to wait long before the Crow brothers tried to sell the recently stolen meat.

At lunch time Cas announced to Gladys he was going to The Smithy and offered to bring back whatever she wanted.

Gladys pulled her plastic menu out of her desk drawer. "Let me look at the menu a minute."

"As if we both don't know it by heart." Cas grinned to himself. "No hurry, I'm going to make a phone call."

Cas dialed the library's number and this time Hannah answered. "This is Cousin Horace," he said confidentially into the phone. "I have another request."

"All right, Horace, though if it takes more than thirty minutes I'll have to do it some other time. We're short handed today. What is it?"

"Is that thirty minutes you mentioned your lunch break?"

"Yes, and I think I hear my partner coming back, so I can leave in a minute. What is it you need?"

"I'm having to stay close to the office myself too right now. What I have in mind won't take more than a few minutes. If you'll meet me at The Smithy, I'll buy your stew or whatever you want and you can take it back to the library with you if you want to. What I want you to do is hold a ring in your hand and tell me whatever you can about it. Will you do that?"

"All right," Hannah agreed. "And I'll take you up on your stew offer. If you can leave now I'll see you in a few minutes."

"Coming."

Cas retrieved the class ring he and Rhodes had found from the safe.

"Have you decided, Gladys?" He called through the door.

"Uh-huh. I'll have a small stew and a couple of rolls. Money's here on my desk."

"Oh yes, I was really worried about that." Cas made a face at her. "Back soon."

He saw Hannah coming from the library as he entered The Smithy. He got his orders put up separately to go and joined Hannah at a table where she had laid some extra napkins. "What do you want to drink?"

"Nothing, I'll get a Coke from the machine when I get back."

"Thanks for coming." Cas pushed one of the sacks toward her and fished in his shirt pocket for the ring. "I'm pretty sure already whose it is," he said as he handed it to her. "But there's nothing like being sure. I'd like to have you confirm that I'm right about it."

Hannah held the ring in the palm of her hand, moving her fingers a little as it rolled on its side.

"It's an old one, Cas. The owner was 'new' when it was," she smiled.

Cas tried to picture Judge Spruce when he was in high school and later, when he had given Muriel the ring.

"He looks like the boy I saw. The one who carried the body into the woods."

She frowned slightly. Her eyes held the question before her lips could form it. "Is he the father of this boy? Is that what you think? It's the feeling I have, too."

Cas nodded. "Yes, I think he is. Can you give me a name, or is that asking too much?"

"I can give you his initials, they're T.S."

"Troy Spruce," Cas breathed.

"Must be, you can see for yourself." She handed the ring to him. "Hold it up a little where the light will hit it better. They're scratched inside the band there. You can see them if you turn it a little."

Cas turned the ring until the light caught the scratches on the inside. "You're right. He must have done it himself. I hadn't noticed them, they're so light. Just scratched in there like that. With what you saw and these in the band I'm sure now it's his."

Satisfied, he replaced the ring in his pocket. "You've earned your stew, Hannah."

Dropping off Gladys's stew and rolls Cas went back to the break room to eat before returning to his application task.

Fortified with lunch, he passed the time writing letters to the applicants for the deputy job. All of them were the same except the three he wanted to interview.

"I guess being chained to this desk has been good for me. I've got some things done I've been putting off. I'm glad to get these letters out to Gladys."

He pricked up his ears when he heard the phone ring and listened as Gladys answered.

"Yes, he's here." She covered the mouthpiece. Then seeing Cas watching through the door she mouthed quietly, "It's Cortez Lorenzo."

"Okay," Cas nodded. "Put him through."

"Sheriff Larkin?" Lorenzo asked when he heard him pick up the phone.

"Yes, I'm here, Lorenzo."

"You told me to call if I hear from the meat men. They called me just now. From the junction, he told me. And I told him I do want the meat. He said he'd be here between four and five o'clock."

"Good. You did exactly right. Who's in the store with you right now, Lorenzo?"

"There's me, my son, and a boy who works part-time after school. There are two customers just leaving, I think. Should I close the store? I don't want anyone to be hurt."

"No one will be hurt, Lorenzo. Get everyone out of there and close up as close to four o'clock as you can since he said they're expecting to be there between four and five. They may be earlier than that. I'll have three men over there. One inside and two outside. Your son and the boy can go somewhere else until this is over but you'll have to stay there to give him the money for the stolen meat. We'll move in and arrest 'the meat man' as soon as he takes the money."

Lorenzo had listened closely without commenting. "I have to give him the money?" Lorenzo asked, sounding unhappy about it.

"Yes, Lorenzo, you do. Because he won't have sold it till you do. But you will get it back. And you won't be in any trouble. Set your mind at ease about that. You're helping us catch a criminal. A thief who has been preying on our neighbors here and in Marble County."

"All right," Lorenzo sighed. "I close the store just before four o'clock and send los ninos over to The Smithy."

Cas called Harlan Glover.

Harlan answered the phone himself and Cas explained quickly. "I'm about to arrest the Crows, or at least one of them. They called Lorenzo and they're on the way here with meat. Probably from the thefts you told me about."

"Okay. I'm going out to their place and pick up those hides I told you about seeing and anything else I see that might help us. I've had the warrant ever since I saw the goat hides."

The first deputy went to Lorenzo's at three forty-five, shortly followed by the other two to watch for the truck in the alley. At five till four Cas walked over and entered the store going from the front door to the back where he could see all the meat department and the doors.

"I am glad you are here." Lorenzo told him nervously. "Your other men are out in the back. I'll lock the door now."

Lorenzo put the closed sign up under the shade where it couldn't be seen from the inside and they waited.

It wasn't long before they heard the Crows arriving.

Cas tilted his head, "That must be their truck from the noise it's making. Must have invested in a glass-pack muffler," he whispered to Lorenzo. "Just go and stand behind the meat counter."

Cas took off his hat, put it on a shelf in front of him and ran his fingers through his hair where the hat had mashed it down.

Quiet reigned in the store as they listened to the approaching sounds. The inside deputy, hat off, was between Cas and Lorenzo posing as a customer when the 'meat man' came in and walked straight to the meat counter where Lorenzo stood.

Cas recognized Jerry Crow, the youngest Crow brother, from the fax picture. His step was confident, not suspecting what awaited him. He called to someone at the back door, "I'll let you know," he waved a hand to whoever it was waiting out there.

Cas stepped behind a display and Lorenzo crossed himself.

Jerry crow turned and approached the meat counter, grinning as he came. "Hi, Lorenzo!" His snaggle-toothed grin widened at the prospect of making a dishonest dollar or two.

With his meat counter between them, Lorenzo tried to ignore the tenseness between his shoulder blades and fixed his attention on 'the meat man'.

"Got some good meat for you here at a good price. You want about the usual? I have a little more, if you can use it."

"No, no. The usual will be enough. Can you get it in all right?"

"Sure. My brother's out there to help me." Jerry went to the back and beckoned to someone.

"What's he need?" Someone called.

"Those first three stacks. I'll come help you with them."

There was no time lost loading the new dolly with meat packages and in a few minutes the Crows had it all stacked on Lorenzo's meat counter.

Both brothers waited as Lorenzo looked at the packages and what was written on them using stick-on labels. He stepped over to his cash register. "Same amount as last time?"

"Yeah, same as before." Jerry answered quickly.

Lorenzo counted out the money. The Crows' attention was on their pay as Cas came closer and the inside deputy moved to arrest them as soon as Jerry had the money in his hand.

The surprise made it easy to get them under control without a struggle.

"Unless you count all the cussing." Cas thought as he checked the Crows for concealed weapons.

The two Crows were already handcuffed when the two deputies came in from the back. Rhodes and Doug smiled at Raines, who had made the arrest.

"There's no one else out there," Doug reported. "One of them must have been driving. The other one in the picture didn't come this time for some reason." Doug looked disappointed. "Tough it's not the whole set, or is it flock?"

"Yeah, they're such pretty things." Rhodes grinned as Jerry struggled with the handcuffs.

Lorenzo stood by, relieved no one had been hurt as Cas promised. He put his hand on his chest and took several deep breaths then looked out the front window. He looked toward The Smithy across the street where he had sent the boys.

"We'll get the whole set. We know where the other one is. We'll pick him up later." Cas made it a promise and thanked Lorenzo for his help.

"Oh, and Lorenzo?" Cas gestured toward the packages. "We'll need to tag this meat and what they've got in the truck. We'll have to store it here until we get the paperwork done. It will be divided between the soup kitchen and the children's home, but we have to get the red tape out of the way first."

"Si, si." Lorenzo agreed, wondering how long it would be before he could get his money back.

Cas left the deputies to their task and took the Crow brothers across the square to lock them up. On the way they loudly protested their treatment at the hands of 'the Pine County Gestapo.'

Aside from a few people who turned to see what the commotion was about, they got no attention for their trouble.

"That meat wasn't stolen! Who said it was?" John was indignant at having his money for the meat taken away from him and being herded across the street like one of the cattle they had stolen. He stopped to look daggers at Cas, who gave him a little prod from his nightstick to get him moving again.

"We're supposed to have a lawyer! You can't do this to us!" Jerry got into the act but kept moving, warily eyeing the nightstick.

"You got no proof of nothing. Not a dad-burned thing!"

Cas touched John lightly to hurry him along and kept

them moving quickly across the street. Their continuing insults fell on deaf ears.

"Work is a four letter word to them." Cas thought. He felt no sympathy at all except for the farmers who had lost the cattle.

Entering the office Cas paused to talk to Gladys. She looked the Crow brothers over with distaste as they stood just inside the door. They were still muttering dark threats and trying to look dangerous instead of merely loud and scruffy. She looked to her boss for an explanation.

"That's the Midnight Meat Supply Caleb and the others have been losing cattle to," Cas explained.

Gladys's face relaxed into a pleased smile. "I know they'll all be glad to hear that. Good work, Boss!"

Cas grimaced at her. "I know you're prejudiced, but it sounds good anyway. And for the record, Raines was the arresting officer."

She continued looking them over. "Didn't you say there were three of them?"

"There are. The other Crow's still on the wing. He seems to have sat this trip out for some reason but we'll get him. Call Harlan Glover for me while I show these gentlemen to their rooms."

By the time the Crow brothers were officially in and settled as they were going to get, Harlan Glover was on the phone.

"Gladys says you got our flock of Crows," Harlan chortled. "Tell me about it."

Cas related the facts about the arrest and added, "But I'm afraid Gladys was bragging. We only got two of them, John and Jerry. They're here as guests of the county but I don't know about brother Jake. He wasn't with them."

"You don't need to worry the point off your head worrying about Jake," Harlan said complacently. "I've got Jake."

"You have? Tell me about that."

"Remember when you called to tell me it was going down? I told you I was going out there and see what I could find and pick up those hides, had the warrant in my hand? I saw the new pick-up truck in the yard."

"Yeah, they hired a little refrigerated van. That's what they brought the meat in this time."

"Business must be good! The truck being there, I knew there was someone in there but I decided to go on in anyway. It was Jake. I went in as quietly as I could, the door was open. He was sitting at an old desk working on a big ledger of some kind."

"You got their records?"

"Yep. I've got the records of their thefts, the amount they paid the packing plant to cut up the meat, and how they sold it to markets like Cortez Lorenzo's there in Maryvale. Business was good and getting better. Depending on your point of view, of course. Oh, and I got the goat hides too, two of them." Harlan laughed, feeling good about it.

"Well, that's a thorn out of both our sides."

"Soon as my man here identifies his goat hide I'll send the other one over for Tinwhistle to identify. That should make him happy. I also have the hides from the last three head of cattle they stole with the brands on them. With the footprint Rhodes got at the stock pond, we've got them for sure."

"I'll talk to the plant too, just to nail everything up tight."

"Yeah, that will wrap it up."

The Crows were not able to post bond and were to stay in custody until they came to trial.

"In the meantime," Cas reported to Harlan a couple of days later, "They're singing like canaries instead of Crows. Each one trying to blame everything on the other two."

"I figured keeping them in separate cells would pay off," Harlan approved. "Jake is pure as the driven snow too, to hear him tell it. He's also trying to act like he doesn't know anything about the connection between them and the school clubs."

"Won't do him any good. We're getting all the details about their giving the goats' heads to the school groups and encouraging them in their devil worship clubs to cover up their petty thievery. Their tale is they never took enough to make a hardship on anybody, and so on and on and on...."

"Not on them, that is. But they did invest in the trailer and rent the refrigerated van, poor devils!" Harlan chuckled at their operation costs.

"They thought they had it made not stealing over two head at any one place and timing it close to when the youngsters had their meetings. It worked for a while."

"The low life trash," Harlan snorted. "Using children! We ought to turn some school teachers I know loose on them."

"Yeah, I know of a couple here who would join the lynch mob with vengeance." Cas chuckled picturing Miss Mayme and Miss Minnie in hot pursuit.

"You said Caleb Martin and Matthew Tinwhistle are ready and willing to prosecute the Crow brothers for the thefts of their cattle and the goat. With the evidence there is against them, thanks to Lorenzo, all three will be put away for a long time. And I notice the weekly papers there and here too are having a field day."

"Yeah, it's like the circus. Something for everyone. At least Judge Spruce will be able to hear this one. You know we're waiting on another judge to hold the inquest on the Davis case."

"I hadn't thought about that. How is the Davis case going? You making any headway?"

"I'm getting there, Harlan. I'm getting there."

"Getting there. Meaning you know a lot of things you can't begin to prove?"

"Yeah, you're right. But I've got the germ of a plan to get the proof."

"Well, let me know if I can do anything to help. I'm sure glad you had your eyes open when you found those prints behind Lorenzo's market. You done good, Cas."

"Thanks for not calling it dumb luck again." Cas grinned. "It's a good thing we've got each other to brag on us. Now, if I can manage to get lucky on this other case, I'll even let you rib me about it."

"You'll get there, sure as I'll rib you. I think I'll go down and see what else this older Crow wants to tell me about the other two that I haven't heard yet. May solve some more county crimes without leaving the building!"

Cas opened the safe and took out the little gold bracelet that had belonged to Denise Davis. The D caught the light from the window. He sat looking at it a moment before picking up the phone.

"Gladys, are Rhodes and Doug still here?"

"Doug is. Rhodes just went out, I can catch him for you."

"Okay, hurry. I want to talk to both of them."

Doug came in, Rhodes wasn't far behind. Gladys shut the door of the office.

Cas looked at the clock. "I know it's time to go home, this won't take long. I want to run something by you and see what you think of it."

Both were curious and Rhodes had spotted the bracelet lying on the desk. He pulled his chair closer.

"Is that the bracelet we were looking for?"

"Yes," Cas nodded. "That's it. I found it at one of the club's meeting places. I know now, that meeting place is where Denise was killed."

Cas outlined the plan he had in mind and finished with, "You, Rhodes, and Doug will handle this with me. Gladys will be here that night getting caught up on some things and Raines will be here on duty. Raines made the arrest in the rustling case. That's enough glory to retire on, and we need him here." He looked up at each of them. "Any questions?"

"Not from me," Rhodes shook his head. "I can't see any other way to get him."

"I wish Shirley could be here to get the experience. Could you use another witness?" Doug asked Cas with a hopeful look.

Cas thought about it. "I haven't decided to hire her yet. I haven't had a chance to get her in here and talk to her. Tell you what, tell her to come by tomorrow and I'll talk to her.

If she wants to go, and I decide to let her, I'll deputize her. That will make it official."

"Yes, sir!" Doug beamed, ignoring all the ifs.

"Now don't get your hopes up," Cas warned. "I haven't said yes yet, and she may not be as anxious to go as you think. Tell her to come in after lunch. That will give us plenty of time to get organized. Don't tell her anything at this point, except to come in. But, we'll see. As for the plan, Gladys and Raines don't know the details either, just that we've got a plan and they are to be here."

Rhodes stood up, ready to go home.

Cas and Doug stood too as Cas continued. "I'll talk to Shirley Dalton tomorrow after lunch if she comes in. The three of us, and possibly Shirley, will meet here in the office at four o'clock."

Doug paused at the door. "Shirley will be here. She'll be glad to get in on an 'if' for something like this. I think she'll make a good deputy."

Cas nodded, followed them out and turned to Gladys. "I've got an errand to run before it gets too dark. See you tomorrow."

The errand was to the old ruins on the judge's property. Cas parked near the barn. He took off the broken half of the door opposite the one hiding the small utility truck and took it to a spot above the meeting place.

He muscled it over to where he'd gone down before he discovered the path. "This should get it down there were I want it."

Cas turned the door loose and let gravity do the job. He hurried down the path and carried it into the meeting place, being careful not to tear his uniform on its rough places. He leaned it across a corner at the back several feet from the table with the candles on it.

He stepped behind it to make sure he could see the table and the bench where Hannah had seen Darrell and Denise sitting, where they were standing when she was stabbed. He also tested to make sure the door wouldn't fall, then wiped his hands on his handkerchief. The trap was set.

CHAPTER 20

It was the aroma of pork chops that brought Cas in the kitchen door on scent alert. He always paused to sniff the air unless Connie had heard him and was there to greet him with a kiss. He had been married long enough to have his priorities straight.

Connie grinned up at him as she came in to put her arms around him. "Yes, it's pork chops. Some nice thick ones Lorenzo cut for me so I could stuff them."

"Ah, with your good dressing and gravy and potatoes too?" He eyed what Connie called her 'potato bowl' on the counter.

"Uh-huh. I'm going to a little extra trouble tonight because I'm going to chicken out tomorrow."

"Chicken out?" Cas backed up a little looking worried. "You mean I don't get fed tomorrow?"

"No, I mean I'm going to put a chicken in the crockpot because it's the easiest thing to do. I'll be working for Lisa Randolph and won't be home in time to do much more than take up the chicken and open 'the can of your choice.' Am I fired?"

"No, sounds good to me. I like things cooked all day in the crockpot."

"That's good. It's easy on the cook, too." She turned

away to finish putting things on the table as Missy came in and started pouring tea in the glasses.

"Hi, dad. Have a good day?"

"Well, it wasn't dull." Cas nodded without elaborating. He washed his hands at the sink before he sat down.

Connie passed the rolls. "Maybe Lorenzo will have another meat sale soon and I'll get something good for the crockpot."

"Uh, I don't think so." Cas said it softly, not looking up.

"What's that?" Connie buttered her roll, "What do mean you don't think so?"

"There aren't going to be any more of those beef sales, Connie."

The butter knife was stilled.

"Why not?" Missy asked.

"Because a couple of days ago, we arrested the fellows he's been getting the meat from. They're the ones who were stealing a head or two at a time here and in Marble County. They were selling some of the meat to Lorenzo. We caught them."

"You mean he's been arrested? Cortez Lorenzo?" Connie was distressed. "But Lorenzo! No, he wouldn't!"

"No. Not Lorenzo. You're right. Lorenzo wouldn't. He didn't. He didn't know he was dealing with the Midnight Beef Supply as Harlan and I called it. He helped us catch the thieves. Lorenzo's just fine. He helped us get the thieves red handed. We caught them with the meat when they brought it in and arrested them when they took the money from Lorenzo for it. The write-up will be in tomorrow's paper. Lorenzo's all right and the thieves are in jail. But there won't be any more of those one day meat sales."

The wheels of reason sped to the correct conclusion in Connie's agile mind. "Those footprints you found! Were they? Did they—"

"Yes, they were made by the thieves. They're also the ones who stole Matthew Tinwhistle's goat."

"Gertrude," Missy grinned triumphantly. "Gertrude's avenged!"

"Avenged, at peace, or whatever Tinwhistle wants to call it. One of Harlan Glover's deputies called Gladys and told her he's already been over to Marble County and identified the hide and took it home."

"The goat, goodness. They stole the poor goat too. But they wouldn't make much selling goat meat, I wouldn't think?" Missy made a face.

"No," Cas agreed. "Haven't heard of anyone having a goat roast in quite a while. They stole one over in Marble County too. It wasn't stolen for the meat. They gave the heads to the clubs like Darrell's. I guess it's possible the Crows ate the rest, they look like they'd eat anything that didn't bite back."

Missy laughed but Connie was still thinking about such wholesale wrongdoing.

"You mean they had the nerve to sell the stolen meat right here in town?"

Cas told them about the Crow brothers and Harlan's continuing troubles with them. "They not only stole cattle, but worse, they used our children. They were behind some of the devil worship clubs. Giving them goat heads and speaking at meetings and encouraging them to get members and do other things like the orgy Darrell tried to get his club members interested in. They did a few mutilations to scare people, to keep them from reporting the thefts right away. To cover up what they were doing."

"Well! They certainly deserve to be in jail." Connie's indignation was vehement but faded quickly. "Even so, I sure am going to miss those beef sales."

Missy laughed at her mother's unhappy face. "Makes pork taste better to me. Just think of poor Gertrude, mom...."

Cas shrugged. "I know the Anderson sisters will miss the sales too. You've got to take the bitter with the sweet on this. The culprits are in jail where they belong."

"Oh, I guess so." Connie conceded but not too happily.

"That reminds me, I won't be home tomorrow for dinner. Save me a piece of that crockpot chicken, will you please?"

"I don't know." Connie gave him a stern look. "Considering what you did to the beef supply." She tilted her head, regarding him, weighing whether he was worthy of a share of the chicken.

Cas tried to look properly worried, stifling a grin.

Missy drowned a giggle in her tea.

"Oh, I guess I'll save you some. But you do get by with an awful lot around here."

"Because I'm the Head of the House," Cas announced loftily, winking at Missy.

"Sure you are," Connie agreed piously. "Just as your Aunt Harry says. I can just hear her. 'Man is the head of the house, woman is the neck and it's her duty to turn him in the right direction!'"

Missy and Cas laughed at the truth in that. And some of her Great Aunt Harriet's other pearls of wisdom that it brought to mind.

Neither Missy nor Connie asked what the late work involved but Connie was apprehensive, knowing it had to be something to do with the Davis case.

The next day Cas worked in his office all morning, leaving only to go to The Smithy for lunch. At two o'clock, Gladys rang his phone.

"There's a Shirley Dalton here to see you."

"Thanks."

Cas went to open the door for her, closing it again before directing her to a chair.

Shirley Dalton was five-seven with shoulder length dark hair, brown eyed, and slender. She was attractive and looked neat and well groomed in a dark suit and white blouse. Cas remembered from her application she was a couple of months away from twenty-two, and just out of college.

"You are interested in getting into law enforcement, are you?" Cas smiled as he sat back down at his desk. "Would that be Doug Freeman's influence showing up?"

"I know he likes what he's doing, but it's not just his influence. I have been interested in working in law enforcement for a long time. I'm taking some post graduate courses that will help me. But," she added quickly, "I can get night classes if I need to."

She impressed Cas as nice, smart, and as he listened, really interested in the deputy job.

The interview went even better than he had hoped it would and he decided to hire her.

Cas took an honest look at the future. "She'll fit in here fine and will be dependable help for us. I'd better grab her before pressure to hire a female gets any worse and there's no one this good to recruit."

"I suppose it did have some influence on me that Doug's happy in his work," Shirley admitted. "But aside from that, it's something I am interested in, that I'll look forward to every day when I come to work. I plan on working a long time." She shot a serious look at Cas.

"I know what you mean by that. I like my work, too. Let me warn you there is a lot of time that will be dull as mud with only routine to break the monotony. This is Maryvale, not Chicago," Cas reminded her.

"I know. It's going to be my job to keep it from being like Chicago." She gave him a smile. "I'll count my blessings on the dull days."

"That's the spirit. Has Doug said anything to you about something we are planning in regard to a case tonight?"

"No." Shirley waited, wondering what he meant.

"Good. He wasn't supposed to."

Shirley thought back, "He told me you had some other applications but you would see me today. I think he tried real hard not to give me any false hopes, but it didn't work. I'm not going to give up until you hire me, turn me down, or hire someone else."

Cas chuckled. "Neither would I, that's a healthy attitude when you're hunting work. Would you like to help us tonight with something we're going to do in relation to a case we're trying to close?"

"Yes! I would!" Shirley faltered, "But can I? Does this mean you're going to hire me?"

She sat on the edge of her chair as he weighed his answer.

"Yes. I am. It will take time to get through the red tape and processing that must be done. If you want to help us tonight I will have to deputize you. Eventually you might get paid for it, though I have my doubts," he added ruefully.

"The only certain thing you'll get out of it is experience. The slow processing and the red tape is the reason I've got to be very careful when I hire someone. Deputy Raines is retiring and the paperwork is going forward now. But it's a slow process. It will be a while before you're officially on the county payroll."

"That's all right with me. It's what I want to do. I'll waive any pay for helping tonight. I'll be glad to do anything I can to help."

"Then consider yourself in processing and come back here at four o'clock. I'll brief you then on what we're going to do. Wear dark clothes and comfortable shoes."

"Yes, sir."

As soon as the outer door closed behind Shirley, Gladys looked through Cas's door and smiled, giving him a thumb-up signal.

"Just what does that mean?" Cas played dumb.

"It means I know you're interviewing and I approve of that one. Liked her the minute she walked in."

"Do you know who she is?"

"My guess is she's Doug's cousin. He said he was going to send in his cousin Shirley and her name's Shirley."

"So you put two and two together and came up with six?"

"Am I wrong?" Gladys narrowed her eyes.

"No, you're right. Why don't you apply for the job yourself?"

"I don't want it," was her candid answer. "I like the one I've got."

Cas laughed, "I'm glad you do. And she's not only Doug's cousin she looks like the best of the lot so I'm going to hire her. And you can't tell anyone till she's been here and on the payroll a month. Understand?"

"Understood!" This was accompanied by about the sloppiest salute ever to be seen in the office.

Cas picked up the ringing phone, "Sheriff Larkin."

"It's me, Harlan. The flock of Crows is about wrapped up thanks to all the evidence we have in both counties and the goat hides identified. Your Matthew Tinwhistle came over and identified his."

"Yeah, Gladys told me. He couldn't wait for you to send it over."

"And you must be a celebrity, catching the Crows red handed the way you did. I'm jealous!" Harlan fussed good naturedly because it was his privilege as a friend and colleague.

"Sure, I'll bet you are! The only bad thing is my wife's already missing those meat sales. But Marble County's rid of the Crows now. They'll have to chase down the next heifers they steal in wheelchairs."

"Humpf, they'd try it! But I'll be out there with my cane!"

Cas laughed, picturing the chase.

"It was good Raines got some action to retire on, too. Did the press come out and interview you, give you some good publicity?"

"Guess you'd call it good publicity. A photographer from the local paper, anyway. He came out and took my and Lorenzo's picture and got one of Raines in front of the store. Lorenzo deserved some advertisement. He's still nervous about getting his money back."

"I hope he's not holding his breath," Harlan chuckled. "But he'll get it if he lives long enough."

"Yeah, he's hanging in there. The photographer took a good close up picture of Raines as the arresting officer and I gave him some information on him and about his retirement. It will be nice for him and his family to have."

"Yeah, that's good."

"The picture of me and Lorenzo was taken in the alley at the back of the store where we happened to be at the time. I wouldn't exactly call it a glamour shot."

"That's all right, as long as you managed to get some recognition. I always thought the good guys should get as much recognition as the bad guys do."

"It'll never happen. I doubt anyone will remember it this time next year."

"I doubt it too, but it gives us something to shoot for. Let me know when you get that other thing wrapped up, or if I can help."

"I will. Thanks."

Cas pressed the disconnect and told Gladys, "Get me Judge Spruce, will you?"

It was a matter of seconds till Gladys rang back, "Judge Spruce is on the line, sir."

"Judge Spruce, this is Cas Larkin."

"What can I do for you?" The judge's voice was distant, but civil.

"I'm going over to the school to talk to Darrell and I remembered you said you wanted to know about it the next time I talked to him."

"What are you going to see him about?" The judge was instantly alert.

"There's only one thing open right now that I would be seeing him about." Cas was as distant and cold as the judge had sounded when he answered.

"The Davis case? But, you've talked to him about that and he's told you all he knows. It wasn't much. I can't see any reason for you to talk to him again."

"You don't have to see any reason. I'm conducting this investigation, not you," Cas pointed out bluntly. "So I'll be the one to decide whether I need to talk to him about it or not."

"There's no need to take that attitude. I simply don't see any point in bothering him at school about something he has no knowledge of."

"I called you because you were upset the last time I talked to Darrell. You asked me to tell you when I talked with him again. I'm leaving now to go to the school and talk with him. I called you only because I promised you I would. Goodbye, Judge."

Cas broke the connection. "That should get him in gear."

Gladys had heard his side of the conversation and raised her eyebrows as he paused at her desk.

"I'm going over to the school. It won't take long, in case Doug or Rhodes calls."

At the school Cas wasted no time in asking Janice to get Darrell from his class and asking John Squires for the use of his office again.

John Squires took one look at his face and gestured him in without commenting. "I'll be in the gym if you need me," he told Janice on the way out.

Darrell was soon ushered in, looking sullen. Janice went back to work at her desk.

"Sit down," Cas ordered, brushing past Darrell to shut the door.

"I don't have anything to tell you I didn't tell you before," Darrell started. "Why did you call me out of class?"

"I'll ask the questions here." Cas sat down, his face grim.

Darrell squirmed and looked away, his jaw set.

"You told me you were home studying the night Denise Davis was killed."

"Yes. I was." Darrell stated it flatly, as if his saying so once should have been enough.

"Brazen brat!" Cas clinched his fist in his pocket.

Aloud, he pointed out, "But there are no witnesses to place you there, Darrell."

"My mother and father!" Darrel objected immediately.

"You've admitted you didn't know what time they came back from the country club."

"Well, I think it was around nine, maybe nine-thirty."

"Well, I don't think so. I went out there and talked to some of the people who work there. Especially the ones who waited on your parents at dinner, and later, when they went into the bar."

He watched Darrell. "They went into the bar after they finished dinner and listened to the band in there. Three people who work there said they didn't leave till around midnight, a few minutes before twelve o'clock. I talked to the band leader and he put the time as just before the last number of the evening."

Darrell's sullen expression was gone. He was apprehensive about what Cas told him as well as the chiseled in stone way he said it. He sat silently studying the carpet between his feet.

"Given the established time of death, there would have been plenty of time for you to go out, meet Denise, and get back home before they got there." Cas waited until Darrell looked up and met his eyes.

He was scared now. Cas knew it. More scared than he was last time he had talked to him. He didn't think his alibi would be questioned. He realized he was not above suspicion just because he's a judge's son.

The heavy silence was relieved by the opening of the door. It swung wide and Troy Spruce stood there, his eyes glaring at Cas. He hadn't bothered to knock.

Darrell let out an audible sigh of relief when he saw his father. Cas almost pitied him.

Cas gestured the judge to a chair. "Come in, if you want to, but don't interrupt," Cas ordered.

"As I said," Cas addressed Darrell. "The witnesses I have spoken with say your parents didn't leave the country club until midnight or close to it the night Denise Davis died. You would have had plenty of time to go out, meet Denise, and get back before your parents got home."

"This is about the Davis case again," Judge Spruce sputtered. "As I pointed out, we've both already told you Darrell was at home studying that night." His brows drew together into what he meant to be an intimidating frown. "Did you get us here just to ask something we've already answered in regard to this?"

"I know what you told me. What you said is a matter of record. But what you say is not consistent with the facts," Cas calmly stated. "You couldn't have got home before twelve fifteen according to witnesses, in fact, it was probably at least twelve-thirty, since you had to drive home. And that, with the witnesses' testimony whether you like it or not, leaves Darrell no alibi for the time that Denise was killed."

Judge Spruce sat open mouthed a second, the red anger creeping up his neck. He nearly shouted, "I would think OUR WORD would be enough."

"Your word? You're a judge," Cas's eyes bored into his. "Are you in the habit of taking a plaintiff's word when it conflicts with the evidence before you? I think not. No, bluffing won't get it this time. What you think, if you actually do think you got in at nine or nine-thirty, won't stand up in a court of law. There are witnesses, both statements and tapes, to the contrary. And since you've insisted on being here let me point out a few other things to you."

Darrell and the Judge sat listening as if they could not believe their ears.

"There was a tire print found at the edge of the highway where we found Denise's body. We took a cast from your utility truck, and they match. The tread, the wear, even to a rock caught in the tread."

Cas turned to Darrell. "And you claim you were not a close friend of Denise's?" He glanced at the judge. "When several witnesses have seen you together on at least two social occasions."

The judge shot a surprised look at Darrell. His mouth opened slightly though he didn't speak.

"No," Darrell quickly protested. "We sat together a couple of times at school. The play, and that movie we got credit for seeing. That's all." He cast anxious eyes at his father.

Judge Spruce suddenly looked like a tired old man, which seemed to worry Darrell more than Cas's questions.

Cas followed up his advantage. He couldn't afford not to at this point. His stony features did not soften.

"There is only one thing that keeps me from arresting you for Denise's murder right now." Cas's eyes held Darrell's as he spoke. The boy's eyes were wide with fear.

Judge Spruce asked desperately, "What? You've been honest to the point of brutality so far. What is it that's holding you up?" He spat out the words.

"I'll tell you. I've known for quite a while now that where we found her is not where Denise was killed. She was wearing a bracelet that night. A small gold chain with the initial D on it. Her mother is sure she had it on, and it was not found on her. It must have fallen off in the struggle when she was killed. Her mother reported it missing when we returned Denise's things to her. She said Denise always wore it."

The judge bowed his head, as if resigned to hear it all.

Cas leaned forward, his eyes still on Darrell's. "I'm starting first thing in the morning, with all the help I can spare from the office, a search for that place where the bracelet fell off. I've got some ideas where to start, some hints about meeting places, and I'm not going to stop until I find it. When we find that bracelet which is the only missing link, we'll know where she was killed. You'd be wise to tell me now, what happened."

Darrell slumped in his chair, staring at the floor between his feet.

Judge Spruce spoke up, decisive now. "Come on, Darrell, we're going home." He got up, beckoning to Darrell.

He put his arm around his son as he ushered him through the door and turned a venomous glare on Cas.

"The next time you talk to us, it will be through our attorney."

CHAPTER 21

At five till four o'clock Gladys knocked on Cas's office door and announced Shirley Dalton.

Cas approved of her dark slacks and shirt as Gladys held the door for her.

"Please don't get up," Shirley said as Rhodes and the others started to stand.

Doug pushed a folding chair toward her and she took it.

"We were a little embarrassed for chairs," Cas explained. "The break-room is where we usually gather. I'm glad you wore dark clothing."

"Yes, sir," Shirley looked down at the slacks. "The main thing I was looking for was the comfortable shoes you suggested. I'll get some more suitable ones, as soon as I get a chance to shop."

"You did fine on short notice and not knowing what kind of assignment you were headed for. Rhodes and Doug know the general plan, but I want to go over it again with all of you."

He directed his remarks to Shirley. "This concerns the Davis case. I guess you've read some of it in the papers, about the young girl who was stabbed?"

"Yes, sir. About her being stabbed and where she was found. Not much else was in the paper."

"We haven't had much to go on. Most of our evidence being circumstantial. If we're lucky, this operation will give us the proof of guilt we need."

Cas proceeded with his plans keeping his voice low even though the office door was closed.

All of them listened without comment, understandably a little edgy and anxious to get started.

Shirley, eyes wide, listened intently. Cas knew without looking directly at her, her hands were clinched together as she leaned forward.

Cas was glad he'd allowed Shirley to go with them. It would get her feet wet working with the group and it was a chance for experience that wouldn't come again soon, at least he hoped not. There was no better way to show her how important it was to work together. He remembered what she had said about intending to work a long time.

He finished reviewing his plan. "All we have to do is make sure the car is where he can't see it and wait to see if he takes the bait. I think he'll be there all right."

He looked at Rhodes. "I've been back out there today, just to check. No one's been out there since I placed the door I told you about. That door will give us a place to wait out of sight so we can take him by surprise," he told all of them. "And I doubt he'll even notice it in the corner in the dark."

He told Shirley the general layout of the place, making his description as brief as possible.

"Shirley, you're getting a chance to get in on some action before you even get into uniform. I'm depending on you as part of the team to back us up when we make our move. You're an important part of this."

"Thank you, sir. I know I'm lucky to get this chance. And thank you for letting me use the practice range, too."

"You should add that training you told me about to your application, too. It would be one more thing in your favor."

"I didn't think about it, I was so busy getting the names of the courses I'm taking right."

"No matter, you won't need more training for a while and you'll have time. This is unusual. But you do have to be prepared. One of the most important things about weapons training is knowing when not to use them. But I'm not going to make a speech. We may be disappointed tonight, but I don't think so. Do any of you have any questions?"

"You said we will be out of sight if he comes in with a flashlight, but you said that door is a half door and it's a very large room?"

"The place is the basement of an old house, but it's a big area. The old door is half a barn door, so it's twice the size of an ordinary standard door. Maybe more. There's room between it and the corner of the room for two of us to hide behind and it will be in deep shadows back there. But it will also be close enough for us to see what he's up to and surprise him."

Shirley nodded.

"Anything else?"

Rhodes shook his head, shifting his big feet to get up.

"Then let's get started." Cas scooped things off the top of his desk from force of habit as he rose, and closed his desk drawer.

Gladys stopped her work and looked up as they filed out, looking serious. "Good luck."

"Yeah, keep your fingers crossed." Cas patted her typewriter's guardian angel decal for luck.

In the parking lot Cas said, "We'll go in my car. Rhodes, you and Doug or Shirley, can drive the other car back with the prisoner." He grinned at his confidence, "Assuming we're going to have one. He will be in handcuffs. One car will be easier to hide. We'll put it behind the barn where it won't reflect light when he drives up the hill."

They stopped at the drive-in window of The Roadhouse and got sandwiches to go.

"And fill these, please." Cas had brought thermos bottles for their coffee.

"Don't want my troops falling asleep," he winked at Rhodes.

"You think we'll have a long wait?" Doug asked.

"I don't think so. I told him all I needed was that bracelet, and I'd launch an all out search for it tomorrow. He's going to be anxious to get hold of it."

Rhodes nodded. "He'll probably start out there as soon as it's dark enough, thinking we won't know where to start looking."

Dusk was turning into dark by the time they got to the judge's cabin and pulled up the hill. Cas parked the car behind the barn, and they walked down the path keeping to the tufts of grass and weeds.

As he used both hands to open the door of the basement Cas observed, "The hinges on this old door make enough noise to raise the dead. There's sure no danger he'll catch us napping."

All of them took a quick look around the place before it got too dark to see anything. Shirley shook her head at the garish decorations.

"It would take a mighty dark night for this to look scary. In broad daylight, it's just a lot of old junk."

Cas made sure his door was steady and at the right angle before deploying his troops.

"Rhodes, you and Shirley get one of these benches to sit on. Take it out to the other side of the slope. When you hear the creaking of the hinges, come quietly and cover the door. Doug and I will wait here until he finds what he's looking for, has the bracelet in his hand, then we'll take him."

Rhodes and Shirley selected their bench and started out with it.

"Looks like a hard sucker!" Shirley whispered after they cleared the door.

"As long as there's no splinters." Rhodes eyed it with suspicion. "I'll dust it off before we sit on it, should have done it before we put our sandwich sacks on it."

Inside the basement Cas pointed to the barn door he'd positioned across the corner. "We'll get over there in the corner when we hear the car. The noise that door makes, we could probably take a nap."

Outside, Rhodes and Shirley opened their sandwiches and ate as the dark got thicker, saving some of their coffee.

"I feel like he'll come as soon as he can, but it could be a while. I just hope he takes the bait. I think Cas is right and he will. He knows he's got to if he wants to save his hide."

They talked about the evidence and what Cas had told them about his session with Darrell and the judge. "Yes, I think he'll be here, all right," Rhodes repeated.

Shirley nodded, though it was too dark for them to see each other. "I'm glad to get in on something like a murder case," Shirley said. "I was happy just to get the promise of a job, much less something like this."

In the quiet, Shirley's stomach growled and Rhodes laughed.

"Okay, so I'm a little nervous," she giggled. "Maybe it's good we've got a wait ahead of us."

"Drink the rest of your coffee, you'll be all right. Anybody with good sense would be nervous. We'll move in behind him when we hear him go in. Cas will take it from there. We're insurance, is all."

"I understand."

"We're too small a group not to be able to depend on each other. Don't be embarrassed about being nervous. When you stop being nervous, you'll be too careless to wear a uniform."

"I can see the truth in that. There's more coffee here and it's still good and hot, if you want some?"

"Yeah, pour me some if you can see how. It's getting chilly out here. Can you manage?"

"Yes, I'm holding the cup against the thermos. The night's as black as the coffee."

Cas and Doug sat in the dark basement, getting up from time to time to stretch.

"There's no way to tell how long we've been waiting.," Doug said.

"Probably not as long as it seems. It's black as a coal mine in here."

Doug drew a quick breath. "You hear that?"

Cas strained his ears. "Yes, it's a car coming up the hill. He's coming."

The adrenaline pumped as they hid themselves behind the old door. Neither spoke, listening intently.

Rhodes and Shirley heard the car. They stood up too, waiting in the dark.

Soon they heard noises outside the old cellar. Then the hinges of the basement door groaned as someone entered.

Inside, a flash of light flickered around the dark room. The light stopped a moment on the goat's head and someone grunted.

Then the light played on the bench near the table as Cas watched. It went slowly toward the place Hannah said Denise had died.

Cas peered cautiously around the door in front of him as Doug watched from the other side. He saw hands searching, feeling around in the grime between the ancient stones.

Looking out on the other side of the old door, Doug held his breath. There were three hands, then four!

One of the hands lifted something shiny and a voice exclaimed triumphantly, "Here it is!"

Cas and Doug gave the old barn door a hard shove and leveled their weapons, Doug holding his flashlight. The two men stood gaping, stunned by the sudden light and the fall of the door.

"FREEZE! POLICE!" Cas's voice bounced off the stones and bare walls as the two culprits stood squinting at them.

Two more flashlights moved in to help light the scene as Rhodes and Shirley came in.

Darrell and Troy Spruce stood still and unbelieving, the shadows around them making the old cellar seem full of deputies as shadows shifted in the light.

Rhodes read Judge Spruce and Darrell their rights while Doug moved to cuff their hands behind them.

"Just a minute!" Cas reached to take the bracelet from Darrell before Doug handcuffed him. He put it carefully in his shirt pocket.

"This is all a terrible mistake!" Troy Spruce began as soon as he found his voice. "As soon as I can see my attorney, he'll get this straightened out."

He stood up straighter and raised his eyebrows at Cas. "This is my property, you know. We are on my property."

It sounded lame. Even Darrell seemed to find no comfort in it. He waited miserable and dejected beside his father as Rhodes directed them to the Spruce's Lincoln and got in beside them. Shirley got in front to drive, looking to Cas for further directions.

"You go first. I'll be right behind you. Good work."

Cas and Doug walked to the back of the barn to get the car. "I hear that on all the television shows," Cas grinned, "And she deserved it."

Doug laughed, proud of his cousin.

It was late when they got back. There was no one around to wonder about it as Shirley parked the Lincoln and waited for Cas to pull in beside them.

"This is really going to be a surprise to the town of Maryvale in the morning," Shirley marveled.

When they marched their prisoners in Gladys was shocked and it was hard for Raines to keep from showing his pleasure openly.

"I want to make a phone call," was Judge Spruce's first request.

Cas nodded. "Use the phone in my office."

Cas removed the handcuffs from Troy Spruce's wrists but did not close the door for him to make his call.

Gladys concentrated on her filing, trying to keep busy and not stare at the judge through the open door.

His face showed his disappointment at what he was hearing form Laurence Fields.

Cas was listening on another phone behind Gladys. He had picked it up to call Connie, but it was not connected to an outside line. He simply held it, not wanting the judge to know he was hearing his troubles.

"The shoe's on the other foot now," Cas thought. He remembered all the times prisoners had had to wait while their attorneys hunted Troy Spruce up to set bail.

Judge Spruce came out of the office, giving Cas a curt, "Thank you," for the use of his phone. Not that it looked like it had done much for his disposition.

Raines escorted Darrell and his father to their 'guest of the county' quarters.

"Gladys, you're about through here, aren't you?"

"Yes, sir. I've been having a hard time keeping my mind on what I'm doing since you got back anyway. There's going to be a lot of shocked and surprised people in this town in the morning."

"I'm sure of that. This is all we can do for now. I'm also sure Laurence Fields will be here first thing in the morning. Let's go home and get some rest."

Cas closed the door behind Gladys. He glanced down the hall where Darrell and the judge were lodged.

"I hope Darrell is as miserable and uncomfortable as he looked following Raines, him and the judge too. Troy Spruce was past due being reminded the law is for everyone, including judges."

He took time to go back to Raines who was on duty to thank him for his help and give him a pat on the back that let him know he was a good man who was appreciated and would be missed when his retirement came through.

Before leaving, Cas took the bracelet from his pocket, thinking sadly of Denise and how little of life she had to enjoy. He took the fragile memento into the restroom, washed it and dried it before replacing it in the safe.

He glanced at the phone. He decided not to call home, hoping Connie had managed to get to sleep. "Sanctuary, here I come," He breathed to himself as he left for home.

CHAPTER 22

Attorney Laurence Fields came to see his clients at a little after nine the next morning. Cas heard his voice and looked up from his work.

"Come into my office first, will you?" He called through the open door.

Fields smiled at Gladys and went in, closing the door behind him. "I don't think this would be a good time to refuse," he grinned at Cas.

"Probably won't change much." Cas warned him. "I assume you're here to rescue the Spruce clan?"

"Yes, I located the judge who is to come for the inquest first, and got him to set bail."

"Which is surprisingly low, no doubt?"

"Well, certainly. But not considering he's a county judge, remember. And I have to earn my money, don't I?" He shrugged. "And a county judge is not likely to run which is one of the main things to consider setting bail."

Cas didn't bother arguing with any of that legal logic and got to the point.

"You're familiar with the Davis case, aren't you?"

"I'm sure everyone in Maryvale is. Denise Davis was killed by a stab wound to the heart."

"Then you are also aware Judge Spruce excused himself from the case because he was close to the victim. Denise was the daughter of his office manager and secretary, Muriel Davis."

"Yes, I'm aware of that. I also know the inquest has not been set, if that's what you were going to tell me next." Fields smiled and there was a few seconds of silence between them.

"There's something you're leading up to," he studied Cas's face. "You surely don't think the judge and his son are guilty of this murder, do you?"

"Yes and no."

Fields raised his eyebrows.

"It could have been a terrible accident." Cas continued, "I can't get them to talk about it. It looks like they're more willing to hang than tell the truth about what actually happened."

Fields listened; he'd known Cas a long time.

Cas leaned forward, his lips a grim line. "And make no mistake about it, if they don't start talking there will be a conviction. Or at least, Darrell will be convicted. I've got enough evidence now to put Darrell at the scene where it happened. The scene where she was killed is on the judge's property, out where the cabin is. They both lied about where Darrell was the night Denise died. I have witnesses who knock his alibi about being home in the sand. Then last night my deputies and I caught them both red handed trying to retrieve evidence from the scene of the crime."

"God!" Fields exploded, knowing Cas was telling him the truth. "I haven't talked to them yet. What do they say about it?"

"Nothing. They've categorically denied everything, even where there is undisputed proof. The first thing they tried to cover up was he was out that night and had no alibi for the time Denise was killed. Then they claimed they, the judge and his wife, were at home and could support his claim that he was at home at the time. Even objected to my questioning him along with the other students who knew her. His alibi was about all he had going for him against the other evidence I had, and it didn't hold up about the time they got home that night. I talked to the people who saw the judge and his wife at the club that night, the ones who waited on them. The musicians playing in the bar, too. I have written statements and a recorded statement that they left there late enough that Darrell would have had more than enough time to meet Denise and to get back before they got home. He has no alibi. We have casts of the tracks their little utility truck made at the scene where Denise's body was found, and as I said, we caught them red handed last night. That's what they're doing here."

"And they lied on record, about the alibi, both of them?"

"Yes. I took statements which they signed. I don't think they gave it much thought, the way they acted."

Cas glanced at the casts on the credenza. "There is so much evidence against Darrell, and the judge trying to cover up for him is so obvious, if there is no other version of what happened, Darrell is as good as convicted."

"I appreciate your telling me this." Fields shot him a grateful look. "You think there's a chance this could have been an accident, then? Not murder?"

"I think, with what I've learned in my investigation, there's at least a chance it might have been an accident. Yes."

Cas rose to see Laurence Fields to the door. "Maybe they will talk to you. I don't have any choice but to charge him if they don't."

"I'll see what they have to say." Fields walked with Cas to the cells, thinking about what he had heard. Before they got close enough to be heard in the cell, he shook his head. "I can't see why they would refuse to tell what happened. Not with what's facing them."

Cas shrugged. "I can make an educated guess, but it's for them to tell you. Here we are." He closed the cell door behind Fields and left them alone.

After their conference and the necessary paperwork Darrell and the judge walked out with their attorney ignoring Cas, who looked after them through the still open door of his office.

Fields turned to Cas, his hand on the outer door. "I'm taking them home. We will meet in my office this afternoon."

Cas nodded, not commenting.

"Cas," Gladys said, not too sure how to put it. "Did Darrell, was it Darrell who did this?"

"We don't have proof of exactly what happened yet but the evidence we have points that way. The most damning thing is we caught them trying to retrieve evidence from the scene of the crime last night."

"Oh. I wondered when I saw them both. The judge must have been trying to help him, to cover up for Darrell. Is that it?"

"Right now it seems that way, but that's between us, Gladys. Until it's been through the courts and decided there is to be no information given out on anything to do with this. Not even that they were here."

"Of course. I understand." Gladys was a little miffed he thought he had to explain that to her. "I was surprised when you brought the judge in with him, that's all."

The call Cas was waiting for came at about three-twenty that afternoon. It was Laurence Fields.

"Cas," he asked quietly enough that Cas knew he was not alone. "Could you come to my office? My clients and I would like to talk to you, if you can get away."

"Did they ask you to call?"

"Yes. They want to make new statements in regard to the case, about the death of Denise Davis."

"All right. I'll let my people here know where to reach me and be there as soon as I can."

At the law office, Field's secretary announced Cas and Laurence Fields came to meet him at the office door. Judge Spruce and Darrell sat near Field's desk and did not look up when he placed a chair near them for Cas.

Cas avoided looking directly at either Darrell or the judge, but he had seen traces of tears on both averted faces.

He fervently hoped the tears meant they had both told the truth at last. He sat down and waited for Fields to speak.

"Sheriff Larkin, this statement has been written out and signed by Darrell Spruce. I'll ask him to tell you what it says in his own words before I have it typed up."

Cas turned his attention expectantly to Darrell.

"I…I," Darrell's voice was barely audible. "On the night this happened," he kept his eyes down as he spoke. "I was home reading when my parents decided to go to the club to have dinner. Mother had been to a garden club meeting and didn't have time to cook. After they left I had trouble getting my mind back on my reading. I decided to call Denise."

"She answered the phone?" Cas had been wondering about the phone call.

"Yes, sir. Her mother got her a phone line for her birthday. I called her on her phone."

"I see." Cas nodded.

"We talked for a while and I made arrangements to meet her a block over from her house. She had been to a couple of the meetings of the club we had organized, and I wanted to invite her to go to the big meeting with me."

"The big meeting. You mean the one where there would be people from Marble and other counties. The one you called an orgy?" Cas pinned him down.

"Yes. That one."

"Wasn't this supposed to be a wild party, with perhaps, sex involved too?"

Darrell kept his eyes down. "We, the group talked about it, yes." He hesitated slightly. "I was going to ask her to be my partner."

"What makes you think she wouldn't be shocked at being asked to attend something like that?" Cas kept his eyes on Darrell.

"I didn't know. But," he didn't look at the judge. "We'd been out on the sly a few times. Our parents didn't want us to date. And when I picked her up, we went by a fast food window for sandwiches and Cokes before I took her to the meeting place to talk."

The silence when he paused emphasized the seriousness of the statement he held in his hand. He never looked at anything but it and the carpet between his feet.

"I put a couple of my mom's tranquilizers in her Coke, so she wouldn't get excited or anything," he continued and mumbled something else.

"What was that? I didn't catch it," Cas demanded.

"I thought the tranquilizer would take effect by the time we got out there, and being at the meeting place, too, I thought she might say she would go and be my partner."

Darrell was the picture of misery. The judge stirred in his chair, but didn't speak, bowing his head to study the carpet as Darrell did.

"He's suffering for Darrell, and his own guilty conscience is working on him too," Cas thought. "It's taking a lot of the starch out of him, having to keep quiet and let Darrell take his lumps."

"You mean go with you and be your partner for sex, too?" Cas pressed.

"Yes. That's what I was hoping."

"All right. What happened next?"

"We finished our food, we drank our Cokes on the way out. We started talking about the big meeting we were going to have. We were sitting on the bench beside the altar."

"The table with the candles on it?"

"That's right. Then I asked her to go to the meeting and be my partner. She looked surprised and asked me, 'for sex too?'"

"And then?"

"I said yes, if everybody else was doing it, why not us?"

"Did she accept?"

"No." Darrell looked up at the window, taking a deep breath that sounded painful. It rasped slightly.

"She giggled. I thought she was just playing with me, you know, teasing. So I asked again. She got up off the bench, and she was laughing!"

"Laughing." Cas repeated the word, remembering Hannah telling him Denise felt no fear, that she was laughing when she saw them.

"Yes," Darrell nodded. "Laughing hard, like she'd heard something really funny. I got up too. I asked her why, what was so funny? And she said—she said…." Darrell turned then to look at the judge, the picture of misery.

Judge Spruce nodded for him to continue.

"She said, 'because I'm your sister! The judge is my father too!' I know I looked shocked, I was! I didn't know whether to believe her or not and she kept on laughing! I reached for the knife on the altar to threaten her. To make her stop laughing like that. But just as I got the knife up in front of me, she turned her ankle and swayed. But she caught herself, and she looked like she really hurt. She looked down. She couldn't stand on her ankle. She couldn't get her balance. She fell against me! She fell on the knife. Hard, all her weight on it. Then in a second, she just sort of-relaxed. I thought she must have fainted, and I eased her down to keep her from falling on the stone floor."

Darrell's haunted eyes saw nothing in the room, only the dark scenes which had been tormenting him. He went on as if having started he couldn't stop talking, relieving himself of the painful pictures in his mind.

"But when I bent down, she wasn't breathing. I thought she had just got the wind knocked out of her and I shook her a little. But she didn't come to. And I held the metal part of my key ring up as I'd seen someone do on television, and there was no moisture, no breath. No breath and no heartbeat or at least I couldn't find any. I didn't want to think, I couldn't believe, it was so quick! I couldn't believe she was, that she was gone." A slight chill shook him.

Darrell's face was haggard and pale. He dashed sudden tears from his eyes, but continued in anguished tones.

"And the knife! It was in so deep, the way she fell on it. Or I, maybe it was because I was so scared, I couldn't get it out. I left it there and took her back to the car. It was hard to do. She was heavy! I was afraid, I didn't mean to hurt her. I didn't know what to do. Then I thought I'd put her in the river behind The Roadhouse. I...I tried to carry her there. But out there in the dark, before I got to the water, I had to put her down. I couldn't make it. And I knew my parents would be coming back. I panicked, I left her there and ran back to the car."

"Don't you mean the truck?" Cas corrected gently. "You ran back to the little utility truck."

"Yes. The truck, we went in the truck. I went back to the truck and got home as fast as I could. My mom and dad came in a little while after I got back."

Cas addressed his next question to the judge. "How long have you known about this?"

"Darrell asked me about it the next day. If she, if Denise was his sister. Then I asked him why he thought so, and all this came out. I told him yes, she was his sister. But all that happened a long time ago, that there was nothing between me and Muriel now. And that Muriel was making her own living for her and Denise. I also told him this was the reason we hadn't wanted them to date or to spend much time together."

The judge avoided Cas's eyes, but his voice was strong. "I'm glad she knew I was her father," he told the indifferent beige carpet defiantly. He looked up. "I gave her that bracelet she wore for her birthday."

"I had a sister," Darrell said, regret softening his low voice. "And I didn't even know it."

"I'm sorry, Darrell." The judge spoke to him as if they were alone. What secrets did they have now? "I'm so sorry. About everything."

Cas watched the drama being played out before him. He turned to Fields as he got up.

"Can I have a word with you, counselor? Bring that statement with you."

Fields opened the door for him. "We can talk in the conference room," he led the way.

Settled at the expensive looking conference table, Cas touched the statement. "Let's work on this. The facts are what we need, not a lot of embroidery."

Fields positioned the statement where they both could see it comfortably. "Right. I need to ask you some things before the inquest, but we can take care of it now."

"What he said about her falling against him," Cas anticipated his questions. "The coroner's report bears that out, that it must have happened just as he said and the ankle and the top of the foot were bruised. I'll show it to you if you want to see it."

They sat side by side working on the statement, deleting all reference to the relationship between Denise and Darrell. The invitation to the meeting and being a partner for sex was left as stated, along with the reaction it had caused. Denise had laughed at the idea of an orgy and the invitation which included sex. They left in the part about Darrell's hurt and embarrassment at her reaction to the idea of being his partner or even attending the so-called orgy. His picking up the knife and her falling against him explained why the knife was wedged in so deeply. The turning of her ankle explained the bruises that were detailed on the autopsy form and verified the sequence of tragic events. The only thing left out was the thing both Darrell and the judge had tried so hard to hide. That Darrell and Denise were brother and sister.

It took only about twenty minutes for Laurence Fields to get the statement rewritten as Cas watched.

"Now, we'll get this typed up so Darrell can read and sign it."

Cas reread the typed statement as they walked back to make a copy. "The facts are all here. I don't see any point in adding anything else."

"And you had nothing to do with this, right?" Fields handed him a copy of the statement.

"Certainly not! It's not my job."

"Do you want to talk to them again?"

"Yes. I'll go back with you."

Fields sat down at the desk and handed the typed statement to the judge, his expression betraying nothing. "I'm sure you would like to read this before Darrell signs it."

Judge Spruce took the statement and started reading. He looked up in surprise a few seconds later, then continued reading.

When he finished the statement he looked up at Cas, trying to find words. "I don't know how I can thank you enough. I was prepared to take it years ago if this got to public ears but I had to protect my wife, she had a bad heart. And no one knew, about this relationship. I'm glad she never knew. I worried about her and then, no one knew after we came here, and we agreed to keep Denise and Darrell apart. We tried to keep from hurting anyone else."

Finding it difficult to speak he simply handed the statement to Darrell to read and sign.

"Sheriff Larkin, if I can ever do anything for you...."

"As a matter of fact, there is something you can do for me," Cas said decisively. "And the sooner the better." Cas had not sat down. He stood, underlining the urgency of his words.

"Of course." The judge stood up then and faced Cas, wondering what he would ask. But he was already committed and nothing would be too much compared to his first born. Spruce was in no position to argue.

"What do you want me to do?" The judge braced himself and waited.

"I want you to take Darrell to your family doctor. And if he doesn't see anything wrong, go to a heart specialist. Will you do that?"

Elated, Darrell had handed the statement back to Fields and stood looking from his father to Cas, wondering now why Cas wanted him to see a doctor.

"Yes, I'll do that if you say so. But why? What makes you think I need to?"

"He's not as strong as someone his age should be. There is something wrong, though I don't know what. When he left Denise there on that path, it was more than panic and wanting to get home that stopped him there. He couldn't make it any farther. He said so right there in that statement. You need to get him to a doctor. One who knows what he's doing. A heart specialist." Cas was intent enough to convince Spruce to do as he said.

Worried now, the judge held out his hand to Cas, who took it still looking grave.

"I'll call and make an appointment as soon as we get home. And thank you." He gestured at Darrell.

Darrell came to shake hands with Cas.

The judge and Darrell left and Fields put an arm around Cas's shoulder as he stood at the door with him. "This will wind it up. People can stop worrying about having a murderer in their midst. You've done an impressive good job, and a compassionate thing here."

"It's a relief to have it cleared up."

"I saw a picture of you and Cortez Lorenzo in the paper," Fields studied Cas's face. "You've more than earned your salary this quarter."

"You'd be surprised how fast people can forget things like that when it comes to underwriting the budget."

Fields relaxed, amused at the frugal budget he knew the county operated on. "I can sure testify to the truth in that!"

Cas smiled, relieved to have done with the case and turned his face toward home. Sanctuary.

EPILOGUE

T he day of the inquest, Cas attended and watched as the facts were presented. The autopsy report corroborated the turned ankle and the force of the fall on the knife. The finding was death by accident.

Cas got up to leave, to get back to his office and his work.

Judge Spruce caught up with him going back into his office.

"Can you spare me a few minutes?"

"Sure, come on in." Cas pushed the door of his office closed behind the judge but did not sit down, glancing at two notes on his desk.

"I wanted to tell you I took Darrell to our family doctor and to the heart man he works with. He told us Darrell had rheumatic fever when he was a child. We didn't even know it. But he's on some medication now, temporarily, we hope, and we'll know how to take care of him now."

Cas spindled the notes and locked his desk preparing to leave as he listened. He took something from the safe and put it in his pocket before he straightened and turned back to the judge. He nodded approval of the trip to the heart specialist but the judge still had things to tell him, so he stood patiently listening.

"I'm glad the inquest is over and I'm grateful for your help. I've decided to retire. I wanted you to know before the rest of the county. I've turned in the papers and got the ball rolling on it. We're going to move to some property my wife has had for some time. Her aunt left it to her. Anyway, it's not too far on the other side of Fort Craig near Rainbow Cove on the river, and close enough for Darrell to live at home if he goes to the university."

He hesitated before adding, "Muriel has a good job and will have a good retirement when she wants it."

"That's good." Cas glanced at his cleared desk.

"I'll walk out with you, if you're ready."

Cas nodded and opened the door, the judge beside him still talking. He talked all the way out to the parking lot.

"I don't know how, with everything else there was going on at the time, you ever figured out Darrell needed to get medical help. Are you a magician, or have second sight?" The judge raised his eyebrows, his question half serious in spite of his smile.

Cas had his hand on his car door and one foot inside. "Yeah, second sight," he grinned back. "And it sure comes in handy around this county. By the way, this belongs to you." He handed something small to the judge and drove toward the exit of the parking lot.

Before he entered the stream of traffic, Cas stopped and looked in his rear view mirror.

The judge was standing where he'd left him, staring in wide eyed disbelief at the class ring in his hand, wondering just how much Cas did know about all that had happened so long ago.

*Turn the page for an
excerpt from*

The
Nelson Scandal

A Maryvale Cozy Mystery

Book Two

Jackie Griffey

"Connie, is Cas there? This is Rhodes."

"No, Cas hasn't got home yet. I was about to call you. It's not like him not to call if he's going to be late. Do you know if he had to stop somewhere?"

"He went on one of our rounds on the way home. I'm going to check on him now. He may have had a flat or something. I'll call you back, don't worry."

Rhodes made record time and was getting closer to the bridge. He pictured it and the road as he hurtled through the dark, lights and siren heralding his approach.

He saw Cas's car's lights first. Gripping the steering wheel hard enough to hurt, he pulled off the road and looked down at the car. The open door stirred faint hope, but there was no movement.

Thankful the lights were still on, Rhodes half climbed, half skidded down to the car, holding to the tough underbrush and outcroppings of rock to ease his descent to the open care door.

He carefully touched the still figure in the driver's seat. Blood oozed from Cas's hairline. Rhodes searched for a pulse.

The Nelson Scandal

available in print and ebook

THE
MARYVALE COZY MYSTERY
SERIES

Cozy mystery author Jackie Griffey likes to read as well as write mysteries and romantic suspense. She and her family, two cats, a Chihuahua, and a couple of wild bunnies live in Arkansas.

Jackie loves hearing from her readers. You can contact Jackie through her publisher at:

JackieGriffey@epublishingworks.com